Colonfay

a novel by

Myles O'Grady

THE PERMANENT PRESS
SAG HARBOR, NY 11963

Library of Congress Cataloging-in-Publication Data

O'Grady, Myles
      Colonfay / by Myles O'Grady
        p. cm.
      ISBN 1-57962-068-X
      1.World War, 1939-1945--France--Colonfay Fiction. 2.
      France--History--German occupation, 1940-1945 Fiction.
      I. Title.
      PR6067.G745 C65 2000
      823'914--dc21   99-34810
                                     CIP

THE PERMANENT PRESS
4170 Noyac Road
Sag Harbor, NY 11963

For my wife, who makes everything possible.

But love has pitched his mansion in
The place of excrement
For nothing can be sole or whole
That has not been rent

W. B. Yeats

Monday

1. Armand & Family

ARMAND DE COUCY, FULL of years and honor (save in his own family), fell out of a tree in his park at Colonfay in the department of the Aisne in northern France. A hornet stung him and he lost his balance. It happened on a Monday and he was buried seven days later. He was not ready to die. Things were left undone. During the course of that week a lot of skeletons fell out of the closet. This is not a history book. God knows what it is. A tale told in a week. Full of sound and fury and all over the place. As many strands to be woven together as a braided rope. Well, it was a French hornet.

The same Monday morning. Armand's daughter, Laure, reborn, with a fullness in her body and all impediments flushed away. This is her story, or stories, for she has many faces. *Laure, Lolo, Laurence.* Depending. Right now she's lying there asleep as the clear dawn breaks over the Lubéron Mountain of Provence. She has a beatific smile on her face and a comforting hand between her thighs. She's dreaming of things a married lady should not be dreaming of. Stolen fruit. Oh, the joy of it! Oh, the succulence of it! A gentle mistral rustling the plane tree is the background symphony to her dreams. The birds are trilling, the bees humming, the sun shining, the scent of the honeysuckle the bottom note to the delicious smell of sin. Free at last! Never to go back. Hell is in the north; Heaven is in the south. Her father's fall will be for her the ultimate release. She despises him. Had she been anywhere near the tree she might have felt like giving the ladder a push. This mild-mannered man who wouldn't say boo to a goose does not inspire much filial piety. Laure has lived too long already with his legacy of shame. Laure, cerebral, wanting not to be, last night liberated with her first unbridled climax.

Laure's husband, Dermot McManus. A free-range Irishman with a lot of miles on him, unintellectual. Activist.

Dreamer. Rolling stone. 'I imagine, therefore I wander.' Opposites attract? And endure? Yes, and pigs will fly. This Monday he's in Gilleleje, Denmark. He's supposed to be on location in Mexico, directing photography. He was there until two days ago, when, discarded by Laure like a Métro ticket in the wind, and having lost his center of gravity, he left for Denmark. Dermot needs a jar of *hyggelig*. *Hyggelig* is a Danish word for which there is no equivalent but 'everything in the garden is lovely' will do. *Hyggelig* is promoted if there's a complaisant female troll around. Marital deprivation may be dissolved in carnal pleasure. Laure would concede that, at times, Dermot has the right to call up the reserves. Those who knew Laure, and knew about Nana the Troll, said "His balls rule his brain" but, sure, they don't know the half of it. He too is saddled with the sins of his father. Plus the lapsed Irish Catholic guilt thing. Overcompensating like a mad fool. Dermot likewise seeking orgastic release.

Dawn in Paris that same Monday. Armand's son, Patrick. He's already at his desk in the Rue du Cardinal Lemoine. He's an insomniac. The grey hours are best for injecting a bit more concentrated tedium into his story of the slug crawling across the ceiling. The ceiling he sees (and he sees it clearly) is in the bedroom at Colonfay. It's not like Proust's chamber, redolent with affection and happy anticipation. He hasn't seen it since 1938 and every day he celebrates his removal from it with a word from the acid muse. He is, as they say, out of the family loop. When he hears of his father's fall, he will ask—Did he bounce? Patrick has almost managed to exorcize the demon of inherited guilt. He's earned remission of his father's sins. He's not unhappy. He's a philosopher. He's got it made. He understands what Beckett meant when he said there's nothing funnier than unhappiness. He's laughing as he selects the word. Melancholia can be *fun!*

The main cast is there. There are extras, some with important roles, like André, Laure's American Liberator.

And others, like Mouse, Dermot's cousin, sometime shrink, fixer, the anchorwoman, though anchorman would be more appropriate in Mouse's case. There's Nana the Troll, Dermot's comfort lady; both the balm and the fly in the ointment. They're dispersed hither and yon. Trying to consolidate them is like trying to gather up the pieces of an exploded fragmentation grenade and reassemble it. Let the bits fall where they may. All fiction is chaos. The magnet is Armand. He fell out of a tree. That's a hard fact. Let's get to him. First, a word about Colonfay where the poison flowers grow. A hidden house in a secret corner of France, unknown that is except to the permanent residents nearby; 'the glorious dead,' planted in military rows with regimental badges carved in the stone markers and, yes, the obscene *'Dulce Et Decorum Est'* on the plinths of the central memorials. Colonfay, scene of battles long ago. And yesterday. The château of Colonfay, the family house that once echoed to the happy sounds of children at play and later to the screams of the victims. A monument to man's inhumanity to man. And woman. And child. Colonfay, and the killing tree. The cedar of Lebanon. The execution post. The wreck buoy on the human chart.

2. Colonfay: the Last Battle

COLONFAY. WAR-TORN, AGAIN. The great storm of August, 1980. It devastated the region. A brilliant white night flickering with incessant sheet lightning and simultaneous cracks of thunder, like the 120mm guns that had often rocked the house in earlier times. It had blown great guns too. The shutters rattled; the house groaned; things jumped about in the *grenier* under the roof. Dawn was a sky that bled. A German Expressionist dawn, blood-red slashes across a green and purple canvas, with a few small daubs of blue, and black clouds like funeral spinnakers racing across the sky on their way to the cemetery.

Which cemetery? Take your pick. Colonfay was between the French war cemetery of La Désolation—*Yes, La Désolation!*—and the German war cemetery at Le Sourd—*Yes, The Deaf!* "The dead are all on one side," as the poet, René Arcos, said.

The monument in the cemetery, erected by the Crown Prince for his friends: *Treu Bis Zum Tode.* Faithful unto death. *Ja*, verily.

"Up yours, Heinie," said Dermot, every time he passed it. Dermot, in 1943, a trained killer at seventeen, remembering the sergeant instructor on the Commando course at Achnacarry, "Mac, I'll see your name on the village war memorial yet!" Funny. War was hilarious. You could die laughing.

Colonfay was always in the thick of battle. The park was violated in August 1914, during that first battle of Guise, and again in October 1917. During World War 1, that they used to call The Great War—*The Great War!*—it was the headquarters of General Lanrezac commanding the Fifth French Army and later that of the German general commanding five armies. The *cave* had been reinforced to make a bunker. During World War II, the house alternated between French, German, British and American tenants. Colonel Charles de Gaulle rested there after his exceptional stand and the park was churned up when Guderian's and Rommel's tanks swept through from the "impassable" Ardennes with their buckets and spades on their way to the seaside at Dunkirk; and again in 1944, by the American 1st Army during the Battle of the Bulge. That was in December when the U.S. 1st Army tried to hold Bastogne and 80,000 casualties resulted.

The house was shat in at different times by Prussians, Russians, Bavarians, British, Moroccans, Americans, and French Meridionals to whom the sound of a shot was an instantaneous laxative. It was desecrated by the brutal and licentious soldiery, with the panelling of the library burnt and the roof ripped open to make an observation post. The retarded village girl had been used and abused in a maid's room, by an entire battalion. It was said that the Crown Prince Wilhelm had been taken aback in the *orangerie* by his friends in the Kaiser's Garde Regiment Zu Fuss. People in the village had the General, von Kluck, dressed in women's nether garments and dancing on the dining-room table.

Dermot: "You lost over two million men in the Great War."

Patrick, son of Armand: "It wasn't all bad. On the other side, Paul Wittgenstein lost his right arm, and Ravel composed his Concerto for the Left Hand for him. One concerto is worth two million men. War's great for music!"

Way back in 1814 Napoleon had slept there on his way to encircle Blücher at Château-Thierry. In 1815 the Emperor had dallied a while on his way to the battle of Waterloo where Blücher, coming to the aid of Wellington and saving the day, took his revenge. In 1870 the Prussians bivouacked in the park on their way from the battle of Sedan to invest Paris. And so on and so forth. Colonfay. You know you're there when you see him at the crossroads. He stands there, the cast iron *poilu*, a soldier of France, resting on his upturned rifle above a list of the local fallen, *'mort pour la Patrie.'* He's a sad sentinel, ignored save on one day a year, your standard economy model war memorial for impoverished small communes, like Colonfay.

Dermot would salute the poilu. *He remembered the Commando sergeant with his brilliant wit but limited repertoire: "Mac, I don't want you to die for your country. I want you to make the other bastard die for his!"*

You would be through Colonfay before you realized it. There's nothing but a line of nondescript cottages leading into the village; a small store with a bar; a church that's visited rarely; the château hidden away behind the church.

Château, castle, manoir, maison de maître. The house at Colonfay was just a big house but it was *'le Château.'* So what was it about this house and its hidden park, planted with exotic trees? Well, it was on the direct route for armies from the east. Huns and Visigoths.

The cedar of Lebanon dominates the park. It has watched for three hundred years the passing of the barbarians and has sheltered murder and mayhem and all sorts of abominations. Reprehensible acts unconnected with war. Blood has fertilized it, and Laure has shed copious tears under it. Armand is but the latest victim of the killing tree. Poetic justice? Who is to say? Now, again, Colonfay devastated. Trees uprooted, slates torn off the roof. Lightning has struck the old walnut tree. The wall to the kitchen garden looks as if a Tiger tank has been driven through it. The small greenhouse is matchwood and broken glass.

The venerable cedar of Lebanon is smashed in its lower branches, one hanging down like a broken arm, all twisted with the sinews white and the tendons stretched. The whole scene is like that of a battlefield after another battle.

3. The Breath Upon the Glass

ARMAND TOOK THE best part of a week to die. It's a long time if you're in agony but it's as the blink of an eye if you're trying to put the pieces of a dysfunctional family back together again. Impossible? By no means. Perish the thought. Impossible is not French.

Impossible n'est pas français. That's what the French say. They say it with habitual modesty and a blind eye to the facts. They repeat it parrot-fashion like children learning their catechism. *"Impossible n'est pas français!'* Yes, well, if you believe that you'll believe anything.

Impossible is not French! If you say something often enough the words may become the action. This is what Armand de Coucy said to himself that mournful Monday morning after the tempest. He looked out of the window at the desolation in the park and the shattered cedar of Lebanon. Armand de Coucy, at the age of eighty and crippled, decided to make like an acrobat. "*I may be* hors de combat *but I will go up that tree and cut off the broken branch.* Impossible n'est pas français!" Well, we know how that Cartesian gem worked out. There's no fool like an old fool, as Granny used to say.

Armand was up the ladder sawing away when the hornet stung him on the left wrist. He turned to slap it with his right hand. The whole body twisted. He was locked into a rigid plastic 'corset' from the neck to the lower back, a consequence of an accident chasing moths at night in the Cameroons two years ago. He had fallen down an animal trap and broken three vertebrae. He was then a stripling of seventy-eight.

The saw flashed away. The ladder skidded along the branch, lost its anchorage and pirouetted in empty air before toppling backwards. A giant hand gave it a push. The old man was flung off and landed horizontally face up. He lay there on his broken back looking surprised and peevish. He tried to move. A pain shot through him. The shaggy bitch stood there looking at him, wondering. She licked his face. She whined. He moved again, tentatively. More pain.

He said, "*Palsambleu!*"

Nobody except Armand de Coucy had said *Palsambleu!* for a hundred years. He was given to démodé expressions. He would never have said the full, '*par le sang de Dieu,*' by the blood of God. Never would he take the Lord's name in vain. He was a passively religious man. Went to Mass some Sundays, gave to the poor. Confessed his sins, which weren't many, but not all. Saintly. Well, yes, they do say that the biggest sinners make the best saints.

"Butter wouldn't melt in his mouth," said Dermot, who had his measure.

"The devil incarnate," was what Laure, his only daughter, thought, and despite Dermot's intercession, she treated him accordingly. "My father, the war criminal," she said as she introduced him formally to Dermot (who had already met him briefly) before they were married.

Dermot thought that a trifle excessive but no doubt she had her reasons and, as your man Blake said, 'the path of excess leads to the palace of wisdom.' Sometimes the path is long and when you arrive at the palace it's a mausoleum.

Was that Laure's problem? Could be. Dermot had had his problems with his father. True for you, we spend our lives recovering from our childhoods. The English poet Larkin was right: 'They fuck you up, your mum and dad.'

Armand was an entomologist, a lepidopterist specialising in moths. He passed out. He came to in a world that revolved, then stopped. He saw himself in different situations, dreamy images in and out of focus; like looking in a steamed-up mirror that was sometimes wiped clear. The breath upon the glass. Images held awhile or in chaotic sequence. Slipped images. Into his consciousness spun a butterfly. It fluttered above him. He thought it curious. A *Papilo podarilius,* called *Le Flambé.* It seemed to have lost its way and was working in the wrong zone. Its inertial navigation system was all screwed up. The black diagonal stripes made it unmistakable. A flying zebra. He had seen it south of Lyon but never as far north as the Aisne. Most curious. He remembered seeing it described in the book *The Butterflies of France* as 'a rare swallowtail butterfly.' Had he seen it described as '*Iphiclides podarilius*'? Maybe. He couldn't remember. The red-tipped wings.

What he kept remembering was Laure. Laure and her little *culottes* with the red piping. Laure lifted up by her Uncle Didier to swing on that branch of the tree. Laure screaming. Running to him, wrapping herself around his leg. Crying, "Uncle Didier does things to me! Make him stop, Papa!" And him saying, "Don't be silly, Lolo. Don't be a cry-baby. It's only a game. Your uncle loves you. He wouldn't hurt you. Go back now." And her running into the house and locking herself into her room in the tower.

Did he know that it was more than a game? Did he want to know? Laure, little Lolo, her need ignored. His denial. Laure, who never forgave him for not protecting her. Laure who held him more guilty than she held her uncle, and who would never trust him again.

4. The Liberator

FOR LAURE THERE was no curse but a blessing at André's house under the shadow of Montagne Sainte Victoire. Who was it said the best time is going upstairs? Right. Oh, yes. And how. Apart from the big death in the north, the small death in Provence.

He's following her up the steep, narrow stairway in his 17th-century house at Le Tholonet near Aix. Showing her the traditional maison de maître. *Halfway up he puts his hands on her hips and stops her. He's touching her.*

She can feel his body behind her. Warm against her buttocks.

He says, "Look up."

She sees the bas relief on the wall of the landing. A tondo. A big carving within a circle, a Madonna, in a pale blue gown, with halo, delicate, beautifully executed. Not a Luca della Robbia but still. It has been created with talent. It's unvulgar. Not like those gaudy madonnas in the churches or at the crossroads. Yet.

There's something about it that's different. It's lascivious. The virgin has a knowing smile, conspiratorial, lewd. Her hands are lowered and are opening her gown at the vital point. It's the Piero della Francesca Madonna del Parto, the pregnant virgin before she got pregnant. Hand in the slit of her gown, daring, playing with herself, inviting. Nothing is more provocative than a saintly whore.

He says, "It was a maison de rendezvous *built by an archbishop for his mistress."*

She says, daringly, " Consecrated sex."

She's excited. She's conscious of his warmth behind her. She'll never understand why she does it. A brainstorm. Unpremeditated. No thought of revenge, of betrayal. No thought. Just a sudden impulse to jump off a cliff. Her body has a mind of its own. Her arm is out of control. It's like a non-drinker suddenly reaching for a brandy snifter and knocking back the fiery liquid. Burn me! She reaches back and touches him. Feels him. She's shocked by her own audacity. Frightened. He pulls away and then comes closer. Lifts her skirt. She helps. She's ready. Ready? She's been ready for twenty years. The dam bursts with a vengeance. The valley floods. The tidal wave sweeps everything away. She's submerged. She's dumped, almost unconscious, by a breaker on the heavenly sands. She comes back into focus. She sees close to her eyes the octagonal tiles, the steps worn by centuries, red, cracked. The strip of polished oak at the edge.

She gasps, "Is this what it's like? Oh, God!"

He says, " Yes, pray for it."

She says, " Madonna!"

She looks up at the Virgin. She thinks Holy Mary, Mother of God, thank you. Her fantasy had been to have someone come up behind her and do this, and never to know who it was. Three hours ago she didn't know his name. Over the door of the studio, Chamfort's 'Les passions font vivre l'homme; la sagesse le fait seulement durer'. The reasonable people survive; the passionate live. Why hadn't she realized it? She's not Lolo any more, or Laurence. She's Laure, complete at last. And free. Free of Dermot, free of the memory of her uncle's fumbling, of her father's refusal to understand it, of her mother's religious fascism.

5. Armand and The Fall

IT WAS EARLY morning when Armand fell, steamy, threatening more rain in between the gusts, the sky now a grey eiderdown, all lumpy but completely overcast. Clouds moving fast from west to east. There was the scent of wet cut grass and a healthy whiff of cowdung which drifted over from the farm next door.

The clock on the church tower in the village, not yet advanced for summer time, struck an uncertain eight. He floated in and out of consciousness and looked up through the branches of the tree at the family château, built by the miller of Guise when he came up in the world, with his shield over the door and the date in iron figures set in the wall, half on either side of it, 17 and 82. Built just before that misconceived Revolution. Improved with the money from local banking, the mine at Lille, the ownership of the northern railway line.

He could just see the top of the iron gates of the park. He imagined seeing the faces of the Germans pressed against the rails. He knew the Germans. They visited regularly. They came on cavalry chargers, they came marching up the drive in their coal-scuttle helmets, they arrived in Panzer tanks, and they showed up nowadays in Mercedes and BMW cars. Nostalgia brought them. To see the old H.Q. They peered in the big iron gates and they said, "*Papi was there, in that big house! Im Schloss, Baby!*".

The Irish came too. First, in 1914, in the uniform of a British cavalryman, then in 1956, in a Ferrari. Occasionally an Englishman from the Natural History Museum would come to talk butterflies or look at his precious library. Aliens. All so different to the French. Connections but no real communion.

He looked at the tower window from which Laure used to shout down at him when she was young. Bloodlines and landscape, he thought, it's what happens to you first, between birth and the age of seven, that decides the way you end. Yes, of course the Jesuits knew that years ago. It's the fragments. The little things. The ceiling in your bedroom. The branch of the tree from which you swung. The first funeral you went to. Your first bicycle. The taste of your first strawberries of the season. The racist conversations.

More drift. Armand de Coucy would confess to being an unreconstructed Royalist, like his family before him. He didn't much care but he would have preferred an autocratic king in Versailles to an autocratic (*socialist!*) president in the Elysée. He maintained that the murder of Louis XVI and the establishment of the Republic in 1792 had achieved nothing except to destroy the stability and the fabric of

French properly structured society. A properly structured society would be a pyramid, with the de Coucy family—and selected entomologists—up near the apex.

The Marshal had been an acceptable substitute for a monarch for a while, until it became too much of a good thing. The Vichyists may have gone too far at times but in the beginning he believed they had the good of the country at heart. Unity, no communists, no freemasons, no Jews. Well, that was a mistake. The arrest of Max Farber decided him. Still, France was France and England the traditional enemy. But better to be saved by the British and the Americans than to live under the murderous Huns.

He dissolved into his library—and Max Farber. The books were nothing by comparison with the butterfly collection, his lifetime achievement, his proper memorial. The universities of Florida and Bonn had been after it for years. But the rare books, some very rare, were valuable, especially the Hübner from Augsburg of 1793 and the Rambur on the *'faune entomologique de l'Andalousie'* of which only eight examples exist. The gem of the library was *'Tome V111 (1901) de N.M. Romanov, Saint Petersbourg,'* of which only four copies were known, and of which he had one, obtained for him by Max Farber in 1938. He had searched the world for it. It was the last book he found for Armand de Coucy.

The last time he saw Max. He wrote it down. It was in the box in the small room in the *grenier*, the space under the roof that ran the full length of the house. For Laure to read. Maybe he put a spin on it to exonerate himself.

14 July 1942: They came and took Max and Karen Farber away this morning. There was a big commotion on the stairs and I looked out of the window and saw about eight gendarmes take them to the bus. They were each carrying a small suitcase. The gendarmes were pushing them along. Oriane, my wife, joined me at the window. She told me to come away from it but I could not. As Max went to step up into the bus, he turned and looked up.

18

He waved. A feeble and resigned movement. Oriane turned away but I held up my hand in a salute. Nobody saw me, I think.

Laure was in Paris at the time and she kept asking where they were being taken and where was Sarah, her friend. Her mother, Oriane, said they were going on a long holiday. I looked at her sadly.

It was the night before last that he came to the door. The maid was off duty and Oriane answered it. She came into my study, where I was cataloguing the last lot of butterflies.

"It's the Jew from downstairs," she said. "He wants to see you. Don't ask him in."

I went out. Poor Farber was standing there, holding this portfolio. He was hunched over, hopeless with anguish. But his eyes were clear. Even angry. Anguished he may have been, for his family mainly, but disgusted also. He was resigned to the fate that had overtaken him, as it had his family. His fine Semitic features were more hawklike than ever. His tall forehead betrayed an intelligence which would not permit any self-delusion. He has found rare books on Lepidoptera *for me, and I have known him, more than once, to advise me against buying a particular volume because he questioned its provenance.*

"Monsieur de Coucy, I'm sorry to disturb you. And your wife, especially." He had heard her remark.

"It's not important, Monsieur Max. What can I do for you?"

"I want you to buy these drawings from me."

"But I'm hardly in a position to buy drawings now."

"No, no. I didn't make it clear. I want you to keep them for me. I have made out a bill of sale, so you can prove that you bought them, in case anyone questions your ownership. It's for five hundred francs, but you don't have to pay it. The bill is made out two years ago, and there's a receipt in with the drawings."

"What's it all about, Max?"

"Don't tell me you don't know, Monsieur?"

"Are they giving you trouble?"

19

*"Can I come in for a minute? Just inside the door? For
your sake as well as mine."*

*I let him in and we stood in the hall. Oriane came out of
the kitchen and looked at us. I was ashamed.*

"What is it, Armand?"

· *"Mr. Farber wants us to look after some drawings for
him."*

"You must do no such thing."

*"Listen, Oriane, I have bought various books from Mr.
Farber. This is just something else. Please leave us."*

"It's very foolish. Think of Didier."

Didier was my brother-in-law. He was an inspecteur des
finances, *and had just taken a post with Vichy. I didn't know
it then but he was a colonel in the Milice. He had ingrati-
ated himself with Abetz, the German Ambassador. He and
his friend, Robert Brasillach, were both publishing pro-
German tracts for Drieu la Rochelle, who had just become
editor of* Nouvelle Revue Française. *I never liked Didier. He
was an ineffectual opportunist type. Polished, like all the
rest of them but a bully.*

"Yes, all right, Oriane."

She left.

*"Monsieur de Coucy," Max Farber said, " I hope this
doesn't upset your wife too much but I must ask it of you.
The shop has been requisitioned under the Aryanization
Law. I expect them to arrest me any day."*

"My dear fellow . . ."

*"It's all right. Don't fret yourself. My brother and sister-
in-law in Hamburg have already been sent away, and my
father, too. I don't know where they've been sent but there
are rumors and they are hard to believe. Father said he'd
be safe because he had an Iron Cross from the first war. And
they boasted that Hitler was afraid to go to Hamburg. Safe!
He was one of the first to be picked up."*

"Tell me about the drawings."

*"Family property, not inventory. My grandfather
bought them in Italy, and they have never been out of the
portfolio since then. Said to be Correggios. Six drawings for
a series called* 'Amours des Dieux'. *Rather more erotic*

*than those paintings in the museums in Vienna and Berlin
and elsewhere. Not worth a great deal even if genuine. Old
Master drawings aren't expensive. Yet. But these have been
a family puzzle for a century. My grandfather had one
painting which he bought at the same time as these drawings. I suppose it is now hanging on the wall of some lech-
erous Nazi. My father had it in his study in Hamburg. We
have each made it a sort of game to trace the others. I think
I have a clue. It's written in the 'history' inside the portfolio.
I think it's your kind of puzzle. We have had fun tracing
those rare editions."*

"We will do it again, some day."

*"I think not. First, we were obliged to leave Poland.
Then Berlin. Now Hamburg and Paris. I think there is
nowhere else to go. I should have gone to America in 1933."*

"What about your daughter, Sarah?"

He turned away. It was too much for him.

*He said, "I'm hoping she's on her way to her godmother
at Cap d'Antibes. I hope they let her past the frontier. They
say they don't want Jewish children, but Bousquet is
rounding them up in Paris. If she leaves, I wonder if we will
ever see her again. Her mother is crying all the time. In
Germany they have a saying, 'to live like God in France.'
Strange kind of heaven. We were hoping some French family
would take her in and keep her safe, but everyone is afraid."*

*He looked up at me and a flicker of hope crossed his
face. It faded when he saw me look away.*

"No. Your wife and her brother. I understand."

*I changed the subject. It's easy to look back and
condemn me. But I was not the only one to consider.*

"Does anyone know about these drawings?"

*"No. I wrote to my father to tell him that I was looking
for a secure hiding place, but he had already been arrested
before the letter arrived."*

"Suppose they open the letter?"

*"Don't worry. Nobody knows I have given them to you.
You do realize they are of little value? Just a family game."*

"Come in and have a drink."

"No, thank you. I must get back. They are afraid every time there's a knock on the door."

I let him out. We shook hands. Impulsively, I embraced him. For all the French. After all, I am not a monster. His cheeks were wet. He stumbled downstairs.

I took the portfolio into my study and locked it in the wardrobe where I kept certain valuables. It was hidden behind my army uniform. Me, a cavalry officer! Trained at Saumur, demobilized at Tours, without firing a shot in anger. The portfolio shamed the uniform more than the surrender in 1940. My wife met me as I came back to the dining-room.

"You haven't taken them?"

"Forget about them, please."

"I wonder what Didier will say."

"Didier will say nothing, Oriane. Because he won't know. You will not mention this to anyone. There is nothing subversive or dangerous about it. They are just drawings of no particular value."

"Can I see them?"

"I suppose so."

I unlocked the wardrobe and opened up the portfolio on the big table. The first drawing did it properly. It showed a man wheeling a woman around the room on her hands. Her legs were around his thighs and his penis, a sizeable member and rendered in precise detail, had entered her equally well defined vulva.

Oriane went white. She shook with anger.

"You see. Jewish art. Pornography. My father is right. To think we have that sort of thing in the house. We should never have let that flat to them."

"We also have a translation of Aretino's erotic poems. Would you like to read them? Don't be silly, Oriane. Correggio makes them respectable. His religious paintings in Parma are in the Duomo and the Monastery. But I will take these to the country where their presence will not induce in you sinful thoughts."

Nothing more was ever seen of Maximilian Farber or

his family. They perished in Auschwitz. Two gendarmes came back and helped themselves to whatever they could carry away, and even brought a van for the furniture. I asked them what they were doing and they said it was only the property of 'un sale juif.'

Max Farber. Disappeared in 1942. Perhaps I could have saved him. If Oriane had not been so violently anti-Semitic it's possible that we could have saved young Sarah. Who knows?

He tried to focus again on the window from which Laure used to wave at him, but he could not fix the memory, and the branches of the big cedar wiped a series of images across it. One dissolved into another and blood rippled across them. The cedar, the oldest tree in the park, and the tallest. The killing tree. He should have had it cut down years ago. But you can't murder a tree.

Under it a group of *Résistants* had been executed by the Milice, the French 'Gestapo,' at the direction of his brother-in-law, Didier. This was in 1943.

And under it Didier had been shot in retribution in 1945. Armand was not blameless for the summary justice to his wife's brother.

Laure, *la petite Lolo*, unaware of the background affiliations, had discovered her Uncle Didier's corpse under the cedar. It had unbalanced the child. She was relieved at his death, but shocked when she became aware of her father's involvement in it. It was a natural execution post. And it attracted shells.

Zooming in and out from dreams to reality, the dominant image was of Laure. Little Lolo. Laure and her unrelenting attitude towards him. Remembering her hysterical fear of his brother-in-law's demands. A real fear, which he minimized at the time. Then her conviction too that he was personally responsible for all the crimes of Vichy, including the disappearance and presumed death of her childhood friend, Sarah, and the agony of Marcel, her first escort at *'Sciences-Po,'* the Institute of Political Science, unwelcome in the family, being a Jew, who was hidden in a wardrobe in the Dordogne throughout that shameful period. The gods may not visit the sins of the fathers upon the children, but the fallout from their acts casts a shadow that stays with the children for the rest of their lives.

Laure, little Lolo, on his butterfly hunt that time. Telling him things about Didier. Pleading for help. "Papa, it's not nice. It hurts! Make him stop!" Armand's embarrassment. His anger. But his excuses. And his impotence.

He was determined to confront Didier but his brother-in-law, now a colonel in the Milice, had discovered a wire-less transmitter in the forester's cabin in the wood on the Colonfay estate. Didier said he accepted that Armand had nothing to do with it but it was on his property and the Germans would not be so accomodating as he, Didier. Were it not for the fact that Armand was married to his sister, Oriane . . . and he left the sentence unfinished but with an unmistakable hint of menace. So how could he have assured Laure that Didier would never do it again? His own daughter. Unable to protect her.

More image slippage to the day in the wood.

A voice from behind a tree said, "Pssst!"

He said, nervously, "Come out."

A man in a strange uniform emerged.

He asked, fearfully, "What do you want? Who are you?"

"A friend of your son, Patrick. He's in London. He told me about the cottage. Said it was deserted, almost a ruin. That I could hide there."

From his voice he was probably English but his French was fluent.

"Who are you? What do you do?"

"It would be better for you not to know. Pretend you've never seen me. But I need a key and others may come here from time to time."

"You know I'm a functionary of the government? I should turn you in."

"Your son, Patrick, would thank you for that. Already he despises you for working for Vichy. If you want to lose him forever, turn me in. There are many more like me in France. Sooner or later, we'll be back in force. Then your friends the Huns won't know what hit them. My job is to report the movements of troops and generals. I ask nothing of you, except that you forget you've ever seen me."

Armand opened the cottage and took the box of butterflies he had stored there. Gave the key to the Englishman. As he turned to go back up the lane, he said, "I will deny all knowledge of your presence but I will not inform on you. Do not compromise me."

"*Merci*, Monsieur. Any message for Patrick?"

"Tell him to come home when it's all over. His mother needs him. And his sister. And his father who loves him."

"That I will, Monsieur. But for God's sake don't say a word to your wife or your daughter. You'll only put them in danger."

Laure now, and The Legacy in the attic. Plus the proof that she never gave him the chance with which to exonerate himself. Locked-up family secrets, tales of shame and glory. Never told because he could not bring himself to admit the shame of it, and some glory that seemed minimal. That and the secret pictorial 'treasure' of indeterminate title and extraordinarily salacious effect. The portfolio. Ticking away like a time-bomb, ready to destroy his reputation. Finders keepers, as the English say. '*Biens meubles*' is the French legal term, meaning any objects you can move you can claim title to. Blood money, Laure would say, if she knew the origin of it. Lord knows what she would say if she saw the pictures.

Armand was clear-headed for moments. Then he had a feeling of panic. She must understand that he couldn't help himself. That he didn't mean to allow her to be hurt.

He must live that long!

He craved her forgiveness. He was not, after all, a murderous fiend. Or an accessory to a child molester. And if he had been misguided at the beginning of the war, he had tried to make up for it at the end. He was too shy a man—

25

too proud and, for a placid person, too angry to explain—when she attacked him on the few occasions that they met.

Only Dermot seemed to understand human frailty. He had been shot at. He knew there are no heroes, only suicidal fools. And, as he said, there are more ways of choking a cat than giving it melted butter to eat. Sometimes you can be on the side of the angels, yet work from inside the enemy's camp. His attempts to get her to soften her attitude towards her father had only made Laure more angry. Of course, he didn't know the dark side of her childhood.

What right had his daughter to criticize him? To accuse him? What did she know about the circumstances? Only what her leftish friends told her. Jews and socialists no doubt. It was not his fault that she had read about him in the book *The Vichyists* published before the full facts were known.

No, Dermot was his only hope. He would come—if it wasn't too late. He could sift the evidence. He could persuade Laure. When she knew she would forgive him. This became his imperative. He would stay alive until that happened.

The lawyer, his lifelong friend Alain de Malherbe, would arrange the inheritance, but only Dermot could make Laure accept it. After all, it was not negligible. This house and the farm and cottages. The building in Paris. The stocks and the gold. And the drawings. Oh, Lord. They must be explained to her. He was only holding them in trust for Max Farber.

Who would get the books? Would Laure keep them? (Patrick, his son, had quit the family in 1940, and spent the war with de Gaulle in London. Apart from one standoff meeting at the *notaire's* over his mother's estate, his son and heir had never spoken to him again. Patrick was a lost cause.) It was all lost in complexity. Ignorance. Pride. Divided wartime loyalties. A misunderstanding, that was it. An unfortunate misinterpretation of his actions. What choice did he have?

As he said to Dermot one day, "If I had been in England during the war perhaps I would have behaved like an

Englishman." The very idea of him behaving like an Englishman was ludicrous. You could see it stuck in his craw. He was full of sin, but he wasn't that bad. Dermot said, "I can just see you in your bowler hat with a neatly furled umbrella and a neatly furled mind!"

He listened to the buzz of the midges and the howling of a dog from the German war cemetery just down the road. *Le Sourd*, The Deaf. And deaf they were, the cream of the German aristocracy, fallen at the Battle of Guise on August 30, 1914. Over sixty years ago. It came back with crystal clarity. It was just before the Germans overran the estate and Armand and his parents moved back into their apartment in the building that they owned on the Rue Freycinet in Paris.

The day the family left, their faith in French arms shaken by the arrival in the library of one of Krupp of Essen's 26cm howitzer shells, the château was captured. They just beat the gun. To balance the score, the retreating French Fifth Army put a shell into the dining-room. Tit for tat, but it changed nothing. You could still see the mark where the south wall had been repaired.

Armand passed out again. He faded out that real *papillon* and faded in his childhood fantasy *Schmetterling*. The fantasy that was triggered by expolosive reality. The shell landing in the park, the haphazard presence of its victim, and, later, inventing the story just to bring in a butterfly, his new obsession. He called it 'The Random Significance of the Butterfly' and it was his first entry in his diary of entomology. It was also his only departure from the cold, scientific facts which would dominate his life. It was a story inspired by his father saying, "A people with a language that can make a *papillon*, a *mariposa*, a *butterfly*, into a *Schmetterling* are capable of anything."

Feldwebel Heinrich Schmutz of the 2nd German Army was tired of operating at the edge of chaos. Limbering up and hauling the 26cm howitzer from Liege to Namur to Maubeuge to Guise inside ten days was no picnic. In a sweaty August, 1914. His face was caked with burnt cordite, his head deadened from sleeplessness and the constant crumps. At last the French seemed to have stopped for a day. Prima! *The gun was settled, the Krupp barrel loaded with shell and cordite and the breech closed and locked. He took his place at the gunlayer's position. The Hauptmann shouted the elevation. The map coordinates were fixed on the château at Colonfay. Heinrich cranked the wheel until the needle was just hairline off the right position on the brass dial. The snout of the howitzer cocked up high into the air. Heinrich saw a butterfly land on the barrel. He was distracted for a second. He thought:* Ach! Ein Schmetterling! Schön!—*and shouted the confirmation of the elevation. He completely forgot to fine-tune the dial. The Hauptmann sneezed and jerked the lanyard at that second. The gun belched flame and hot cordite. Heinrich Schmutz said,* "Scheisse!" *as he was thrown away from the jumping recoil. The loader, a bit of a wag from Kassel, shouted,* "Cordite burning brightly, Sir!" *The projectile, inscribed this time not with a quotation from Kant but with* 'Gott strafe England' *was hurled away to descend a bare hundred meters on the far side of the château, in the park, quite near the cedar of Lebanon. It threw up a geyser of dirt and filled the park with black smoke. It did very little damage, unless you count the loss of a British liaison officer who had wrung it out and was shaking the drops off next to the tree.*

Armand, lying there, immobile, tried to bring order out of it all, but it eluded him and he abandoned himself to a not-unpleasant state of hallucination. The dog lay against his thigh and looked up once in a while and barked. There was a constant ache but no severe pain. He tried to move his fingers. They worked. He dug them into the muddy soil. His fingernails scraped up the earth on which he lived and to which he would soon go. The land of his fathers. Land from which they were still digging out shells from the First World War. Land which had been in the de Coucy family continuously since the seventeenth century. Now it was the end of the line. Patrick had no children and Laure was determined not to have another. Her one child, a daughter, Penelope, had died not long ago. Suddenly he felt cold. The pain became severe. His whole back was hurting. He wished for an injection to anesthetize it.

The park was totally enclosed by woods. No one would come until Colette, his housekeeper, came back from the village, maybe at ten o'clock. He hoped she would look for him and not just leave his lunch on the kitchen table.

When she did find him, he kept repeating—*Faites venir Monsieur McManus. Telephonez Maître de Malherbe.*

Little did Armand de Coucy know it, but when he stirred up the hornet's nest the sting of one in the remote hamlet of Colonfay would have a fallout in southern France, Denmark, Ireland.

Well, as we noted, it was a French hornet.

The farmer and his worker lifted him gently onto a door and carried him into the house. He was delirious. They put a mattress on the long table in the dining room and he lay there. They managed after great exertions to change his wet clothes for dry ones and they lit a fire to raise the temperature even though it was hot outside. When the SAMU—the *service d'aide médicale d'urgence*—arrived they first blocked his body with sandbags.

When they prepared to move him onto a stretcher he came out of his coma and insisted that he not be taken to hospital. He was vehement and kicked to such an extent that they were afraid he'd do himself terminal damage. They called the hospital at St.Quentin and were told that a doctor would come immediately. To leave him alone. The *maire* of the commune was summoned because he knew him well. He could make contact, if anyone could, with Laure and Dermot. Patrick's whereabouts were unknown, except to the lawyer, Alain de Malherbe, whose office would only say that he was somewhere in the Midi, due in Aix en Provence on Tuesday. It would be Wednesday at least before either Laure or Dermot could be reached.

Immobile as Armand was, when conscious, his head angled, he could still see out the window to the park, and the thing he focused on was the cedar of Lebanon. It continued to dominate his thoughts and as he lapsed in and out of the dream world he imagined himself still under the tree.

6. Laure and Her Fall

THE MIDI OF France. Maurepas, a village in the Lubéron of Provence, in between Avignon and Aix.

Laure, Armand de Coucy's estranged daughter, came awake reluctantly. She was swimming with an amorous serpent in a lake of cream. A shaft of light on her eye. Her black hair spread across the lace pillow. Nude, one arm under her, an alabaster body and long. Her upper back exposed to the waist. Her head on her other outstretched arm. Her classical features, pale and still unlined, in repose. She was forty-seven but could have been thirty-five. The black cat walked on her face. She shrugged him off. He came back, protesting, waiting to be fed. The big ginger cat stayed curled up by her feet.

The Provençal sun through the half-open shutters was too bright, too soon. It spotlighted an errant branch with the orange trumpet flowers that were trying to creep in the open window. Scent of honeysuckle, mint. Pigeons cooing. Doors rattling in the mistral. The Judas tree scraping the walls in the courtyard. A dog howling in the distance.

On the empty side of the bed, scattered art books. Two on Pontormo, one on Parmigianino, annotated. A notebook with scribbled drawings of certain pictures, and comments. Bedside table, also piled high with books. The flotsam of a late night catching up on abandoned work. She was trying to finish the new book on Mannerism which was overdue. The publication date was timed to coincide with an exhibition at the Grand Palais in Paris. Laure de Coucy (*épouse McManus*,' as they put it on all documents, relegating the

30

husband to his proper subsidiary place) was an expert on Italian Mannerism, the intellectual painting and architecture by certain artists between 1520 and 1600.

It was not an élite pretension with her. She was not conceited about it. It was simply her mental escape from the trappings of the world of law for which she was trained. She was 'Laurence' in this, the expert, and in this academic persona, with daunting abstract intelligence, she knew her stuff.

Was this predisposition to obsessive pursuits genetic, like collecting butterflies? Could be, partly. She was a compulsive student. Sublimated sexual impulses? Unquestionably. Escape? Most certainly. Escape from the constant religious strictures of her mother, her daily lessons in 'proper' comportment, her perverted warnings against the physical. Of men. Sex! Filthy! Daily Mass, hidden body, good works. Escape too from the rigid confines of that slice of society which excluded anything modern. No emancipation here. Escape from the daily evidence of her mother's slavery to her father, a man who took as his natural right to be waited on hand and foot.

Dermot, too, becoming the heavy husband, seeming the replacement father, older, criticizing. 'Lolo' to him, his little girl too, as if he had any right to use her childish pet name. The cell door, the chains that bound, dried out the soul—and other parts. In her Laurence role she wasn't taking any of that *merde*.

The tragedy of Penelope, the wild and wonderful Pen, light of their lives, the glue that held the marriage together and whose sudden death froze in time all communication between Dermot and herself.

Art history was an exciting, solitary source of discovery. It fed her imagination. With some people escape was the cinema; with Laure it was paintings. She wrote her own scripts in her head. She entered into the pictures. The trick had once returned her to sanity. Sometimes she published her findings. Occasionally she lectured. Above her head, a contemporary copy of the Poussin *The Nurture of Jupiter*. (They were not Mannerists but Poussin was her God and

Claude Lorrain was his Prophet.) On another wall a poster of the Rosso Fiorentino's *Deposizione* from Volterra. Now awake, and still the liberated Laure, body-aware and happy, she said, *'Bonjour!'* to the boy in the Bassano poster of *The Flight into Egypt* just to the right. He was leading the donkey and looking down at her. She always talked to him. So far he hadn't replied but she knew he heard her. She shook herself into action. She had to work today. Yesterday was wasted. Well, no. And not the evening! Oh, no!

Going to her cousin Clémence's dinner at Vaugines. Tuesday, the funeral of Tante Marie. Holding Clémence's hand and the agony of a lunch at her uncle René's house, *La Fontanelle*, at Montdidier les Murs. Today, she was determined to get down to it, the work, she meant. Unless. Unless André came across.

André was yesterday's bombshell. Rocket? No. *Tsunami*, that was the word. An underwater earthquake erupting and a giant upheaval on the surface.

A rogue wave that drowned her. Washed out her inhibitions. Drowned her fears. She had kicked over the traces.

Her friend Pascale has an apartment in the Provençal village of Maurepas and Laure had promised to help her choose a table for it. It was the Sunday market at l'Isle sur la Sorgue. So she went with her to find one. Pascale has uncertain taste and Laure is endowed with all the virtues supposedly. She has an unerring eye. Pascale is working on Laure's new book. She's a retired journalist and she's doing the captions and some of the editing. Pascale is an unpredictable genius. A bouncy little woman, fey and often childish. But brilliant. An owlish woman with a completely round head, and thick glasses behind which sparkle a fearful intelligence and a child's intuitive understanding of the human condition. She has an antenna which picks up instantly the fraudulent and the phony.

Pascale was a communist, until Hungary. She and her husband, Michel, both at the Sorbonne. He active in the *Résistance*, Pascale sticking little French flags on the backs of German soldiers in the Métro. Michel went to a station in the Auvergne. To meet a contact. Saw the man on the opposite platform. Didn't see the Gestapo following him. Waved. Carted off to Buchenwald. Endured the long march from the camp as the Russians advanced. People dropping out, dying, all the time. Worse than the camp itself. Even today he can't speak to Vichyistes, collaborators. Is reserved with Laure about her experiences because of her family's Petainist background. Pascale is uncompromising. So is her friend in the local village of Lourmarin, François, the retired ambassador, the man who lives in music. But Pascale knows that Laure has broken the family ties. She knows too that her friend can never break the biological and genetic components.

They crossed the Lubéron at Bonnieux, Laure trying not to look at Ventoux in the distance and noticing only the splashes of broom, like yellow explosions all over the hills. Sunlight and shadows on the twisty road, rocks overhanging in the Combe de Lourmarin. The hairpin bend, looking back over the ravine of Buoux, a jagged cleft in the earth that Dermot says looks like a *vagina dentata*. An Irish poet with a dirty mind. Pascale understands him. There was a wild mistral gusting, the branches of the trees in turmoil, the noise of a million waves breaking on rocks, an insane dance of the leaves. The car was buffeted.

Pascale insisted on shopping for vegetables in the Place de l'Eglise.

Laure complained, "All the people in the world I want not to see will be there."

The place was still possible. Just about. But the professional liars had their eyes on it and soon it would be overrun by the media kids. Now it's mostly Germans and Swiss and Belgians searching the tables in the street for useless objects, old locks, bugles, biscuit tins, old helmets, stolen silver, junk.

A squeal, "*Fay-leeks!* Here's a brass box you can keep your condoms in!"

Another squeal of '*Prima!*' from Felix.

Laure said, " *Quelle horreur!*"

Pascale shrugged, *"Des Boches.* Quote: When I think of Beethoven, Bach, Goethe, and Wagner I can't hate the Germans."

Laure said, "Today, I can."

They sat outside the Café de France, half hidden behind the plane tree, and listened to the vapid conversations of the tourists.

- Let's sit here.
- Yes, do let's.
- In the sun?
- No. In the shade.
- But I like the sun.
- I prefer the shade.
- No, I like the sun.
- I like the shade.
- This looks all right.
- Yes, half in the sun.
- And half in the shade.
- The sun is very strong in Provence.
- Yes. The sun's strong.

Pascale said, "Stimulating, no?"

Laure said, "Live and let live, as the English say."

Pascale said, "That's not a very French concept."

Laure agrees. But she wishes she could look upon the human race with a less jaundiced eye. All she asks is to be allowed to wander alone through her inner world of books and pictures, diving into Stendhal and losing herself in Caravaggio. She's an unhappy island. No common touch. Afraid of human contact. Too much of that when she was young.

Frozen, waiting for the thaw. Yearning. It's coming.

Pascale sat up. She touched her arm.

"Look! That's class!"

A young girl with suntanned, polished thighs in well-cut khaki shorts. Long slender legs. American legs. Coltish. Golden hair cropped like a boy's, razor-cut and shaped to the head. An arrogant head, high cheekbones, regular features, clear, grey eyes. Man's white shirt. Showing the long neck, an oblique fringe hanging down over the forehead. Understated. Standing out because there was nothing garish or aggressive about her.

She strode across the Place like a general reviewing troops or a girl who had since birth been used to looking down on the groom from a high saddle on a thoroughbred hunter.

She was *free!*

Laure felt a pang of envy. Even she couldn't deny the truth of Pascale's admiring comments. A northern blonde but with style. *Pas moche.* She was glad Dermot wasn't there. He liked them with a pedigree.

"They're better over the sticks," he said. "Great jumpers."

He pretended he liked them young and boyish. Sex objects! Small-breasted, lithe. Firm flesh and golden pubic hairs, he said, jokingly, unfeelingly, but it fell flat. Laure is dark and well-endowed. It hurt.

The girl was followed by a distinguished man in drill slacks and a business shirt; with rimless glasses and the look of someone who, as Dermot might have said, keeps a weather eye on the leech of the mainsail on Long Island Sound. No, he'd be wrong. This one was too sensitive, slightly tortured. Lean and austere. Slim, hooked nose, cerebral type. Lawyer? Academic? Essayist? *Washington Post* journalist? No espadrilles but normal polished loafers. Plain steel watch and carrying the *New York Review.* Yes, American. Sensitive. He saw her looking at him. She was embarrassed. But suddenly bold. He held her gaze, interested, the signal. The girl dragged him away. He looked back once. Maybe she doesn't hate all the human race. Maybe not all men are brutes. What would it be like? Maybe—the pilot light was lit. When would the afterburner cut in?

They paid and left. Pascale went into the paper shop; Laure walked down the narrow street lined with stalls selling junk jewelry and suchlike. She stopped at a stand to look at some peasant outfits. They were surprisingly original, subtle and stylish. Castelbajac in l'Isle sur la Sorgue.

She was touching a skirt when a voice out of the distant past said "Laure!" and there was Clémence, her cousin, standing behind the clothes rack and with dawning recognition, blushing with awkward embarrassment. Instinctive clutching and kissing. Confused jabbering.

"It's you, Clémence!"

"Yes, it's Clémence, Laure."

Clémence, the wild one, eccentric, who had married an Englishman and, though no one in the family knew it, a Jew. English! And a Jew! A rich investment trust type, riding to hounds, stalking stags in Scotland, Sassooning all over the place, as Dermot put it. Clémence, who had worked in the French Embassy in London and saw her escape route. What now?

"What are you doing here? Why aren't you in England? Where's Jeremy?"

"In Hampshire, no doubt. With his horses."

"And the children? "

"Giles at Ampleforth, Camille at St. Mary's, Ascot. Catholic schools to let them learn about the enemy. Proper little English children. Abandoned by their wayward mother."

As Clémence talked, The Man came up and kissed her quickly on both cheeks. He turned to leave, but he looked hard at Laure and the girl standing behind was eyeing her coldly from the background. Her antenna had picked up his interest in Laure and there was a hint of possessiveness in her appraisal. It was the couple she saw outside the Café de France. Laure was too embarrassed to ask Clémence who he was but felt happy that she could establish that later.

"Now, what are you doing?" she asked Clémence.

"I've had enough, Laure. Quite enough. I'm divorcing."

"No!"

"Are you surprised?"

"No. I'm only surprised you could stick it out for so long. I mean, who could you talk to?"

"Oh, everyone. Provided it was about schools or horses or property or Prince Charles's desire to be a Tampax inside Camilla."

"But you liked it."

"Yes. Well, it was different. A different prison."

"I remember you saying you were going to marry a rich millionaire."

"Yes, well. Conservative balls, house parties in Scotland, Trevor Square. Money is the root of all boredom. Give me my little *cabanon* in France. Listen, Laure. You must come to Maman's funeral. On Tuesday. That's one of the reasons I came back now. She always asked about you. You were her favorite. She was so proud of your success."

"What success?"

"Survival, for a start. Defiance. Look, we have to talk. I tried calling you in Paris, and Maurepas. You *must* come to the funeral. It would make her so happy. And come to dinner tonight."

"Oh, Clémence. After all these years. I can't. I'm going back to Paris tomorrow."

"You must."

"No, I'm sorry, Clémence. I can't face that lot again."

"After all she did for you? She practically brought you up during the war. It's not asking much."

"Isn't it?"

"No, it isn't. After all, she was an exception."

"Yes, but she supported Uncle René against my mother. And she hid Grandfather."

"What would you have her do? All that's long ago. I hate them as much as you. Come to dinner and talk about it? I need you to be there, for moral support. And Maman would expect it of you. Do you remember that time in the wood?"

Yes, she remembered. She was a wartime refugee at her maternal grandmother's home of *La Fontanelle*.

She was seven. Chased, in panic, her legs like lead, the two louts from the village trying to take their revenge on the people in the château. Falling, torn, screaming. His thing, all red and purple. Her scratched thigh. His finger inside her. Her aunt coming on them like an avenging angel. Beating them with her stick. Her grandfather's anger, having them put away, the gap between peasants and the family widened even more. The nightmares. Aunt Marie sleeping with her, guarding her, teaching her. That did it. She was a child again. Back at La Fontanelle. Motherless, friendless, abandoned, for her own safety, they said, but it didn't matter. She'd rather be in Paris with her parents and her brother. Aunt Marie helped her through the long years. Aunt Marie, a war widow, selfless, converting her sadness into abundant care for her daughter, Clémence, four, who had never known a father, and her niece, Laure. The awful time when they took her to Avignon to go back to Paris and she threw herself on the rails because she didn't want now to leave Aunt Marie.

Yes, she owed her. And she remembered the other childhood shock when the gallant *résistants* came to take their revenge. Laure's recurring nightmare. She was still seven. The age of reason, it's supposed to be. The First Communion. The year between August 1944 and August 1945. An impressionable age. Certainly the impressions come back sharply. It was a year when she moved about from pillar to post. *Une saison en enfer*, as Rimbaud put it. It was a bad year for vipers and scorpions and other venomous creatures in Provence. The *épuration* at Montdidier-les-Murs.

She was sitting by the fountain playing with the cat when they came. She was still wearing the petticoat made from the American parachute that they picked up in St. Tropez when two Americans landed in her paternal grandmother's rose garden there. The sound of the truck. They pushed in through the gate at the end of the avenue of pines, carrying shotguns and a submachine gun. A sullen crowd and dangerous. The vengeful peasants of the Midi. Settling scores and claiming to dispense justice. Eliminating witnessess to their own behaviour. One was the tenant farmer who wouldn't pay the rent. Another the mad baker who worked with the Germans and was now filled with righteousness and a need to earn his place with the heroes of la Résistance. *They all got medals.* 'Ils se couchèrent Pétainistes et se réveillèrent Gaullistes'. *She ran inside. Her Great-Uncle Pierre, 'Pay,' met her as he emerged from the study. He handed her the book he was carrying and steered her gently into an armchair. He stood at the top of the steps and looked down scornfully. Then he looked away and surveyed for the last time the old bastide from which had been issued the five volumes of carefully crafted words on Greek civilization. He said "I am Pierre de Montriveau. I imagine you want my brother. He's not here. He's in Switzerland. Kindly leave.* Allez-vous-en! *he said. His tone did not please the so-called* résistants *who have now, like scorpions, crawled out from under the stones with a sting in their Stens. "You'll do," said the leader, and motioned him out. They prodded him with the guns, but they didn't look at him. They were guilty and embarrassed. He led them behind the house into the courtyard and she heard the bark of the shotguns and the chatter of the automatic weapon. She stumbled out and found him lying on his back on the gravel. She knelt and touched his hand. Blood had soaked his shirt but he still had a look of disdain on his face. Acceptance. Inevitability. Her Aunt Marie came and took her away, shielding her face from the torn flesh of her gentle great-uncle. She kept the book in her hand and it was bloodied when she fell down beside him. It was his own translation of Sophocles's* Ajax. *'The gods may judge me but not these men.' The executioners slunk away. The platanes moaned in the fresh mistral. The Dentelles de Montmirail bit into the clear sky of Provence and Mont Ventoux reared up, topped by white limestone and its gaunt crucifix silhouetted in agony on the barren ridge. Calvary, again.*

They met that evening at her cousin Clémence's little house near Vaugines. Sat outside in the balmy air, it saturated by the sweet scent of the broom growing on the hill behind, the landscape falling away over the valley of the Durance to the Trevaresse and beyond the outline of Sainte-Victoire, crouching in the distance, all planes and recessions of greys and blues, viewed through a misty filter. Clémence, nervous. Her daughter, Camille, over from London for the funeral of her grandmother, missing her boyfriend at Eton, sulky.

From inside the house came the sound of a lone cello. In the stilly night the Schubert *Sonata Arpegione*, then Brahms, then a rare piece, which made her wonder. Filling the night, speaking direct to her heart. The perfect touch. Unreal. The warm night air, the scent of the broom, the soft landscape, the purple sky, the music. The cello, played with certainty, deep and clear.

Laure wondered aloud, "Who?"

Her friend and collaborator, Pascale said, "I don't know."

The old retired ambassador, François, said, "A master."

She was about to go and investigate when Clémence came out pulling a man after her. André. The Man from l'Isle sur la Sorgue.

He smiled. She blushed. She was glad it was too dark to see.

Clémence said, "This is André. A friend of Georges. He's a painter. Be careful. He'll have you posing for the origin of the universe."

He held her hand for a long time. It tingled. She shivered.

He protested, "Don't listen to her. I'm no Courbet."

She said, "If that was you playing, thank you for the music."

He asked, "Did you recognize it?"

She said, "The Schubert and the Brahms, yes. I had trouble over the other piece. Eighteenth century. Could it be the *Caix d'Herveloix Suite*?"

"Bravo!"

"Where did you learn to play like that?"

"Oh, you know I always had big ideas. Jewish boys are expected to play the violin but it wasn't big enough for me."

"It's my favorite instrument."

"Oh, I hope not."

He smiled, "You are certainly the reason I came to dinner. I saw you in l'Isle sur la Sorgue. I know all about you. An intimidating person. All brain. A French *intello*. Emphasis always on the wrong end. Living your life with the head not the heart, in fiction, in pictures of fantasy. But you have great legs."

"For the *vieille de village*."

"The best soup comes from an old pot."

"*Merci!*"

But she laughed. She sat carelessly. Not provocatively. She wouldn't know how. She had poise but no artifice. She adjusted her dress.

"Don't move," he said, looking at her through a frame of his hands.

"Hey, wait a moment."

But he was mock serious, wagging his finger, warning.

"Why? There are not that many moments left. There will never be another tonight. There is only now. Now. And, by the way, I'm not impressed by intelligence. As Mister Aristotle said, there's nothing in the intelligence that didn't pass first through the senses."

Later. To the house at Le Tholonet, under the shadow of Montagne Sainte Victoire. Liberation.

Tuesday

7. Dermot's Revenge

IT HAD BEEN A polite nibbling sort of dinner and Dermot felt as out of place as an abortionist at an Irish convent. The elite of Morelia, Mexico, were putting on the mono-grammed feed bags and carefully avoiding any unseemly or interesting topics. They were at the Villa la Florída and, courtesy of Mouse, his location scout, who was an old friend of the owner from her days in Mexico City, he was at the host's table.

Morelia is the social Everest of Mexico. The hostess fluttered nervously, the guests muttered approvingly. The platitudes came tumbling down. It was all very refined. The food was almost too precious to eat. There were little minia-ture potatoes (or were they turnips?—he couldn't tell from the subtle flavor but judging by the color they had the blight and if there were any fewer there would have been a famine). Oh, he thought, these were very nice and very polite people. They were so nice and so polite, yes, and so dedicated to being attentive to Dermot, being a new face and underprivileged by virtue of the fact that he had to work for a living, that they went (painfully) out of their way to make the meat-and-potatoes rough diamond feel at home.

"Do you have food like this in Ireland," asked the lady on his right.

"Ah, no. Begod, pig's head and cabbage is all we get. And kalcannon on Sundays if the potatoes aren't rotten. And the pig isn't sold."

Mouse across the table roared again. Approved.

Her ladyship laughed condescendingly.

"But you speak French?" she asked.

"Not a word, milady."

From across the table, Mouse listening to this inter-change with some amusement, interjected.

"Don't you believe him. He's a cantankerous Celt but he's well-read in three languages. Been house-broken in the best houses of *la vieille France*. Married to a distinguished French lady from a distinguished family, *la vie de château*.

and all that. Monarchists, you'll be happy to learn, princesse. Slightly to the right of Gengis Khan.

"So why is he so *gauche*?"

"Ah, answer me that and we'll all be in your debt. His mood swings are most unpredictable. At the moment he's in his anti-French mode."

This one had said her name too was rather famous. They all had the *noble particule,* at least. It was '*madame la baronne*' this and '*monsieur le comte*' that. It was so rarified that when his call to France came through he jumped up quickly and shot out like a racehorse out of the gate, full of wonder at the banality of the rich.

Laure's voice cold and flat. "What do you want?"

"Just to hear your voice."

"Why don't you call Nana? I found a letter you wrote to her."

He went cold. Hesitated for a moment.

"What letter?"

"A letter you wrote after she had been here in November. In my bed. All about your lusting for her and lying in front of the fire and wanting to be with her all the time."

"That was a fiction. A total invention. I'm a short-story writer. It was never sent."

"Of course. And the nude photographs? This is not a fiction. I'm leaving you. You can stay in Paris until you go somewhere else. But I never want to see you again."

"Wait. I'm coming back."

"Don't. I've had enough."

And she put the phone down.

He went straight to the cottage in the garden and walked around in a state of shock. Emptied. The whole marriage thing had been uneasy but it was his sheet anchor. Stress every day but he had accepted the strain. Now the anchor was about to drag. The cable was ready to break.

Still, no wonder he chose locations as far away from France as possible.

Why Mexico? It was not his favorite country but Mouse, the location scout who knew everything and every-

46

body, knew a Spanish colonial town that offered the right backgrounds for the advertising shots. He hated the job. Corruption, pollution, violence, the *federales*. Foul food in Puerto Vallarta. Ripe sewage. Diarrhea. And cigarette ads that he was making to spread cancer for a German tobacco company.

He thought you'd have to be drunk all the time to support life in Mexico. He identified with Malcolm Lowry, the author of *Under The Volcano*, the autobiography of a drunk in Mexico, alienated from his wife and his own society and hell-bent on self-destruction. He was a satisfying creative role model.

Dermot thought, 'Like me, except I'm dry nowadays. You'd need a good supply of mescal to live here. The only foreign residents who could abide the place came from Toronto and Los Angeles. Well, he could understand that. He'd been in both places.'

No more! he said to himself as he walked around in his disconnected state. This is the end. Out of the business, out of the marriage, out of everything that went against his nature.

'I'm a writer,' he told himself. 'An artist. I don't have to act like an accountant.'

A hollow laugh sounded in his brain. The excuse was invalid.

The whole exercise had been a disaster. He should never have taken it on. Mexico came close to Pakistan and Ireland for the places he could stay away from without any sense of deprivation. He saw it as a vast shantytown, dusty and decrepid and populated by surly and unprepossessing natives. A jabbering of tourists, the men in Hawaiian shirts and their 'brides' in gaudy Bermudas. Brides of sixty yet. The Spanish death thing everywhere. Death in Ireland too hung over him like a permanent cloud. Would it never disperse?

1938. Late summer in south Kilkenny. Slievenamon, 'the mountain of women,' brooding there through a misty veil with purple folds. Slack water. A high tide. The River Suir up to the top watermark on the green wall of the quay. Under the bridge, a rowing-boat swinging to its painter through an iron ring set in the wall. Long eelgrass swaying under the surface, thick as a forest of cobras and full of menace. Dermot sits there in the sternsheets with an idle fishing rod over the transom. He's looking down at the red-haired girl, Mouse, who is lying on her back with her legs up over the thwart. He's mesmerized by the beauty mark high up on the inside of her thigh. His thoughts are sinful. He has a pubescent's urge. He looks away into the water. The tide starts to turn. Something catches his eye under the bank. Something white. It comes into view. A hand sticking out of a dark sleeve. The body floats free. He's frozen with fear. The corpse nudges the boat and comes to rest under the gunnel. He lifts his hand inboard. Mouse sees there's something wrong. She sits up and looks over the side. She screams. He jumps ashore and pulls her after him. He sends her away for help and she runs towards the village. He feels sick. It isn't real. At first he's afraid to look again. Then, almost defiantly, he goes back into the boat and takes an oar and pushes the dead mass back into the weeds and mud. He plants the oar in the mud to stop the thing floating free again. Finally, mustering all his courage, he reaches into the cold water and pulls the body half out onto the bank. It slides up easily. He's filled with dread. He recognizes the old Norfolk jacket. He pulls again and twists at the same time and although the body will not roll over completely the head flops across and the eyes stare at him with glassy sadness. He is still kneeling there in the mud holding the two lapels of the coat and looking at the unshaven face when they come from the village. The rough stubble will never again graze his cheek as his father plays the game with him. He will remember the shattered head where the bullet has emerged and the slack jaw and the agony. And the High Mass with himself as an altar boy and the whiskey priest and he will remember the words said as they carry the coffin away: Sure, didn't he ask for it, the West Briton?

So Dermot ran and he never stopped running, from Paris to Rangoon, from Melbourne to Morelia, until he ran right back where he started from, the prison of his own instability. And the rest of his life he looked for the things that had been taken away from him—his childhood, his security, a boat, a home that was not a prison. He ran away, always looking for duplicates, for substitutes, for distractions. On the way he ran into some people running, apparently, in the same direction, like Laure, but sooner or later their paths diverged and he was left alone, a solitary runner.

He didn't return to the dinner table in Morelia and they knew something was wrong so Mouse excused herself and went to his cottage. She stood in the doorway and looked at him. Silently. Appraisingly. Unsympathetically. Analyzing, deciding.

He sat on the bed, head down, now lost. He told her about Laure.

He said, "It's Laure. She's jumped ship. Or kicked me overboard. I'm alone, all alone. Orphan in the storm. Sunk."

Mouse quoted, "Courage, she said, and pointed towards the land."

"Not funny, Mouse. I'm alienated. Outside it all. I can't even look at the crew any longer."

"No, Dermot. That's clear. You hate the job. You hate the photographer. You hate the models. You hate the hotel. You hate Mexico. And you don't like yourself. No wonder Laure left you. You are now the Compleat Misanthrope."

"Yes, I find them all repellent."

"The strange thing is you actually like people at times. Even the French. The ones here are perfectly nice, polite and interested in you."

"At the moment I go mad when the people here talk to me. All the men have pokers up their arses. And when the crew ask me for direction I walk away. The job is sick. Sick. A new cigarette brand for chrissake!"

"How do you feel about Laure?"

"I don't know. She's fine. Special. I love her. But the marriage has been dead for ever. A virgin when I married her and she stayed a virgin. Locked up tight. Couldn't be touched. *Leave little Lolo alone!* Except at the beginning when I think she forced herself and before the death of Penelope. Very offputting. Then, with gritted teeth, dry and desolate. Afterwards, hysterics. *Leave little Lolo alone!* Acting as if it was dirty. Wouldn't see a shrink. Became almost suicidal at times. Wanted to but couldn't. Like a young hunter that couldn't take the fence. Went up to it and always shied away. Wanted escape and found a new prison."

"Did she have a puritanical mother? Ultra religious? Taught her that sex was unclean? For procreation only? Or was she abused when young?"

"Dunno. She refused to talk about it. Hated her mother. That woman was certainly religious. Went to Mass every morning. Her father was very withdrawn. Very well mannered but totally unemotional. No communication there. A nice man but cold. Last century ideas of paternal authority. Nothing, family, daughter, son, allowed to intrude on his moth-collecting passion."

Mouse said, "Classical. How awful for her. But you seem to get along together. Everyone thinks it's an ideal relationship. Not me. Chalk and cheese. The cultural gap is too wide. But I can't conceive of you splitting up. You must get along on some level. The vertical cerebral?"

"A state of suspended animation. An armed truce. No verbal contact most of the time. A constant anger. *"C'est ridicule!"*— that's all she can say whenever I suggest something. Antagonism. At times like that she's Laurence. I mean it. She calls herself that. A holy terror. Make a good camp guard. Laure, Lolo, Laurence, you never know which role she's playing."

Mouse lectured, "Same person, different personalities. Soon they'll try to prove they're different persons. Multiple personality disorder or some such drivel. We shrinks gotta make a buck. Merely different facets of the same personality. Protection as needed. Authority when we want to project it. We all do it to a greater or lesser extent. Little Lolo is like a hedgehog curling up inside itself and showing

50

spikes to the world of predators. That's you at times. She can be absolutely charming. I like her. She's inhabited."

"That's another role. In company, she switches on the compliments. Knows how to flatter. With a fine French veneer of good manners."

"Oh, cut it out! Think a little. Be kind. Defense mechanism, that role switching. Age regression as Lolo. Back to the child to deter unwanted attention. Don't touch me! Frustration leading to domination as Laurence, the expert. I know more than you! Charm, a need for admiration, for affection. Dissociative Identity Disorder, the book calls it. Crap. Elementary psychobabble, mate. Three faces, three fees. Whacko! Well, she's French. And you do have some pretty shaky habits and irrational ideas. No one could live with you."

"Yes, Doctor. French is what she is. Unless something's French it's no good. We're all idiots because we haven't been brought up the right way and we don't have their corrupt attitudes. Or their culture. Berlioz, Balzac and a lot of pretentious bollocks."

"The old joke. When God made the world and all the others complained about Him giving all the good things to France, the Alps, the Pyrénées, Burgundy, The Mediterranean, the Atlantic, etc., and He thought and said, 'You know, you're right.' And to compensate He made the French. Sure, they're different. Unboring. And you're being neither fair nor sincere. She has an enormous problem and you haven't helped her to overcome it."

"Maybe you should have married her, Mouse."

"I wouldn't mind. But I think she's completely hetero. Needs to be penetrated but can't do it. And you put it in elsewhere. No wonder they say your balls rule your brain. Still, I don't blame you. But you're hardly a pillar of support. Always away".

"Nothing to stay for, only strife. Fuck the French."

"That's today, boyo. Tomorrow they're the salt of the earth. Civilized. Yer man Cezanne. Matisse. Bonnard. Baudelaire. Verlaine. Flaubert. And Rimbaud. Your heroes."

Mouse continued, "She makes no concessions?"

"Seldom. Everything I say, she questions. Everything she does, I find to be done the wrong way. I get fed up with the constant put-downs. The Irish are all clodhoppers. I can't watch the international news because she's not interested in it. Only French politics and half the ministers and mayors in jail for corruption and presidents tapping telephones of likely mistresses and ordering the sinking of Greenpeace ships. Everyone does it, she says. My books are trash, better written by some French type years before. No such thing as celtic or anglo-saxon or Scandinavian art. Jack Yeats? Bah! Munch? Bah! All her friends, little ugly swarthy types, dishonest creeps from the Louvre. Condescending, with superior smiles. No backbones, any of them, but swollen heads."

"I always thought they were a fairly conceited race. And unscrupulous. But her put-downs are merely resentment. Hitting back. You failed her. What do you do that most irritates her?"

"Well, I admire the wrong women. If I comment favorably on a girl she sneers. My God, she says, you have terrible taste! *Elle est moche!* Especially if the girl's tall and blonde and Scandinavian or American. Not suffering from duck's disease like the French. Only the Latins have that special God-given superiority. That magic. That mystery. They have as much mystery as the peroxide in their blonde hair."

"Well, she's insecure. You shouldn't admire other women. It's not nice if Laure's repressed. These other things are rather trivial. Not the real reason for the clash. Intelligent people should be able to reach compromises."

"Not me, Mouse. I loathe that word. Like moderation. I want to break out. It's constant hard labor. Cultural incompatability, that's the problem. Sexual too."

"What about the Danish pastry? The Amazon I met?"

"Nana? She's Swedish. From Malmö. Married to a German. Alsen. Lives in Hamburg. Just has a house in Gilleleje, Denmark. Pretends to be Danish because it's more acceptable than Swedish or German."

"Nana. What a childish name. Nana, here's your banana! I'll bet she eats it, too. What on earth do you see in her? Just sex?"

"Christ, Mouse, I need to relax at times. Get out of the conflict. Nana's full of sin but she's untamed and I like that. The exact opposite of Laure. Open. Fun, too. A gypsy like me. Another walking wounded. Vulnerable. And a walking invitation to every man in the place. Need to be wanted by everyone. I can't stand her mood swings for more than a week at a time, but for that week it's a narcotic. No cultural one-upmanship. Even though I know she sleeps with others apart from her husband and I mind like hell. I even think I've slept with Nana immediately after she's been with someone else. In many ways she's an innocent child. Not responsible for her actions. Treated as an object, a beautiful object since her early teens. Always on display. A status symbol for rich old men."

"And you're not even seriously rich! Why does she go with you?"

"She says she loves me. She does, at the time. But it rolls easily off the tongue. Love is a very transient emotion with her. The duration of it is measured in millions. Pounds, dollars or D-marks. I'm a distraction. She's bored with her husband. Her third. He's filthy rich but mean. Watches TV, travels economy even though he owns two hundred buildings in Hamburg. Nana is addicted to luxury. With me she travels first. But I'm not strong enough to take her. Nor rich enough. I'm a diversion. But then life is a diversion."

"Kafka said it first, Dermot. You resent Laure because she has a different culture."

"And she's locked up tighter than the vault of the Bank of England."

"Ego and ownership, laddie, apart from passion deprivation. I think Nana's your antidote at the moment. Physical release. Get the dirty water off your chest. Your whore. The town pump of Copenhagen. You don't owe her anything. Run wild. Remember the old navy rule: when in doubt, panic. Go and get a fix. Think through your cock again. It's infantile but. Forget the job. I've got your list of final shots

53

needed. We'll get them done. I'll leave a message on your answering machine in Paris when we pack up. Take the transparencies to the studio in Zurich. They have your scribbles. The client won't expect to see anything for two weeks at least."

"I don't know where to go, Mouse. No base any longer."

"Where's Nana? Jaysus, that name. She should be in a kindergarden."

"In Denmark for the summer."

"To Denmark you go. Then, isn't it about time you stopped jumping around like a blue-arsed fly and went back to Ireland? Stay there for a while. Talk. Walk the highways and byways. Find yourself. The house at Piltown is available. Eileen O'Connor will look after you. I'll go back there on my way to Switzerland. Get the place ready."

"That's not a bad idea. Maybe I'm ready for it. Face the demons."

Dermot hadn't been back to Ireland since he made a fast visit just after the war to sort out a legal problem connected with the sale of the house and tenancy of the farm. That time acting on impulse decided to call on old Paddy Harrington. He would fill in the gaps in Dermot's knowledge about his father. He got more than he bargained for. He fled, determined never to return.

Sitting in the Harrington farmhouse, watching the flames and listening to the old man, who must have been seventy-three. Paddy's father bought the farm when the estate was forcibly broken up in 1923, or maybe 1924. The Bessborough Hunt used to meet up the road, outside the main gates of Bessborough House.

Paddy said, "It must have been May, 1918, when Michael—your father, came back. I remember the lilac was in bloom and thinking of Rupert Brooke's poem. I nearly recited it but one look at him finished that. I went to Fiddown Station to get him in the pony and trap. He limped along the platform dragging an old Gladstone-bag. I wouldn't have recognised him if I met him in Sackville

Street. He was different in all sorts of ways. Diminished. Shrunk. And he wouldn't talk. He just hauled himself into the trap and sat there huddled in the corner. Like a wounded dog, I thought to myself."

Dermot protested, "But he was wounded."

"Oh, he was indeed. Two bullets on the Somme in '16 and a bayonet in the thigh somewhere else. Scratches to him. I'd picked him up after he broke his collarbone at a point to point and it looked as if he'd lost one eye, and when he came to he said, 'I'll be alright now Paddy: one eye and one arsehole.' No, it was the gas that did it. That was at Passchendaele. That's what finished him. A miserable thing. Shrivelled his lungs and destroyed him altogether. They gave him a one-hundred percent disability pension and when they do that they expect you to have the decency to die before you draw it too long. But still.

"There was something else.

"We went slowly up the Long Walk, t'was a grand day, with the big beeches murmuring, and the rhododendron bushes coming in from either side, and the smell of decomposing leaves and mossy dampness, and the scent of the lilac, and always the steaming horse manure.

"It must have been better than the smell of rotting corpses and I thought he'd brighten up because he used to love a gallop down there. Nothing would bring him out of his shell. When we came out of the wood and the house was there on top of the rise I pulled up. Not a peep out of him. He hardly raised his eyes.

"He was bent up, all six-foot-four of him, under the front of the trap, you'd think it was a parapet, shrunken into himself with misery, staring ahead unaffected by the old house. You had the feeling that he didn't much want to approach it."

Dermot insisted, "Well, he didn't much like the place, you know. He was always saying Ireland was a kind of Purgatory through which poor Irishmen passed before escaping to England or America."

"Is that a fact? Is that all you heard him say? 'This village,' he would tell you, 'Piltown, do you know what it *means in Irish? A hole. Draw your own conclusions. Apt, it is. We're living in a hole.' Then he'd take off on one of his flights of rhetoric. 'What comes out of the hole? Bubbling out of it is misery. And guilt. We're all flawed by the misery and the guilt that boils up out of the hole. It's pure and undiluted. One hundred proof misery. And the watershed never sinks much below the surface. Always in good supply. It's the spring of Failure. Not the water of life; the reverse. Drink it before the age of three, as the priests say, and I give you a failure for life.' Another of his favorites was the Upas Tree. 'Ireland,' he would declaim, 'is the Upas Tree of Europe. You know (turning to all the ignorant yahoos around) the Upas Tree is a Javanese tree so poisonous as to destroy all life for many miles around'.*

"Or, 'The land in the valley?' he'd ask, 'Tis like glue. It sticks to your feet and you can't shake it off no matter whether you go to Paris or San Francisco. Oh, you may think you've shaken it off but back it comes at different times through your life. It's like elastic. It lets you go for a certain time or distance but then, Wham! it snatches you back from whichever heaven you've found. The Land of Saints and Scholars? The Land of Blackguards and Robbers.' Yes, he was a Jesuit in reverse. Always preaching doom about the valley and the village."

"But you expected him to jump for joy when you took him home, Paddy."

"I despair of you. You've been too long in America where they never look under the surface. You know he was a sailing man. There's the real wind direction and the apparent wind direction. The apparent is what you see by the direction of the burgee at the masthead. But that's influenced by the speed and direction of the vessel and it's not true. He was like that. Apparently he hated the place. In fact, he loved it.

"And that day it was at its best. A clear, fresh day with pale sunshine and a few harmless clouds. Slievenamon reared up with its peak in the sun and the shadows passing across the purple folds in it. It's like the Montagne Sainte Victoire at Aix. Always there, always different, always friendly."

Dermot smiled, "A pity we're not a visual race. We need a Cézanne. Jack Yeats didn't capture it the right way."

"Yes, lad, you're right, if a trifle over-sophisticated."

Paddy went on, "And the Waterford hills, all covered in trees, soft and blue. And the Suir rippling slowly through the valley. The demesne of Bessborough. And over there Curraghmore. He knew it all like the back of his hand. The best land in Ireland. Hadn't he hunted over all of it? And fished every hole in the river? And, to hear them tell it, poked every girl behind every wall in the county. You couldn't drag him away if you tried. I slowed the horse to a walk going up the Long Walk because I had seen him, many's the time, tired and happy, walking The Conqueror, that great stallion with the provocative name, back from a meet.

"And I've watched him, unbeknownst to him, looking at the house and the trees and the round pond with the waterlilies, and seen him tearing around with his sheepdog, Sailor, who wouldn't leave him for a minute. You wouldn't believe it, being a rational man, but I've seen that bitch looking up at him and crying, when he came back, with the tears running out of her eyes.

"It was in his blood and every time he went away he was pining to come back. Like the rest of us. Maybe you left too early. You wouldn't understand. But whatever he said about Ireland or Piltown or the house, what he was really saying was 'tis a curse that's a blessing and the soil of it goes up through your feet and once it's in you you never lose it. All these facile comments by our national geniuses like Shaw and Joyce and O'Casey are all very well. 'It's the sow that eats its own farrow.' Yes, it is. But that's not the half of it.

"You never got on with him. Of course you didn't. He wasn't an easy man to get on with at the best of times. And after the war he was frozen inside himself. He didn't have anything to give you except how to ride and how to fish and how to read. He gave you that. And the genes. It's a pity you never bothered to know him. If you had, you'd know his life was blighted by what happened in Flanders."

Dermot insisted, "What happened is what I'm trying to find out. A lot of people went through the same thing and came out of the black tunnel at the end. Even the ones who were crippled for life. And he did recover, more or less."

"You're a hard man. Like him, unforgiving. He wasn't sorry for himself at all. He didn't want your sympathy. He just wanted to be left alone in his—sadness? melancholy? anguish? loneliness? I don't know."

"But you do know more than you're telling, Paddy."

"Yes. Perhaps, Dermot."

"Well?"

"Go back a bit. He grew up with the Yuill boys, Bertie and Vere, Lord Duncannon, and their sisters, Lady Irene Congreve and Lady Gweneth Yuill. He was almost an adopted son of the Earl and Countess of Bessborough. Your maternal grandfather, after all, was his Agent, after he lost most of his property. Mike stayed with them in London, when he was at Stonyhurst, and that gave him an English slant on things too.

He hunted with them. He raced point-to-point against them and the Beresfords at Curraghmore. His best friend before the war was Norman Leslie who practically lived at the Big House. He spent weeks of his holidays with the Greers at the National Stud. He joined the 12th Lancers and went to France when most of them went with the Irish Guards. Look at what happened.

Eric Greer, twenty five, a colonel commanding a Battalion of the Irish Guards, and his brother, both killed in 1917, the same battle as your father got his gassing. Norman Leslie killed at Mons in 1914. Lord De Freyne and his brother George both killed the same day in 1915, and buried in the same grave. Dermot Browne, Robert Gregory of Coole, Basil Blackburn, John Hamilton and Eddie Stafford-Harman, killed the same day. Peter Connellan, at Armentières in '14. James Brooke, Maurice Dease. All his friends."

Paddy paused.

"And Archie Yuill, the next in line in the Yuill baronetcy.

58

Who would inherit the earth. The sun around which the entire Kilkenny hunting universe revolved. Loved by everybody. A natural leader.

Your father came back to an empty world. A wreck of a man and probably thinking he had no right to be back."

He stood up and started to walk around the room, picking up books and pictures and putting them back down again, obviously agitated. He relit his pipe and finally seemed to make a decision. He sat down and looked at me as if deciding whether to go on or not.

"You can't stop now," Dermot challened him.

"We'll see. Let me come at it in my own way again. What I'm saying—all right, all right, I'm repeating myself— is he was not the holy terror that went off in 1914, that's a fact. Everybody remembered him as harum scarum. And fun. And outgoing. And here's this bundle of misery casting a curtain of gloom on everthing. And it wasn't the wounds."

"What was it, Paddy?"

"Now hold your horses. I'm trying to give you the picture and put it in proper focus for myself as well. Ease off."

"Sorry."

"Not at all. Patience isn't one of your family's trademarks. But I have to get it right."

They were sitting by the fireplace of the farmhouse at The Paddock. It used to be the Home Farm. It was familiar. Dermot expected Mrs. Harrington to come in with a big round of home-made bread.The kitchen was modern now but the great fireplace remained. Paddy Harrington was born there. He too grew up with Dermot's father and his aunts. But he had to work on the farm and he was lucky to get a scholarship to St. Kieran's College in Kilkenny and afterwards he went to Maynooth. But there was something out of gear with him and his confessor decided that the lusts of the flesh were too much for him. Instead of taking the cloth he wound up a classics master at Blackrock with the Jesuits.

Something happened over a boy and he became a literary editor of the Irish Times, writing poetry and hitting *the bottle. He still was writing the odd script for Irish radio. His own sister, Edith, had been the best horsewoman in the county, and rode at every Meet.*

Paddy took up where he left off. "Listen, you left here when you were ten, I think. Didn't I take you to Fiddown myself? So you should know the background a bit. Nothing was clear in Ireland in 1918. All I'm saying is he was a changed man and it wasn't the wounds that did it. There was a deeper wound."

Dermot complained, "But the gas didn't do him much good. After all, he got a one-hundred percent disability pension. He must have been nearly dead. And they gave him a medal."

"Ah, you're right, of course. He was a wreck physically, with his lungs shrivelled up by that mustard gas, burning him all the time, and coughing and wheezing like the Rosslare Express. I'm not saying he wasn't affected by it. Of course he was.

"The medal? Yes, he got an MC on the Somme. Military Cross. He wouldn't talk about it. Except once. He was ashamed of it. When he was well gone one night and someone kept at him about it, he put his drink down and pounded the table and he looked at the man and he said, "They handed them out with the rations. So many per unit. MCs for most people and DSOs, Distinguished Service Orders, for a few. The higher the rank, the more decorations. The more men you killed, the higher the honor. Look at Butcher Gough over there in Tipperary. General Sir Hubert Gough, KCB, Knight Commander of the Bath, MC, DSO and two bars. Sent back in disgrace from Ypres. He didn't kill enough of our chaps that time.

"And don't forget all our other Ascendancy heroes. We supply the generals. Field Marshal Sir John French, our new Viceroy, he killed enough of us until they pulled him out as a Commander in Chief who despite his own name couldn't even talk to the French. They covered him with medals and orders and gave him fifty thousand pounds to put in his hip pocket and the thanks of a grateful King for making such a cock-up of it. Sir Henry Wilson, Sir Stanley

Maude, well, he was at Gallipoli, Sir Bryan Mahon, and all the others who are now back on their Irish estates. For a while.

"Here's how it happened, once and for all. I was cowering in a trench until the barrage ended. I was shit scared. Our own barrage, supposed to creep up in front of us. Expect six percent casualties from our guns, General Rawlinson said. I'd moved a platoon into the middle of no-man's land to have a head start when the balloon went up. I was bloody sure no one would make it to the German front line from our own. We had eight fifteen-inch naval guns for a front of twenty eight miles. You'd think they'd find a target away from me.

"One landed too close and blew in the trench. I dug myself out of it through the mud and was lucky enough to find a hole and a body to stand on. His guts came out when I put my weight on his back. I cursed him. I climbed out and straightened up, to see if I could.

"I was stunned. I was covered in mud. When I stood up, not thinking, I was in a daze, and suddenly there were these seven jerries, right in front of me. I still had my revolver in my hand and I was just thinking to throw it down, I was so tired, when they put up their hands and shouted 'Kamarad'. They thought I was the Angel of Mons rising from the earth, with a full regiment about to surface around them.

"And I just had the wit to drive them back. You have to understand something. They weren't all dedicated killers. They were a Bavarian Reserve Regiment. They'd had a million shells thrown at them in the past few hours.

"The bloody things didn't go off, a third of them, and they didn't cut the wire the way they were supposed to for General Rawlinson. 'Don't worry, chaps,' says he, 'There'll be no Germans around when you walk into their positions.'

"That's all there was to it. Seven jerries equals one Military Cross for your hero. A split second later and they'd have had me in the bag. The Second in Command, shitting himself and leading from the rear, got a bar to his DSO, and Haig got a count of seven Bavarian pioneers to offset against fifty seven thousand front line troops he threw away that day.

"For days we were collecting the wounded from mud, sliding them back on ground-sheets. Some of them drowned when we left them lying in trenches waiting for orderlies to take them back. And the jerries let us collect them from no-man's land, and helped us. I tell you, there were no willing heroes. Except the dead. Now that's the last time I want to hear about it. It doesn't matter a fuck who won the war. It could have been stopped in '16. But the glory boys wanted a victory. Four hundred thousand British corpses on the Somme and another four hundred thousand at Passchendaele for nothing. Everything else is a lie."

Dermot said, quietly, *"I suppose it was quite a speech at the time. Not too well known then but it's all old hat now."*

"Yes, everyone knows everything except what it's like. The price of everything and the value of nothing."

Dermot asked, *"Did he say anything else about the war? I only remember finding his medals one day and playing with them before my mother took them away. Mons Star and two or three others."*

"Not much but what he did was explosive, too, to coin a phrase. But I would ask you to remember that he was going through another hell. His hair all fell out. It came back later. I'm wondering if it wasn't an effect like chemotherapy, the poison might be the same base. He couldn't sleep at night. He'd walk the roads and the woods. He told me one day the scream of the vixen was the most frightening thing he'd ever heard, worse than the screams from the wounded on the barbed wire. He stayed well away from everyone. Like a bear with a sore ear. He took to the bottle and he sat in the corner of Anthony's bar not talking to anyone."

"What snapped him out of it, Paddy?"

"Arrah, yer a great fella for simple answers to complex questions. You're not at all Irish. Sure, we like to take our time and talk around it. You know the old one about how do you get to Waterford and the answer that you can't start from here; you have to go to Carrick-on-Suir first, but sure the road's grand. That's the way we are. I thought you said you were a wordsmith? Ease off a bit and I'll be after telling you."

He was playing the stage Irishman. Obviously, he wanted time to phrase it delicately. For a man who had taken all the prizes in Greek and Latin at Maynooth, he was laying it on with a trowel. Dermot stood up and poured himself another cup of the black tea.

"Take your time, Paddy," he said. "I don't have to be back in London till Wednesday."

"A party at Mount Juliet, that's what broke the spell. That and a little incident at Knocktopher when the I.R.A., nearly shot him. There was what you'd call a big fallout from it, and you're part of it yourself.

"The first meet of the Bessborough Hounds was on Boxing Day 1919, just before the so-called war of independence. Everyone who was left alive was out. There were a lot of gaps in the ranks. It was quite an event. Fasten your seatbelt and put on your earphones and watch the big screen. Don't blame me if you don't like the scenario. I'm thinking of it as a script for Irish Television, so I'll tell it that way. It's a reconstruction of events as I heard them from the lady in question and a few others who were at the party. Brendan MacMahon and Gerry Redmond saw most of the action.

Let us fade in on the crossroads at the Main Gates of Bessborough House. Horses held by grooms are prancing about, snorting steam in the cold weather. Huntsmen in pink are standing around drinking their 'stirrup cups.' Some are mounted. There are quite a few locals watching the scene. They would follow the hunt on foot as far as possible.

There's the sound of hounds braying, hooves stamping, shouts of grooms, and a sudden cheer.

Let us jump on the title: The Young Master is Missing.

Then we cut to a Rolls Royce that has just arrived. The chauffeur opens the door and out steps Lady McConnell, Letecia, known to intimates as 'Lally,' of Mount Juliet.

She is a woman of about thirty, immensely tall; golden-haired, statuesque, and commanding would describe her. A crowd gathers around her and her laugh can be heard above the other sounds of the meet. The chauffeur then opens the boot and we see that it is a well-stocked bar. The Master and other officials and friends join her in drinking. The grooms are invited to participate.

A big chestnut is led up to her and she is given a leg up to sit sidesaddle. Her glass is handed up to her and she toasts the assembled crowd. In her black, divided, full-length riding habit, bowler hat, and white silk cravat, a tall figure on a tall mount, with her head thrown back in laughter, she is a presence. A devil-may-care.

Now let us cut to a long shot of a rider approaching down the Long Walk . . . it is Mike McManus. He is walking his horse slowly, timing his arrival for the departure of the hunt. Lady Lally sees him and gallops off to meet him. She turns her horse to join him and leans across to kiss him exuberantly.

Let's hear the sound of a hunter's horn.

She slaps his horse on the rump and takes off, leading the field at a lively pace.

Now, here we see two horses grazing by a style. Two riders are sitting side by side on it. They are Lady McConnell and your father, Mike.

L.M: Welcome back, Mike. I missed you.

M.M: You didn't miss much.

L.M: Still feeling sorry for yourself. Stop it. Bill's due back this week with one leg and half his face burned off. He'll never ride again. And here's you still spluttering a bit but otherwise sound in wind and limb. I hope. When are you going to prove it to me? Tonight? We'll have our first post-war thrash.

M.M: I'm not up to it, Lally.

L.M: If you don't use it you lose it. I'll expect you this evening.

She leans over and grabs an intimate part of his anatomy. Next we see a rollicking dinner party, everyone merry and not quite sober. Lady McConnell stands to propose a toast.

L.M: We have an old friend back. I'd like to propose a toast of welcome to Mike and his to his rapid recovery. Especially that.

Much laughter and a chorus of—To Mike! Speech, speech!

Lady McConnell dashes down the table and hoists him to his feet because he is obviously on the point of bolting. All escape routes are blocked.

M.M: Bad cess to ye all. Can't you leave a man in peace? But thanks. We have a smaller table than before and a lot of absent guests. If you'll allow me to I'd like to propose a toast to them. To Maurice, and Richard, and Basil, and—he stops almost unable to continue—Norman and Dermot and Peter and Eddie and all the other absent friends.

A voice at the end of the table said: You forgot the Young Master, Archie, Mike.

MM paused and then said, quietly: No, I didn't. Not by a long chalk.

After another long pause, ambiguously: Not for a moment.

He sits. There is an embarrassed silence before the table becomes animated again.

Now let us cut to the bedroom. It's morning. We see Lally and Mike, in a state of undress, lying on the bed. There's the remains of breakfast on a tray. She is stroking a long scar on the inside of his thigh.

L.M: Another few inches and you'd be a gelding.

M.M: I'm beginning to think that would have been a pity.

She looks closely at the wound scar and then bends.

Now let us return to the respectable drawing room. They are both properly dressed

L.M: What was all that about Archie last night? Everyone was shocked. We thought he was one of your best friends. Same regiment and everything. Together on the Somme, weren't you? Were you near him when he was killed?

M.M: I shot him.

So, let us freeze on the horrified face of Lady McConnell.

And so, son of Mike, we fade out.

Dermot said, "Whew!"

Paddy asked, sarcastically, "Well, will you give me a job writing film scripts? Or are they not dramatic enough for you?"

He stood and staggered a bit as he went to the table and poured another stiff drink.

"Too dramatic, Paddy. Unbelievable. To be honest I find it all a little corny and, if you'll forgive me, sentimental. Slushy."

"Maybe so, but I think it's the gospel truth. I told you you might not like the scenario."

"How do know it's the gospel truth? Man murders baronet in front line trench, sounds slightly imaginative to me."

"Not murders, Dermot. Executes. This is a semantic point which exercises us a lot in Holy Ireland these days and evermore."

"Elucidate, Professor."

That's what Paddy told Dermot. The narrative was his father killed Archie Yuill to save him from the ignominy of a court martial and being shot by a firing squad as a coward. He did it to save the family. But he couldn't live with it afterwards. And he was cast out of the group.

Suddenly, Dermot remembered. He went cold. His voice cracked as he talked.

"Yes, it was a nice try, Paddy. But there's another possible scenario. He was ordered out of the dugout. He was in a funk. He refused to go. Yuill threatened him with a court martial. He shot Yuill. Then, in a panic, he climbed out of the dugout and confronted the Bavarians. They surrendered. He took them back. He got an M.C. He said Yuill had been killed charging the Hun front line trench. Yuill was awarded the D.S.O., posthumously. Everyone came out smelling of roses. He was a coward and a murderer.

Paddy was upset. He looked at the floor.
"Where did you get that idea?"
"I remember when he was rolling drunk one day. He
kept repeating, 'He wanted to have me court-martialled.'
I asked—Who?
He said—Archie. He wanted me court-martialled. I had
to do it."

The summing-up for Dermot had to be about delusion.
Misplaced loyalty to the British. Growing up dependent
upon them for crumbs thrown from the rich man's table.
Allowed to mix with them, through the servants' entrance
now, even if it wasn't always obvious, and liable to have the
door slammed in your face. Then to be finished as a man by
the war in France, in the British army, to which he as an
Irishman owed no allegiance and for which war his country
had no blame and no responsibility. To be cast adrift, an
alien to his own people because of his misguided belief in
the decency of the occupier. His awe of the gentry. His
loyalty to the Lord and the siblings.

He paid for that. So did Dermot.

Dermot, hating everything about Ireland, resolved never
to return. His father got one thing right. That place was a
sort of Purgatory where poor Irishmen suffered before
escaping to England or America. Or France? Well, in this
contest for nightmares, so far: France 2, Ireland 2.

Mouse checked the airline schedules and saw there was
a flight out of Morelia to Mexico City early the next day,
and a connection to Frankfurt and on to Copenhagen. Good
old Mouse. She kept her cool, her *sang-froid*. No bitching.
Fuck the consequences.

He turned in. Tossed about restlessly. Guilty as hell this
time about quitting in the middle of the job. Leaving her to
hold the baby. Again. Mouse. His one ally, his wailing wall.

Apart from being his first cousin Mouse Grover was,
perhaps, his only true friend. The tower of strength in times
of stress. She was his senior by two years, a little creaky in
the joints but still active. She was efficient, spoke the lingo

67

and could arrange things. She was a qualified psychologist and could handle obstreperous models. She was a cushion between him and the crew. Dermot was there as an artistic director. They were shooting test pictures.

He was a poet by choice, but he said it came easier when he wasn't hungry. So he was for hire as a creative consultant, an expert in new product development. He was expected to turn shit into gold for commercial exploitation. He was at the end of that line too. Commercial suicide loomed high. He had done something which was truly deplorable.

He had agreed to work on the development of a new cigarette brand. The worst of it was the client thought he was a genius. Praise that was like a knife cut. Eternal shame. A million dollars development fee to create a new brand 'for young blue-collar workers of low self-esteem' With a dishonest gimmick. And the knowledge that it would appeal to kids. Still, it would fail. He knew that. If they made a cigarette that would cure cancer they'd get the promise wrong.

Now, in Mexico, at the end of his tether. The whole project had been a washout and it was his fault entirely. It was a location job on which everything had gone wrong, including the locations. Big Manolo refused to release the equipment at Customs in Puerto Vallarta until Mouse fixed it with the proper backsheesh. Three days wasted and already over budget by sixty thousand dollars. The models, with one exception, were a bunch of old scrubbers that they picked up in Los Angeles; the photographer, an old friend, was a cut above his station. He could read and write and was not terribly interested in taking pictures. His cameras broke with no possibility of repairing them. Aeroplanes had to be chartered to cart them around and although the insurance called for twin-engined machines they had to scrape over the Sierra Madre in a single-engined Cessna with six up and a load of equipment, climbing over the mountain like a pregnant prawn, as Dermot said.

When things go wrong on a location job the problems multiply until every solution leads to an even greater catastrophe. You are trapped in the vortex as the pictures become totally irrelevant and the costs spiral out of control. Even the weather, which was his excuse for going halfway round the world for shots you could have got in the next county, turned sour.

All he wanted was to be back in his wooden yawl, with no inane conversation and the creaking of the timbers and the slap of the water against the hull and a few ecstatic moans of Nana from the transom berth. By the end of the last supper he was walking around with a look of misery and anger on his face.

Mouse kept him in line, more or less. She was a stern taskmaster. Now that the crisis was upon him and Laure had left him he would bail out and let the chips fall where they may. To mix the metaphor properly he had every intention of picking up his marbles and leaving the commercial game.

Somehow the night passed. He took himself in hand and thought of Nana's beauty spot and went over the Pole to Skagen.

His last view of Morelia the next morning was the hideous zoo. The taxi went close to the wire mesh fence. Behind the fence stood the disconsolate wolves. One, standing apart, looked at him with hopeless eyes. He felt inexpressably sad. He wanted to stop the car and release him. The wolf represented all that was noble and free. His loathing for their keepers encompassed the whole population of Mexico.

8. The Mouse that Roars

MOUSE. HER FATHER, Colonel Grover, DSO, retired from the King's Own Shropshire Light Infantry, farming near Church Stretton, bought the McManus family house near Piltown, County Kilkenny, Ireland, leaving Dermot with the freehold of the farm which he let to Mouse for a peppercorn rent.

Mouse, now slight and stooped, hacking cough from chain-smoking cigarillos. The sort of huntin,' shootin' and fishin' woman you'd find manning a one-pump petrol station in the middle of Tierra del Fuego or in Ladakh. (She had, of course, driven a Jeep from Panama down to the tip of Tierra del Fuego. Hadn't everyone?) Loved by everyone in County Kilkenny, despite her known sexual orientation.

Your man Mouse has a good seat in the saddle, they said.

At the beginning of the war, she joined the ATS—the womens' army. They soon commissioned her and put her into the 'dirty tricks department,' inventing infernal devices like lethal catapults, variants on the famous 'cheese-cutter' and ingenious booby-trap devices. At the war office she met a Wren, and got her compass swung and discovered the considerable deviation.

After the war she went to the Tavistock Institute and got a grounding in psychology. She joined Unilever and soon found that she wasn't put on earth to delve into housewife motivations concerning low suds in washing powders and sexual perceptions in the squeezing of washing-up liquid containers. 'Reversion to the breast' syndrome for ice-cream finished her. She left and through war-time connections joined the library service of the British Council. That's where Dermot found her, in Athens.

Mouse, the lacrosse-playing convent schoolgirl, Captain of Games, unconventional, eccentric, champion of Dermot since they were children together. She was in and out of his life with long gaps between meetings.

In 1955 Mouse was chafing at the bit in the UKIS. A poncey outfit led by a pompous ass. Dermot lost touch with her except for the annual Christmas card. He invited her to the wedding in Paris in 1957 and she came. She kept up a sporadic correspondence with Laure. They liked each other. She was godmother to Penelope, their daughter. He met her again at an opera in Batignano, near Grosseto, in Italy. Her ex-Wren friend, Gwendoline, another eccentric, had a house at Campagnatico, the next hill village. Dermot had allowed himself to be inveigled into an evening of too-experimental opera in an old convent. It was enlivened by the soprano falling out of an olive tree. He heard Mouse roar. It was the high point of the evening. He used to keep a boat in the old harbor in Porto Ercole before they built a boat park full of plastic called a marina and he'd drive up and stay with Mouse and they'd talk books and pictures and eat good pasta. He took the yawl back to Scandinavia where they still raise the ensigns at the sunup gun and lower them at sundown, instead of leaving tattered old rags of convenience hanging over the arse-ends all year.

When Dermot left the international agency and set up as a consultant in Lausanne, he needed someone to keep the business on the rails. Someone trustworthy. 'Keep the secrets in the family,' the old Italian safeguard against the tax inspectors. Mouse was happy to take control. Untaxed Swiss francs went a long way in Ireland. She went back to the house three or four times a year. Kept inviting Dermot and Laure but they never accepted. Dermot said he was afraid to face the ghosts. Laure thought Ireland too sad. Mouse became Dermot's Administrator, Accountant, Location Scout, Stylist, Foredeck Crew, and Nanny. She was indispensable.

And Mouse Grover adores donkeys. She likes looking at them better than at people. Limpid eyes, resigned, and no foibles. She finds them more sympathetic than the mercantile morons she's forced to deal with on Dermot's behalf. Or the so-called intellectuals. The asses know, she says, that nothing ever happens. She collects strays in her meadow down by the river Suir in the County Kilkenny in Ireland. They're in clover. Mouse is the best man on Dermot's team. Pillar of strength. His cousin, the only one in the family he's close to. Since childhood. His manager. His apologist. Shrink. She's an original. Is beyond disappointment because she has no great expectations. Fatalist. Smokes cigars, is at home in fatigues and wellingtons. Slouch hat. Copper hair, ploughed-field face. High cheekbones and the stance of a thoroughbred. Slightly lopsided from falls from horses and nights in wet cockpits during Fastnet Races.

ye belies will of steel. No studied eccentricity. edate, tranquil, like her donkeys, but Semtex on fuse at times. Like Dermot, all his life. ring some of his more memorable rebellions.

The Confession Book. The Jesuit, Father Aloysius, SJ. Dermot's cousin. His father's age but his first cousin. The Science Master at Stonyhurst. To which seat of learning Dermot was scheduled to go. A miserable, mean-minded character, cadaverous, with a smell of carbolic and sanctity and a dew-drop at the end of his poky nose. Hairs in the nose and the ears. A permanent five o'clock shadow. A Zurbaran Inquisitor. He was a brilliant young scientist at Cambridge but got a vocation and became a Jesuit at thirty-five. Came to stay twice a year. Dermot made to serve at Mass for him. Go on, keep the peace, son, says his father. Hits the bell a good wallop at the right times. Knocks it off the step. A glare. Slips a marble under the priest's foot as he comes down the steps with the wafers. He falls flat on his face just inside the marble wall and the chalice is thrown into the congregation, wafers all over the place. Drains the dregs of the altar wine as he hangs up his surplice. Made to say the Stations of the Cross. His father not a practicing Catholic except when Aloysius or Dermot's aunts are about. His mother a Protestant. Converted to get married according to the rites of the Roman church. Laughed at it. The parish priest, the whiskey Father Tobin, coming round to demand, demand mind you, why she doesn't go to Mass every Sunday. His father ejecting him with a boot up the arse. Not helpful to Dermot in the village. With the village schoolmaster, Tiger Twist, ex-IRA, taking it out on Dermot for his father's British military service and his mother's Protestantism. The Confession Book, kept in the lavatory. Referred to as 'The Chapel' and next to the pantry door. This a long, narrow room, tongue-and-groove panelled and painted cream. Brown linoleum. High up, a skylight, opened by a system of pulley with the rope cleated on the wall next to the well-polished mahogany seat. The huge floral ceramic bowl (Thomas Crapper, London, Patented) flushed by pulling down a brass rod on the wall which led up to the galvanised tank high up near the sloping ceiling. Smell of urine-rusted pipes. The old print of the Charge of the Light Brigade *and his father's army cap on a hook next to it. Oilskins. Wellingtons. A wash basin and a jug of water. A table with* The Confession Book, *ruled for date, name and address, or regiment, ambition. Asinine remarks like, 'La vie, c'est pas de la tarte but Mary McManus's tarte aux pommes is heaven! Signed Cieran Boyle, Major.' The* Confession Book, *into which Dermot wrote when Father Aloysius, SJ, was at breakfast after Mass, under Ambition, 'To join the IRA and blow up Stonyhurst. To stick a rusty corkscrew up Father Aloysius's backside and give it a good twist.' When this brought a cold eye, fixing the flushing mechanism so it wouldn't work and then shouting to his mother—Some dirty scut hasn't flushed the lavatory. The joy of seeing the miserable priest sneaking out the back door. Dermot will pay for it later at Stonyhurst. Later, seeing his cousin Brendan coming out of the Chapel all flushed and going in and finding the Jesuit still in there adjusting his clothing. At dinner that night innocently asking his father, "What's masturbation?" and the priest going scarlet and his mother stifling her laughter. His father, sternly, "Nothing you should know about. Where did you get that?"*

"Well, in the philosophy book it talks about Diogenes masturbating in the marketplace and saying it was a pity hunger couldn't be assuaged so easily. I thought it might be what Father Aloysius was doing in the Chapel today."

"Dermot, leave the table immediately!"

"Why, what have I done wrong this time?"

"Go!"

Like now. In Morelia, Mexico. After Dermot up and left her to pick up the pieces. An obstreperous commercial infant this advertising shoot.

Mouse is in her room in the hotel, choosing clothes and props for the next day's photograph. The model is Cara. Stoned exhibitionist. Sheds her clothes with zest, dances around in just transparent panties. Strokes herself.

Cara is typical of the breed, especially those who are nearly over the hill. For legal reasons the models must be over thirty. Cara is twenty-eight but that's close enough. Showing signs of wear and tear and the fear that comes from knowing that your one saleable commodity is wearing thin and can't be retreaded and you have nothing to replace it. Slept her way to the bottom. Like most of the blonde stereotypes, the Mark 1 Swedish-clone model from Minnesota out of the tatty model agencies in Los Angeles, her elevator doesn't go all the way to the top. Or, as Dermot says, her lights are on but she's not working. Hence the crutch of hash and happiness pills. Right now she's over-dosed on Ritalin on top of marijuana. Flying. Loopy.

Mouse says, idly, "Cara in Irish means friend. Not lover, macushla."

Cara giggles, "What's the word for lover?"

"Doesn't exist. No lovers in Ireland. Great hate, little room. Yeats, alannah. Your man Willie. Reinvented Ireland and the faeries."

"Fairies? You mean fags?"

"Hush! Shame on you. No fags in Holy Ireland. Except the priests."

Cara's confused. She stands in front of Mouse who is sitting. Mouse hands her a white tent-like dress.

"Here, climb into this."

"Must I, Mouse? I'll look huge."

"For the picture. White in a dark tunnel. Lighting up, the flare, the orgasm."

"Oh! Wow! Great! Wow!"

"Yes, well, basta. Curb your enthusiasm, Carissima. Nice name, Cara."

"It's OK. Italian. Wop father and la mamma. From Udine."

Mouse helps her on with the dress. Smooths it over her shoulders, lingers on the hips. Cups the buttocks. Murmurs appreciatively.

Suddenly, as though she's losing her grip, rips the garment up and off, crumbles it violently and throws it on the chair.

She says, "I've had enough of this fucking exercise! Let's have a drink. Drown our sorrows. Any bloody rig will do for these idiot shots."

Mouse is as intolerant as Dermot at times. Lots of grey matter between the ears. Ex-tennis champion. Good on the foredeck, taming the flogging canvas in a gale of wind, Dermot says, or riding hell for leather in a point-to-point. You don't fool with her. She's seen it all and finds it all predictable. Rolls with the punches of life and keeps a horseshoe in her verbal boxing glove.

She says, "That fucking Dermot! The irrefragable bastard! Leaves me holding the baby every time. And it's always an abortion. Rubs the crew up the wrong way and I'm supposed to stroke the egos till they purr like kittens. I hope he's satisfied now. The project's a washout. Bad cess to him!"

Cara pouts, "Why is he so difficult?"

Mouse, who knows her audience is as thick as two planks and who realises that Cara's infantile questions would drive a saint to sin let alone Dermot, is given to expositions delivered in a machine-gun staccato voice, problems and their solutions described with a bit of philosophy thrown in, mostly for her own edification, or just liking the sound of her own voice, declaims sarcastically as she pins up the folds of the gown at the back.

"Difficult? *Dermot?* You must be joking. He's a lamb. Eat out of your hand. He'd give you the shirt off his back. Of course he gets these tantrums. Not more than once or six times a day. It's the job, baby. Makes him sick. He knows he shouldn't be doing it but he needs the loot. An old yacht to feed, a well-heeled wife to keep up with. Well, past tense. His conscience doth make him irritable. A daycent bogtrotter with the mud still on his boots versus sorayfeened French drawing room. He's a reformed lush on a dry drunk. Oral type. Suck it and see. Needs a dummy. He doesn't know it but he's a spoilt priest. Asking for absolution. Agnostic but I'm sure he's doing the Stations of the Cross while he's on the job. Original sin plus. He's always swimming against the tide. Can't think, functions on an intuitive plane but won't accept it.

Keeps trying the impossible. Stretching himself, he claims. He should take the brakes off and let her rip. Can't relax. An Irish poet trying to be an intellectual, trying to keep up with the Duponts or de Coucys as the case may be. Trying to force a cultural quart into a leaky pint pot. To complement his overeducated and overcultured spouse. Who doesn't know it's more important to be good in bed than to know Hegel. This job is a real cock-up. He has to deal with dummkopf clients in Germany, models with the brains between the legs instead of the ears—*oh, no, not you baby!*—smartass English photographers who always know better, better being easier. Dirty French labs that spill their red wine on the negs. Swiss art directors whose cockeyed layouts look as if they were produced on the side of an Alp to the sound of cow-bells. Besides, he has me to deal with. And his French wife. Who just abandoned him. A multicultural collective of problems. So he blows his stack. And hates himself afterwards. Guilt? Oh, baby! Not to blame him."

Cara asked, "You're not married yourself?"

"Me married? No. Tried it once and didn't like it. I'm not motivated that way."

"Me either. I'm married but I find women touch me better."

"Yes, of course they do, but remember this one's no chicken. And you can't teach an old dog new tricks. Chickens, dogs, what the hell am I talking about? It's all mixed up. Cheers! *In culo alla balena*, Carissima!"

"What's that mean?"

"And you an Italian? In a whale's arse. Italian saying for good luck. Bottoms up! Not literally. Sit well away, over there. Get thee behind me, Satan. No, not there!"

Cara is impressed with the sophisticated European spouting French and Spanish and German at the dinner table and dropping the *mot juste* when demolition of inane conversation demands it. With no attempt to modify her language in times of stress but uttering the f-word in such a stylish way that it could be the Archbishop of Westminster starting the Lesson. Scandalous. Irreligious. Given to blasphemous sayings delivered in a monotonous sermonical voice.

"Fuck me, said Mary Magdalen, more in hope than anger, and John the Baptist, being a man of action, grabbed her by the two cheeks of her lily-white arse and dragged her on like a Prussian boot."

That sort of improvization. Oftwhile bursting into song with the Ball of Kirrimuir when the tone becomes too utterly toffee-nosed.

"They were shaggin' in the haystacks, shaggin' in the ricks, ya couldna hear the music for the swishin' o the pricks . . ."

The ludicrous juxtaposition of Cheltenham Ladies' College with the Officers Mess on a Saturday night. Followed by a smile in the embarrassed silence and an "Oh, sorry. I didn't realize there were *ladies* present!" Has a very low threshold of boredom and intolerance.

But no. No showoff unless exploded into action. Too confident for that. Unobtrusive, superior. So self-effacing you'd hardly notice her at a dinner party but when the little ladies of Fulham or the Seventh arrondissement of Paris or Morelia tried to outdo each other with pretentious drivel about food and wine or their antecedents she was likely to come out with some pithy comment or sacreligious rhyme. Made even Dermot wince at times.

The Scotch bottle nearly empty. Cara now stoned and pissed. Mouse still declaiming.

"They say the onlooker sees most of the game. And pretty bloody silly it is at times. Tiddleywinks. Here I am in Morelia, Mexico, picking up the pieces again because Dermot's in another crisis and cheesed off at everybody. Never again! I'll have to make the usual excuses if the job winds up a mess. Thank God and all His saints it's over after tomorrow."

Cara pleads, "Stay on. Come back to L.A."

"Me, a faded old hag in the city of teenage angels? Perish the thought. I ought to be ashamed of myself for even dallying with you. But I'm not. I'm only half Irish. The unihibited half. It was a gym mistress in the convent who taught me not to miss half the fun. Those fucking nuns! Hail Mary! Ciao Gloria! No guilt, me. No saying the beads. Take what solace you can get in this vale of tears. But L.A.? Lalaland? No, thanks, kiddo. Dese old bones must go back to Europe and mind the shop while my sybaritic boss goes playing with his *poule* in Denmark. Besides, my dear, I have a relationship going in Italy. I'm neutral outside that."

Cara, maudlin, "We could have fun."

Mouse looks up and smiles.

"Oh, no doubt we could while away the tedious hours but let's not magnify moments of mutual rapport. Ships that pass in the night, baby. A bit of turbulence in the wake but it soon disappears and leaves things calm again."

"You're hard, Mouse."

"That I am. A hoary old dyke hell bent on inflicting punishment. That's hoary, not horny. You enjoy, and the divil take the hindmost. I have my donkeys. They bray for me. Hee-haw. Just like some people. Double-barrelled Etonians."

9. Laure Says '*Pax*'

AT THE CEMETERY of Montdidier-les-Murs. The funeral of Tante Marie. Laure looked up and shivered. It was August but Mont Ventoux seemed capped with snow. She crossed her arms and wrapped around herself. She was chilled. She wondered why she was trying to ward off non-existent cold. She knew that even in summer the bare limestone of the mountain looks like snow. There was no snow up there this morning. It was sirocco weather, heavy and ominous, but a nervous *föhn* was hammering her mind. It was a day of contradictions. It must have been the cemetery and the open grave and all the death business. All the burial operatics.

"Ego sum resurectio et vita; qui credit in me, etiam si mortuus fuerit . . ."
Intoning tonelessly. The little threadbare priest. In Latin, by royal reactionary command. The shiny cassock. The huge boots, cracked. His matchstick legs and the hole in the heel of his left sock. Standing at the very edge of the cavity. Maybe, she thought, he'll slide in. No chance. No levity there that day. Last time she was there it was the bishop himself who officiated. Proper dignity. Recognition of class. Respect for the benefactors up at the château. How are the mighty fallen. Tante Marie would be the last person to require solemnity. She had wanted to die for a long time. The first time in 1945 when her husband was killed.

Laure stood apart. The family froze her out. A powerful *froideur*. Glacial. That's the way she wanted it. Keep them away, if necessary with all the Polar ice cap. God alone knows why she went. Well, God and Clémence, her cousin who caught her off balance. She felt nothing but resentment.

Impatience. Plain lust. Most inappropriate. To be back in last night's situation. The replays of the first and second nights with André. The other death. *La petite mort.* Everybody else was doing it. She thought, 'When they die they resurrect things. The wrong things. Words that ignite.'

"Requiem aeternam dona eis, Domine . . ."
The Provençal accent struggling with the unfamiliar words. A dead language for a dead-and-alive group. The chief mourners. There's Clémence, her cousin, Tante Marie's daughter. And Clémence's daughter, Camille. Sixteen. From England for the funeral. Short skirt, leggy, bored. Did she do it with Philippe? Or was she, Laure, the only wanton? Uncle René. Standing upright, despite his years. Distinguished. Red rosette in his lapel. Most of the others had little red ribbons. A moth-eaten lot. Remnants of a bygone era. Clinging to the wreckage.

The holy family. They meet only at funerals. Like this one for Aunt Marie. Everyone's favorite aunt. Almost the last of that generation. Thank God. She doesn't even know some of the mourners. She recognises a few. *Hauts fonctionnaires*, a *chef de cabinet*, an *inspecteur des finances*.

Jacques, son of René, failed to get into l'ENA, the *Ecole Nationale d'Administration*, step-ladder to greatness, now working in the cabinet of the minister for industry and proud of it. Condemned to a second-string life of obedience and anonymity. Robert, the really dumb one, who married the daughter of a rich industrialist and edits the magazine she bought for him. *Hotel particulier* in the Marais and a château in Burgundy. She's the outsider. Brought up in America. Always used to ask, 'Are you making a lot of money?' Martine, wife of a *conseiller d'Etat*—a spoiled bitch, Dermot said when he met her.

Sixteenth and Seventh arrondissement types whose wives meet on the Rue du Bac and know people at '*le Quai*.' They buy their Camembert at Barthélémy (*"à point pour ce soir!"*), their bread at Poilane and their ice cream, naturally, at Berthillon and dropping names, *"Valéry's coming to dinner!"* meaning ex-President Giscard. Everything correct. The cousins and their deferential wives. Some of the twenty thousand products of the *grandes écoles* programmed to run the country. As it was in the beginning is now and ever shall be, for ever and ever. Amen.

It was Gide who said *Familles, je vous hais!* Well, she thought, I'll say Amen to that hatred of families.

Mont Ventoux looming up above them. She hadn't seen it from there for thirty years. But it's stamped on her memory. It flashed up like a subliminal message. It dominated her childhood. It's what she saw when she opened the shutters in the morning. When she closed them at night. Hardly big enough to reach out to the clips on the wall. Cold in the moonlight. Rearing up all day, the barrier to freedom. Sinister. Looking down at you and daring you to escape. Impossible to ignore.

Mont Ventoux. Crouching there, like a sleepy alligator, with a white scaly back. It's ugly. Not like Sainte-Victoire. You can't imagine Cézanne painting it. It's not even a volcano, waiting to erupt. Just a long, shapeless, boring heap. Couldn't be a travel poster like that cliché Swiss Matterhorn. A terrestrial hiccup. A giant white slag-heap.

As if someone had hammered a big pimple down, length-
ened it, left it squashed with a ragged spine.

She wished it would topple and cover the small valley
and the commune of Montdidier-les-Murs. Do an Etna.
Smother the area in black lava. Incinerate the past and all
who were in it. She wished it would obliterate the house, the
cemetery and the family grave. She hated mountains, especially this one. It had been an obstacle between her and
Paris, the safe zone. She hated snow, didn't ski. Didn't have
anything to say to people who do.

"Kyrie eleison, Christe eleison . . ."

The priest droned on. She looked up again at Ventoux.
Cold. Like her, some say. She has a natural authority, they
say. Controlled. Cold? Controlled? Well, it just goes to show
you. *Il vaut mieux entendre ça que d'être sourd,* as Granny
used to say. It's better to hear that than to be deaf.

*"Fac, quaesumus, Domine, hanc cum serva tua
defuncta . . ."*

The priest did go on. She willed herself away from
Mont Ventoux and dissolved to other mountains. Parnassus
and Delphi. Monte Grappa, that's in all of Bassano's paintings. The hideous Alps that only Turner could render less
awful.

The *Mourre Nègre* is different. She could just about
stand the wooded peak she saw from the kitchen window in
the village of Maurepas on the southern slopes of the
Luberon. It's just a hill, only a thousand meters. A friendly
pile with a politically incorrect name, soft and quilted, with
a gentle line and no bare patches. She could walk up it if she
felt so inclined. God forbid. She wouldn't even climb up to
Montmartre. The Mourre Nègre is the highest point on the
Grand Lubéron, and the range falls away in a finger pointing
east. To Italy. And it's a barrier between her and Montdidier-
les-Murs.

This fortified farm is the house that Dermot bought
because he liked the name. Built in 1626, after the massacre
of the Vaudois in 1545. The villages running in blood.
Killed because the 'heretics' wouldn't go along with the

priests. And in the house, the old English baronet dead in 1944, at the same time that the gallant *'résistants'* killed the parson and his wife in Lourmarin because they complained about their murderous ways. The house was a hunting lodge, the home of the *Lieutenant de Louveterie*. It's called *La Louveterie*—the wolf house—and Dermot identified with Jack London. It's in a village where the compass on top of the tower of the mairie is out by ninety degrees and the indigenous by a hundred and eighty. He boasted, It's the only place in the world where the sun rises in the north and sets in the south. It could be Ballydehob. Where the church clock stands at one minute to four because the yahoos have stolen the mechanism and flogged it. Where the WC Public is kept locked in case anyone wants to use it. A village of vandals, where the *maire*, full of his own importance, struts like a little turkey cock. The Little Dictator. Where the extra little *sous-préfet* in Avignon backed his every bloody-minded irritant. *La France Profonde*. Profonder than this you can't get. Dermot had a warped sense of humor. And a low level of tolerance. She supposed they had that in common. That's about all. He gave up on the village and left the house to her, staying resolutely in Paris, when he discovered that they were all collaborators and used to drink with the Germans during the war. He wanted to drop a 3" mortar shell into the courtyard of the mairie when the municipal council was meeting there. Then the retired little functionary from Neuilly moved in next door and brought an architect from Rabat to design a Hollywood set complete with pool under their kitchen window. Raw poolhouse and *'plage.'* Designer shrubs. The old village filled with retired fearful diplomats and UN parasites. They bought up the village houses and all the women started to look like refugees from Surbiton or Foam Lake, Saskatchewan. Cars with Swiss and Belgian numberplates cluttered up the parking. There were no Hollywood starlets around the next door pool. Nothing to make Dermot say, as was his wont, "I'd rather be up that than up a dead policeman." They say the Irish make good lovers and bad husbands. Well, the second part was certainly right. He lived for excitement.

Was only just under control. Raging inwardly like a still-active commando. Now the house had the collection of old master drawings that they acquired over the years. Nobody knew it. The whole vaulted *cave* is a gallery with the pictures hidden behind sliding doors. One of each of the Italian Mannerists. Except Correggio. She wrote a book called *Distortions: How to look at the Mannerists*. She had nearly finished the next one on Parmigianino. Parma. That was her spiritual home.

"Dominus vobiscum. Et cum spiritu tuo . . ."

André was waiting for her in the village. When she could decently leave the burial. Get on with it, Father. Her urge made her wish again she had not come. And feel guilty because of it. She was in love with him. What started as instrumental sex had turned into a spiritual need.

"Et ne nos inducas in tentationem . . ."

And lead us not into temptation. Not until this afternoon, she thought. It was not the dead she minded today; it was the living. They stood around like a bunch of lead soldiers, regulation masks of solemnity clamped on their regulation faces. The mechanics of administration. She stood head and shoulders above them.

A porta iunferi. Erue, Domine, animam ejus . . .

She looked at the headstone. She focused on the Cross at the top and the word inside it.

PAX.

Well, yes, she thought, peace at last. But you should have thought of that before. *Pax vobis* to the rest of us. Instead of the constant turbulence, the unrelieved tension of our childhoods, the legacy of referred guilt and embarrassment over your words and your actions. All the dead Montriveau are there. The Montriveau of La Fontanelle, the château near Montdidier-les-Murs in the Vaucluse of Provence. Ten kilometers from Avignon, less than that from the Fontaine de Vaucluse, where Petrarch wooed his Laura. The Sorgue. Sorgue itself, a place that witnessed the worst act of man's inhumanity to man, French style. Not all the water of the Sorgue would wash away the murderous culpability. The day they came walking through the vineyard, a sorry herd, prodded and pushed by the sadistic guards. Staggering, falling, dragged on. Her uncle pulling her back to the house, saying, "Forget it. It's nothing. Just some criminals." But she saw an old woman, limping. She stopped, looked at Laure and her uncle, shook her head and limped on. Laure would never forget that face. That accusation. The indelible vision.

Paris was liberated on August 24, 1944. De Gaulle marched down the Champs Elysées. Thousands lined the route. Cheering wildly. Seven hundred were not there. They were locked in a train that crossed the frontier that same day into Germany. Vichy organised it. Frenchmen rounded up the victims. The journey to the Nazi death camps normally took three days. This one, Le Train Fantôme as it came to be called, took 57. It left Toulouse on July 2. There were 640 men aboard for Dachau and 60 women for Ravensbruck. For eight weeks it meandered around, to Bordeaux, where it was strafed by Mosquitoes, to Angoulême, where it was turned back, and on August 18 it arrived near Avignon, but the bridge over the Rhône had been demolished. The detainees were forced to march seventeen kilometers, through the vineyards of Chateauneuf-du-Pape to Sorgues, and another train. Those on board had been without food and water for days. They drank their own urine. They were infested with lice. They were forced to take turns lying down in the cramped cattle trucks. The allies had landed in the south of France. Near Montélimar the train was attacked by the RAF and nine people in the first wagon were killed. It stopped at Valence on August 24. On August 25 it crossed into Germany, near Metz. It was a French train. The driver was French. During the war some 250,000 were deported, about 75,000 of them Jews. But this was at the end, when France was almost liberated. The Allies had control of the air; the gallant Résistants *claimed control of the trains. No one lifted a hand to free them. Sorgues, where the train stopped for the last time, is less than 10 kilometers from La Fontanelle and the Montriveau.*

PAX.

There they lie, stacked on top of each other or side by side. Gone but not forgotten. Not much room on this headstone for many more but there's only one left. Only Uncle René remains. The patron. The old son-of-a-fascist, defender of the misguided faith. Carrying the family's legacy of lunatic superiority on his stooped shoulders. Obsolescent loyalties, ridiculous beliefs.

The Montriveau. She's one of them but only on her mother's side. Her mother, Oriane, was one of six children of Hubert de Montriveau, her maternal grandfather. But they claim her because of her childhood at La Fontanelle. The war years branded her.

PAX.

She reflected, 'Well, you're asking a lot.'

"Some of them should roast in hell," Dermot said, but he's an intemperate type, and doesn't understand the French.

They were wrong and they were fighting a rearguard. Fighting with the weapons they had. Words.

Verbal dum-dums, they used. They ripped the psyche with words instead of the flesh with bullets. But the words were made flesh on trains, in camps, in ovens. Weren't they just. Dermot saw some of the words written by her grandfather and published in l'Action Française at the time of the roundup of Jews in the Vélodrome d'Hiver in 1941.

'Those who are sorry for the Jews are wasting their sympathy. They are responsible for all our troubles.'

Dermot quoted Yeats, 'Did that play of mine send out certain men the English shot?'

Did they pay for it? Not enough. Laure put the figure her family had killed at 15,000. Minimum. Up there with Leguay, Bosquet and Papon.

PAX indeed.

Back to it. There's not much of it about this July 1980 morning. The priest droned on. One by one they trooped up

85

to the open grave and took the *goupillon*. They sprinkled a sign of the cross in holy water on the coffin below. She waited until they finished and pushed in. They closed ranks. They tried to prevent her but she was fierce in her determination. They had asked her to desist. Not to participate in the religious ritual. "Only the immediate family," they said. What they meant was, 'you're not with us any longer.' She thought, 'I'll show them.' She refused the brush off. The priest looked annoyed. An infidel.

"*Requiescat in pace. Amen . . .*"

She's a lot of the things they say but she's not a hypocrite. She gave up religion a long time ago. When she heard that Cardinal Baudrillart, archbishop of Paris had prayed publicly for a German victory and was an active collaborationist, she stopped going to Mass. And this happened while Marcel was kept hidden in case Bousquet sent him to join his parents at Auschwitz.

She heard the murmur of resentment. She's done it again. She stood over the grave and dropped a sprig on the top of the coffin. A small olive branch. Tante Marie would understand. She paused for a few seconds, unfeeling, then turned and pushed back between the *inspecteur des finances* and the *prof de philo* with his docile wife. Her uncle René, Marie's younger brother, Greek scholar, writer of unreadable tomes, pompous, censorious, glared at her. Yes, she thought, what a family. She added up their reactionary habits, the things Dermot wouldn't at first believe and then roared with laughter when he recounted them to his friends.

Oncle René is a modern man. He finally bought a dishwasher for Tante Adrienne. He resisted it for years because, as he said, one of his pleasures in life was to sit in a comfortable chair after dinner, with a glass of cognac and a good cigar, and to listen to the sound of his wife in the kitchen washing the dishes.

"What do you think of that?" asked Laure.

"Sounds like a harmless pleasure to me," said Dermot, and the fat was in the fire. Grand-père Jacques insisted on

his marital rights. He made Grand-mère Héléne wear his new nightshirts until they stopped itching. He was a bit of a dandy. He sent his shirts to London to be laundered because he claimed the English were the only people who knew how to starch a collar properly. There was always one hamper of laundry on the way there and one on the way back. Who says the French don't admire the English?

Grand-mère Hélène was famous for her melons. In a country where all melons were exceptional, hers were spectacular. No one could touch them. She made sure of that by checking that none of the pips found their way into the purses or pockets of her envious guests. She cleaned out the pips herself and she made sure that the cook didn't give any away. There were ladies who tried to sneak into the kitchen and bribe the cook to do so.

Laure thought—Uncle René. He's in for a surprise, that one. She withdrew to the back of the group. All standing about with severe looks, exuding sanctity, in correct uniforms like a lot of crows. She in her casual dress of jeans and multicolored sweater. Not crows. Ravens. Nevermore.

Suddenly, Dermot's mongrel tied up at the gate broke loose and tore through the legs of Uncle René, nearly toppling him, the old man held up by his son, Jacques. The hairy bitch stopped at the pile of earth and squatted to pee. There was an audible intake of breath. She found the leash and hauled the irreverent animal back. They turned and looked at her in disapproval. Anger even.

She said—*PAX*, and smiled sweetly.

Tante Marie would have smiled too. A little dog's piss in the grave wouldn't worry her. Love from Dermot. It was his dog and she loved him too.

Strangely, for a moment Laure missed his support. Her absent husband. It was so demeaning to have to find excuses for his constant absence. This time he's paid for humiliating her. They turned back, shutting her out. *PAX* is not for nonconformists. Not for Laure de Coucy, *épouse* McManus, adultress, lover of Jews, traitor, socialist, *républicaine*, betrayer of the family Catholic tradition.

She left the cemetery and walked up to the village to give them a chance to escape. She would come back later. They wouldn't want her around to embarrass them. The less they saw of her the better. But she has an invitation to the house. For some reason they insist on her presence at lunch. She's not looking forward to it. But she intends to go out not with a whimper but a good loud bang. It brought back memories. The last funeral she came to in this cemetery. Great-Uncle Pierre. '*Pay.*' After his execution by the gallant *résistants*.

10. Armand, the Moth Man

ARMAND DE COUCY chased moths. It was his only interest. A lifetime passion since he was a student. Lying there on the table, conscious part of the time, and to forget his cramped situation he did a mental inventory of his collection. The drawers filled with boxes of similar moths. Dull, but he wasn't impressed by exoticism. Size and color meant nothing to him. He couldn't put together one of those flashy boxes that are all the designer's rage nowadays. He was not an enthusiastic amateur, waving his net about in the Alpine meadows, like Nabokov.

He was a scientist, an authority. Until his accident in Africa Armand had been an intrepid hunter of the night moth wherever it might lurk—in the jungles of the Cameroons, on the mountains of Ecuador or Sarawak, in Madagascar. He was to be found at night in the steamy swamps, his light fixed to a tree to attract the quarry. He was dropped by helicopter onto remote mountains in Nepal and left there for weeks. There was not a moth with whose sexual organs he was not intimately familiar, this being the means of identifying *lepidoptera*. He had discovered over five hundred new species.

His collection of over a hundred thousand was the most valuable of its kind in the world. So was his library. He was on the advisory board of the National Museum, a friend and benefactor to the British Natural History Museum in London; an illustrious and mild-mannered man to whom people wrote soliciting information and advice from Siberia to Tasmania. Apart from the odd telephone discussion with other experts in the *métier*, and occasional meetings in the museum, he was completely self-contained.

A true gentle man. Cultivated but totally oblivious to others. Rather daunting. You wouldn't address him unless you had been introduced. He regarded all words not about butterflies or rugby to be unnecessary. A raucous laugh would attract a glance of such disdain that it would freeze the culprit for days. A mite boring? Who cared about this boring fellow? Actually, very few outside his entomologist colleagues. Not his daughter, not his son.

Only Dermot. They enjoyed a strange rapport. It may be that they were both nihilists. Or they pretended that life was a huge joke and that there was very little worth worrying about and that there was no real difference between a sinner and a saint. History was bunk and heroics questionable. They exchanged weary looks when the conversation turned to trivia and most things fell into that category.

Dermot had a soft spot for him. He liked eccentrics. And he recognised that whereas he himself was a flashy, uncultured character, Armand had class. The Irishman's pulse didn't race at the thought of a rare night moth the way it did at the sight of a red-haired girl in a miniskirt but *chacun son goût*, as they say in France. Some people chase butterflies; others chase skirts. All things considered, you'd put Dermot in the latter category. Before he grew out of it.

Armand remembers clearly his meeting with the first McManus.

He's ten. He can hear the guns of von Plattenberg's Regiment of Guards in the distance. It's exciting. The sentries are nervous. General Lanrezac, commanding the French Fifth Army, is in the house and his staff are in the farmhouse next door. He sees clearly the rider coming up the drive. An elderly cavalryman in British uniform, with a soft cap and polished riding boots. The man dismounts. He says, "Young man, get your father. I'm here to see General Lanrezac." Armand follows them to the dining-room where a busy Lanrezac is poring over maps and issuing orders. The English officer, a Captain McManus, says (in accent-less French) 'Field-Marshal Sir John French sends his compliments but regrets he cannot help you. His army was chased by von Kluck and badly mauled at Le Cateau while the French army withdrew and left his flank open. He's pulling back to the south and west. He cannot protect the left of the French Fifth Army and he has forbidden his 1st Corps to counterattack von Bülow. His troops are too tired.' Lanrezac's anger is something to behold. Armand cowers behind his father, even though he is proud of his French general. Lanrezac spits out—Dieu me damme! Le salaud! Ces emmerdeurs d'Anglais! Trop fatigués! Merde! His instinct is to shoot the messenger. He is going to try to stop the Germans and save St. Quentin and he's desperately short of troops. Morale is low. The British officer, Irish as it turns out, red with embassassment, because he disagrees with his Commander in Chief's decision and it shows, salutes and starts to withdraw. He's on the side of his own boss, General Smith-Dorrien the commander of the 2nd Corps, who wants to fight, even though they have been badly mauled at Le Cateau and the French withdrew without telling them, leaving their flank unprotected. He always refers to the minute field-marshal as 'That short-arsed little bugger!' As he reaches the door, he turns and says, "Mon Général, the British will fight to the last Frenchman!" Lanrezac, the créole, looks furious. Then he smiles. "You're Irish, McManus. Not English! Bon! Allez! Et bonne chance!" Some chance. McManus hoists Armand up on the horse. He slaps the hunter on the rump. Says, "Giddup, Potheen!" Armand had just taken him to the water trough in the park near the cedar of Lebanon, slid out of the saddle and returned to the house when he hears the sound of an express train coming down from the heavens and both rider and horse disappear in a geyser of dirt and black smoke. They scrape up what was left and bury it temporarily in a corner of the park. They send bits of equipment and harness to the British Headquarters. General Lanrezac personally scribbles a note to Sir John French. 'You've lost a good man. He was Irish.' Much later, after the war, when the deep crater has been overgrown with grass, Armand digs up a bent cap-badge with the insignia of the 10th Lancers. Much, much later, playing grown-up, Laure clips it on her handbag.

The image slips to the first meeting with Dermot.

1956. The day a red sports car came up the drive, shaking the village and bouncing its exhaust off the trees, a prancing horse badge on its hood. Out of it swung a long, dishevelled type with fair hair and a lived-in face with lines like furrows in the top field. Out of the other side came a rich gypsy girl, endless legs and thighs, red-gold hair and freckles and a wild, laughing face. He introduced himself as Dermot McManus and the girl as Nana the Troll. He asked if he could see the place where his grandfather had been killed in 1914.

Then it clicked. Armand remembered that the British cavalryman had been called McManus. They stood in the overgrown crater next to the cedar. The girl walked around, swinging her hips and taking photographs of the house and the park. He told Dermot that the only thing he had found was a cap badge.

"10th Lancers," Dermot remarked. "He must have been sixty, if a day. Silly man. Have you still got the badge?"

"No. My daughter, Laure, took it. When she was a child she put it on her handbag. Perhaps she's still got it. She used to hoard."

"Where is she?" Dermot asked.

"In Paris. She's a lawyer. In the cabinet of Chevalier. He's now a député. Why not call her? Laure de Coucy."

"That's a good idea. I'm just over from New York to sort out the French company. We need a change of lawyers."

And that, as they say, put the cat among the pigeons.

Dermot departed, the spinning wheels of the Ferrari throwing up the gravel of the driveway, and himself singing lustily:

It's a long way to Tipperary
It's a long way to go
It's a long way to Tipperary
To the sweetest girl I know
Goodby, Picadilly
Farewell Leicester Square
It's a long way to Tipperary
But my heart's right there

Armand wasn't invited to the wedding in Saint-Sulpice and he only saw his granddaughter, Penelope, when Dermot brought her to the apartment in Paris and once when Laure was away and he brought her to play at Colonfay. When Penelope was killed, it seemed that all the joy had gone out of his life. He was closer to Dermot, but Dermot had become a hard man.

11. Dermot: His Blackout

PARIS. THE CITY of Light when the lights went out. April in the Sixth Arrondissement, the time they put up the equestrian statue at the corner of the Rue du Cherche-Midi and the Rue de Sèvres. César's huge Centaur in welded iron. Half man and half horse but with certain liberties taken with each. This one has a man's legs at the front end instead of just a man's body over a horse's legs. And two sets of sexual equipment, front and back. Stallion-rigged human and animal. Testicles like cannon balls. The horse's rump presented at the ready, with the raised tail welded up of sundry tools and the biggest a spade, no doubt to keep the pavement clean when he fired out nuts and bolts. The whole hind quarters elevated like the guns of a battleship ready to fire a salvo. Dangerous at both ends and uncomfortable in the middle, as Oscar Wilde said. He could see it from where he sat bleary-eyed outside the little café. He thought of battleships. Guns elevated. Ten fourteen-inch salvoes bombarding the Huns. He had come back from Cologne on the early Lufthansa flight and taken a taxi to the Carrefour de la Croix Rouge. You get up early for that flight and after a heavy dinner with leaden conversation and a restless night and a cabin filled with the sickening stink of men's perfume he was disconnected. Lightheaded. Queasy. Anything was light after Cologne. Concrete, sex shops and the Maria-Ablass-Platz. Saint Germain was like a glass of champagne sparkling in the morning sunlight. It was a fast fix of heaven. Yes, he admitted, it's corny. But it's the way I feel. To live like a God in France, the Germans said, and right they were. Nothing like this on the FrauBertaKruppStrasse, Heinie. Everywhere else is 'la banlieue de Paris.' The Carrefour de la Croix Rouge bright with the morning sunlight. The girls from the Académie Julian in the Rue du Dragon sitting outside the little café, laughing and showing their thighs, portfolios full of drawings, but giggling about more important things. They said hello to him. They knew he was waiting for one of them. Her best friend came up and said she'd be out shortly. It is the year of the shortest skirts in a long time. A French girl in a shroud would be sexier than most in a mini, he reflected. It's the eyes, frank and insolent. A gangly blonde stood at the bar with a pigtail down to her derrière, a bottom barely covered by the little wraparound skirt. She stood first on one leg and then the other with a constant shifting of the buttocks, strapped-in orbs, moving up and down like slow pistons, long lines of thighs and calves, taut sinews and muscles temptingly defined. The shopgirls from the fancy boutiques in the Rue de Grenelle dressed to the nines as walking advertisements for their brand names. A few conceited account executive types and a blue Porsche with all the spoilers, a pimp's car or an art director's, and everyone happy and still brown after the rentrée a month or so ago. Paris. Fleshy girls and physical Paris: the unfailing reward. He sat there, watching the cars shooting out of the Rue du Vieux Colombier, horns blasting like bugles sounding the charge, turning to go down the Rue du Four or across to the Rue de Grenelle, and the sun lighting up the wide crossroads. An occasional whiff of fresh morning air stirred the senses and blew away the heady mixture of exhaust fumes and cheap synthetic perfume that the trendy shopgirls affected. It was all very intoxicating. He was happy. He was waiting for Penelope. He made visual notes all the time. He was a poet by instinct and an international marketing consultant, a creative guru, by profession. So they said but he still found it a jokey tag. He looked, and saw what marketing people don't see. Paris is an open city; a wide sky is painted across the nineteenth-century buildings, mostly six floors high with the zinc roofs. Paris stone, golden, steeped in centuries and luminous, elegant windows, fluted half-columns, delicate black iron balconies, like the lacy underwear of sexy French women, the 'porte jarretelles' that symbolize the naughtiness of Paris. An open invitation. Light and airy. Everything is here and you never get used to it. And Penelope. He was impatient to see her. He was always impatient to see her. Yet he could have sat there all morning. He looked at his watch. She came rushing across the Rue de Grenelle in her funny hat with the upturned brim and her metal hawsers jangling on her wrists and her hair in her eyes and he stood up and opened his arms to catch her as she fell out of breath into them. Everyone sitting there laughed. They approved of the great love affair between father and daughter. She was a bubbly, laughing girl, freckled with mischievous eyes and a funny tip-tilted nose. Full of life and popular. The only one of the family without serious hangups. He wondered how they had managed to produce someone as happy and unneurotic as Penelope. Half Irish and half French. Maybe the two halves neutralized each other. They sat there and she accused him of flirting with her girl friends. He admitted it. It wasn't entirely false. "Look," he said, to change the subject, "I got something for you in Cologne. A Nikon auto-focus." She shrieked. She kissed him. The other girls came over and sighed with envy. They were taking photography as well as painting. His day was made. The light was back in his life again. She picked up her belongings and followed the others back to the school. She said she would go to the famous store FNAC after to get some film and would be home about three. Then scampered away, all legs and flying hair. He was happy to see she had her mother's legs, long and shapely, even if she was careless with how much of them she showed. Her dress didn't cover her; it exposed her. He paid and crossed the 'carrefour' to the Rue du Vieux Colombier and the morning sun shone like a searchlight through the towers of Saint Sulpice. It was dazzling. Like driving into full headlights. He walked through the Place and the fountain was sparkling, the water falling like silver foil over the rim between the crouching lions, and the fluted columns of the church soaring elegantly in two layers to the towers on either corner. Apart from the dizzy effect of the sun, he was out of focus from the short night and the early morning flight. He ran up the stairs and the mongrel barked inside the second-floor flat as he fumbled with his keys. The hearty aroma of slow-cooking lunch filled the stairwell. The mad woman on the third floor was shouting into her telephone just inside the door. "Mais dis donc, c'est pas vrai, tu as raison ma chère," and all the infantile ejaculations that made you wonder if the language of Racine was that rich or vocabularies that small. His phone was ringing as he opened the door. The hairy bitch was jumping all over him. He ignored the phone. Laure was not at home in the upstairs flat. She seldom was these days. They had not lived together for years. He unpacked, showered hot then cold; carefully stowed his Hamburg rig, blazer and grey flannels, striped tie and the rest of the uniform. Into Saint-Germain anonymous style, old jeans and a cord jacket. He fed the dog and put the lead on her and went out. He went through the Place and into the Rue des Canettes and down the Rue du Four to the Boulevard Saint Germain and down to the Palette in the Rue de Seine. Jean-Francois was bustling about. He waved to indicate that the corner table was free so he sat outside having a salad and a Badoit. He became aware of a presence. "That's not the Cork Examiner *you've got there, Dermot." The familiarity irritated him. He turned slowly. He knew it was a London advertising type. "Cronin," he said, "what are you doing here?"*

"I'm here to save your immortal soul," he replied.

"Doesn't seem to be much in your line. When did you get religion?"

"Oh, give them to us after the age of sixteen and we've got them for life," Cronin answered. Dermot went back to his paper and left as soon as he had finished, not waiting for a coffee. As he crossed the street at the Place Saint Germain he saw and heard the fire engines turning out of the Rue du Vieux Colombier and tearing up the Rue de Rennes. Ambulances and police cars were taking the corner fast with screaming sirens. There seemed to be something going on higher up the street towards the Tour Montparnasse. He had a hollow feeling in his gut. Apprehension that made him almost breathless. At first they would not let him near the scene but he burst through and nothing would stop him. The first thing he saw was her portfolio with the wolf cutout on it. Then the remains of the camera. Attached to the mangled body. She was untouched above the waist, with her big eyes open and a questioning look on her face. Her left leg was gone below the knee and her right horribly torn. After that he remembered nothing until he woke up in the hospital. They said he went beserk and had to be dragged away from her when they carried her to the ambulance. She lived, but she would be a cripple. Fortunately, she died two months later. He insisted on being released immediately and a kindly policeman drove him home. He climbed the stairs and let himself in and the dog stayed in the corner, whimpering. He went up to the top apartment. Laure was lying on the bed and she waved him away violently. "Please," she

said hysterically, "go away. Leave me alone." Apart from the grief for Penelope she was reliving the nightmare days of her childhood at La Fontanelle. She could not believe that similar consequences could arrive again. It was more than she could take. Even now they were apart. He was sick. Something worse than being inconsolable is not to be allowed to console. A desolate aloneness. Just nothingness. Except the pain that surged up and overflowed without warning and never stopped. He tried to write it out of his system. It didn't work. All the joy had gone. The second loss was just too much to bear. The first? The body under the bridge. Well, it never faded.

France 3, Ireland 3, in the nightmare stakes.

12. Armand's Priorities

ARMAND WAS TELLING Dermot about his war again.

"I was on my way to Grenoble on the train. I had a pass to go there because Oriane and the children were staying with René's wife's family. They had a big house at Montbonnot and a smaller one in the garden. He was a doctor and very well known. Immune from persecution, I thought. I thought it would be safer, expecially for the children. No one knew what would happen in Paris towards the end of the war. The train stopped in the little station of Saint-André-le-Gaz in the Department of Isère. We were taken from the train and lined up on the quai. They were French *miliciens*. They asked whether there were any Jews amongst us. We all said no. Then they made us expose ourselves."

"What we used to call a 'short-arm inspection'" Dermot had commented.

"Two were circumcised. They were taken away. They screamed that they were not Jews. It didn't matter. The *chef de gare* advised me to leave. I started to walk to Grenoble. It was forty kilometers away. As I left I heard the volley as they executed the two. I was lucky. I escaped."

"By the skin of your penis," Dermot had murmured, in extremely bad taste. "What happened next?"

"I got a lift part of the way on a farm cart. The farmer made me open my pack to show that I had nothing incriminating, I remember. And I remember the date because the day after I caught my first *'Baormir Glabraria'* on the pines."

Dermot said, "That's right. Only the important things deserve to be remembered."

Laure said later to Dermot, "Don't be silly. It's all nonsense. He had a special identification card signed by de Brinon and countersigned by General Karl Oberg, Höherer SS und Polizeiführer. I found my mother's demand for a laissez-passer. It has written in her own handwriting, *'Je certifie que je suis de pure race aryenne et n'ai aucun antécédent juif.'* It, too, was stamped by his friend de Brinon. I still feel ashamed when I think of it."

She never missed an opportunity to put him down. Then Dermot to defuse the situation, quietly mentioned his own experience at that time.

In Armand's eyes, the English could do no right. Dermot was Irish but he wore a British uniform. Royal Marines. Combined Operations. Armand could never understand that. The sinking of the French fleet at Mers el Kebir had been the last act in the Anglo-French historical conflict. Pointless to say that the British couldn't afford to let the French fleet join the Germans. Or that de Gaulle himself had said to Churchill he'd do the same under the circumstances.

13. Dermot: Butterflies and Bullets

DERMOT SAID, "ABOUT that time, in October, 1944, I landed at Milos in the Cyclades in Greece. Trying to knock out a German gun battery."

"The English stole the marbles from the Parthenon," Armand had interjected with a sly smile. "Lord Elgin."

Dermot said, "Yes, and you got the Venus from Milos. But you're right, of course. We had no right to be in Greece shooting at your friends, the Germans." And he raised his cup to his father-in-law.

The French. Fighting each other but seldom the enemy. Betraying their own and the agents of the Special Operations Executive. The D-Day troops thinking they'd rather be fighting the French instead of the Germans. No respect. Or trust.

Dermot meditates. Butterflies or bullets. Milos. That was a night. First they sent the battleship HMS King George V up from Alexandria to bombard the place with 14" guns. Just to tell them we were interested. To leave our card. All afternoon they fired ten-gun salvoes at the German 6" gun emplacement on top of the hill and commanding the sea around the island. A spotter plane kept reporting that all the shells were landing in the target area. So they turned to go home convinced that the gun position had been obliterated. As they left the Germans straddled them with their first and only salvo. They beat it out of there fast. But even a thick-headed German would know we'd be back. The captain of the battleship was mad. At night he stopped the ship and mustered the marine detachment on the quarter-deck, ready to land them with the ship's boats. Someone in Alexandria or the Admiralty put a stop to that nonsense. The ship was going out to be flagship of the British Pacific Fleet. They might have lost a third of the main armament and half the close-range stuff. But there we were in transit for Ceylon and Burma after the D-Day show. The powers that be decided it would be good for us to go and practice on this totally unimportant target. So off we went with some Special Boat Squadron types in two coastal forces motor launches and they put us ashore in canoes. A half-assed operation. The krauts laid on a welcoming party for us. We didn't even get up on the breakwater where we were supposed to land. Two sub-sections with nothing but Lanchester submachineguns and rifles and some 36 grenades and we were going to climb a steep hill and take a well-entrenched gun emplacement manned by Germans. Some hope! They waited until the SBS chaps got 'round the corner into the small harbor and then opened up with everything. They wiped out the lot. The fireworks lit up the harbor as we ducked below the wall. The lieutenant, Commando Craig, said, "Let's get to hell out of here." So we left with our tails between our legs and paddled like hell to the motor launch. Butterflies or bullets. All things considered, I'd rather face Baormir Glabraria butterflies any day but there was more honor in facing bullets. Later, in the jungle training camp in Ceylon, after a slight contretemps during an exercise with live ammo, when the tripod of a Vickers Medium Machinegun collapsed and nearly wrote off a sub-section, the Captain of Marines, whose joy was not unconfined, said "McManus, they're calling for volunteers for more hazardous operations. Life expectancy, six weeks. I've volunteered you. Next of kin will be informed. Get packed." So I was with the 42 Royal Marine Commando in Burma. February 1945. Kangaw in the Arakan. It was the 'Chaung War,' in the mangrove swamps. I was in an assault craft searching the chaungs. Chaungs are creeks, some wide and some narrow. There were crocodiles, mosquitoes, snakes and stakes with trip wires to detonate mines. There were booms festooned with grenades. It was stinking hot and the smell was foul. Even being in the chaung terrified me. There was black mud in the mangrove swamps and there were Japanese. They were not prepared to surrender. One morning there were three hundred corpses floating in an area of a hundred yards and crocodiles amongst them. A very unsettling sight after breakfast. I saw a bald-headed Japanese hanging on to the net on the side of the landing craft and thought he was trying to surrender. I bent down to help him aboard. The Jap pulled a knife out of the water and struck at me. So I shouted "Banzai, you bastard!" and pushed my revolver down into the man's face and fired into his beady left eye. The Jap fell off and I pushed him away with a boathook. It was easy. I

did it without thinking. I felt nothing but relief. I was eigh-
teen, but I had met one of the five survivors of a merchant
ship that had been torpedoed by a Jap submarine. They beat
the crew insensible and then dumped the bodies into the
shark-infested sea. Twenty others were roped together and
towed behind the submarine when she submerged. I saw
three survivors out of the three hundred villagers dumped
on an island with no food or water and left there to die.
Then I was wounded in the thigh, and sent back to Ceylon
where I transferred to sea service on the staff of the Vice
Admiral second in command of the British Pacific Fleet,
and was attacked by kamikazes at the Sakishima Gunto
during the Okinawa campaign and later bombardments on
the coast of Japan. During this period in the flagship I
became friendly with an American cypher officer and after
the war wound up with him in an advertising agency in the
Graybar Building in New York. They sent me to Europe
where I floated around, putting out fires in the local offices,
and that's how I came to Paris—and Laure. It was not quite
as exciting as shooting at Japs. What did the French know
about crocodiles and snakes?

Now Dermot's in Denmark. He spent the night in the
yawl. He's in his spaced-out poetic mode.

A white day. He thought: White as an altar boy's surplice.
The sea mist an umbrella of brightness held over the flat
water, with the sun a silver halo to the east. The glare was
cut by a natural fog filter.
The fishing boats were up on the slips; the erect masts
of yachts probed the fluffy whiteness above; the long line of
wooden posts, with cross bars, like Shinto arches, staggered
into the sea from the beach and disappeared under the
deeper water offshore. An old private jetty. Seagulls
standing on one leg or restlessly picking about.
He thought: A safe haven from the recent storms. He
stood on the breakwater looking up the Sound. He was half-
awake; disconnected by the wakeful night in the boat and

the whole unfamiliar scene. Weightless, unbalanced, barely tethered to the earth. Remote from himself, an onlooker with the narcosis of the north. He felt he could walk on the water.

He thought death should be like this; a white euphoria, immaculate, sea meeting sky and no horizon. Light, transparent, unreal. A veil of tranquility. A good day to die. Well, a small death. Make it soon. The pure white Baltic after the soiled black Pacific of Puerto Vallarta. Natural linen after slimy satin. Innocence after decadence? No, that's too much. The slight moisture of the air deep-cleansed the pores of sweat and indolence. The grimy deposits of cities are flushed away. A bracing caress after a suffocating sauna.

"Le fond de l'air est frais," as his concierge in Paris says. The bottom of the air is fresh. The French too have a way with words. Away with the French.

His senses were awake now, hungrily awake. Waiting. Anticipating. Scent of fish, seaweed, ozone. Then a fragrant presence; the proximity of flesh with a faint note of Miss Dior. Beech woods and meadows and mossy caverns. Especially the last. Violins up and under.

She propped her bicycle against the wall and danced up the steps. He reached out behind and touched her hand, without looking. Building the tension. She moved close to him. Silence. A current flowing between. Soaring. They met on a mountain and each meeting is a peak. A Matterhorn, he says, but it's too subtle. Alone on the glacier before they shatter the surface and start the inevitable avalanche. (Yes, there's a certain problem of image-slippage here. From sea to mountain. But home is the sailor home from the sea, and the hunter home from the hill. The fog cleared, the metaphors will roll back up the Kattegat between Denmark and Sweden.)

"Ethereal," said Dermot McManus, finally. "No other word for it."

"Yes," said Nana. "Can we go to the boat? I don't must be seen here." *In her excitement she used interesting English construction.*

"Listen," said Dermot.

And he turned and murmured in her ear as the sea surged up on the shallow beach under the wall. Chuckling, hissing, kissing the soft maidenhair at the water's edge and covering it with a tongue of foam. And he moaned throatily with the fog-horn's moan, it sighing, thrusting and fading, but never ending. Warning, supressing, yearning. A cello and piano sonata by Schubert. His lips brushed her neck.

She shivered. "Come on," she pleaded. Urgently. "I don't have much time."

"Tagesignal: En tone hver 20s," he said, holding her back and timing the fog-horn with his wrist-watch, quoting the Pilot Book and making the Danish retch sound almost French. "56ø07',7N. 12ø18',7E. Magnetic. Slight variation, increasing annually. A few degrees of deviation. That's us. Our coordinates for the fix. Mark the positions on the chart one right on top of the other.

"Oh, prima!" she said, laughing. "One on top of the other. The missionary position! What are we waiting for?"

He turned. They came together in a sudden frenzy. Like always. They ate each other's mouths. They stumbled as one over the iron footbridge. He stopped and made the sign of the cross over the structure. He's superstitious about bridges. Well, later you may understand it. They clambered over the small boats to get to the yawl. They stopped every little while and touched each other. Lightly, lips and cheeks only. Climbing to new altitudes. They said nothing. The touch said everything.

He slid back the hatch cover and they went down into the cabin. Waft of wood resin and varnish, linseed oil, sail lockers, Stockholm Tar. Heady. He held her as she jumped down from the engine cover and his hands slid up her thighs. Skin love. Oblivion.

Later, in the reconsecrated cabin.

He said, "Some comedian said, 'Sex is everything when the flesh is highly semiotized.' Maybe you understand that. I don't. Some other fool, probably in the University of East Anglia, or Aarhus, wherever that is, said, 'Sex is by no means everything. It varies from only as high as 78 per cent of everything to as low as 3.10 per cent. The norm—listen to this, will you—in a sane, healthy person should be between 18 and 24 per cent.' What do you think of that?"

"We're 110 per cent. You're the best lover I've ever had. A sex maniac."

"Score out of ten?"

"Eleven. But it's only because of the danger. Because we can't do it all the time. If we were together the score might sink to zero."

"Do you believe that?"

"No. I don't know. I must go," she said. "I came to get the bread. Sven will wonder where I got to. I saw your mast-head light last night but I couldn't get down. It was a long night."

"Too long, always too long," Dermot said. "And too hard. Crippling. As your man said, in the dark night of the soul it is always three o'clock in the morning."

"What are you doing here anyway?"

"Dear God, Nana. Didn't you notice?"

"Apart from that."

"I broke ranks. I cut and ran. Again. For good."

"Again. For good. Of course."

She went around gathering up the things discarded in a frenzy. The gold bracelets, the lace, the denim skirt, peasant's blouse, silk scarf, the ballerinas.

Dermot sat on the transom berth and grabbed her hips. He talked to the beauty mark on the curved V.

"This time for good. Nothing would induce me to go back to that place. I thought we'd take the yawl to the Med. Back to Greece. Civilization. Maybe the Turkish coast. Where was I? Oh, yes. This." He kissed the spot. "The beauty mark. The starboard-hand marker just north east of the entrance to the totally-enclosed harbor. A compulsion. Revelation, compulsion, benediction." He kissed the spot again. "Commercial suicide, nicht? *Who cares?"*

"You're mad. What about money? Your wife, Laure? And Sven, my husband?"

He noted the order. Money, wife, husband.

She said, "I must go. Come to breakfast at nine. Bring shrimps."

"Is that all?"

"No. I'm hungry."

"I love you."

"Yes. You love my cunt. But that's all right."

"No, it's more. I can't leave you alone. I want to make love to you all the time from now on."

"I fuck. I don't make love."

"Don't you?"

"You know I do. Oh, why do you come back? I can't stand it when you leave."

"I'm staying."

"I'll bet."

Dermot McManus and Nana 'Troll' Alsen, as she then was. Running away from reality, people said. It's obscene, they said. (Little did they know.) Still playing games. But not playing with a full deck. The wild card was missing.

The French Legacy. Soon be time to put it on the table.

He went about cleaning up the cabin. His cathedral. All Honduras mahogany and teak. Fitted together like a Stradivarius by Oscar Schelin at Kungsor, Sweden. Tree wood and no plastic.

The boat is the other thing that possesses him. His escape vehicle. Designed for him; built for him; created to make him in one place at least, 'sole Master under God,' as the Lloyd's policy says.

He found her gold chain necklace under the gimballed table. Heavy enough to use as the cable for the light Danforth anchor. He hung it on the bulkhead next to the instruments.

He thought, 'She's left it in some funny places. Lost and found in four-poster beds in 14th-century fortress hotels in Portugal. In the Carlyle in New York and the Dolder Grand in Zurich and Blake's in London and the Lungarno in Florence and The Copper & Lumber Store in Antigua and the Auberge Provençale in Eygalières and and and . . . . In boats, aeroplanes, cars. Scandalous behavior under the *eyes of truck drivers on the autostrada through the Appenines. Country roads in Tuscany. Beech woods in Denmark. Courtyards in ruins in the Lubéron . Beaches in Greece. At Terme di Saturnia, the sulphur springs, waking to the smell of brimstone and saying if this is hell, God, you made the right decision. Saturnalia.*

No limits. Every which way. Always new and different. Acrobats. Giving the intellects a rest; snatching victory from the enemy, convention. Infantile. Unserious. Silly games. Talk about hearing the chimes at midnight. But no lawnmowers, golf handicaps, art lectures, home-made marmalade, sociology.

People said, "They're children. Unstable, immature. He's in love with her beard. She's flaky. Ping-pong brain. Will she ever grow up?"

He thought, 'That's us. Isn't it nice we don't have to grow up just yet?'

How did it start? He was on the top of the Eggli, the mountain at Gstaad. Snow and skiiers. Sitting at the outside restaurant, stealing a weekend after a Friday meeting in Geneva. 'Share of mind' and 'market penetration.' 'Perceptual segmentation,' for Christ's sake. The meaningless buzzwords of the professional liars. A prelude to another marital confrontation in Paris. He sat at the end of a long table with his back to the wall, doodling lazy headings in a notebook.

Trying to figure out how to handle the domestic situation. Not wanting to go back to the fray. Thinking aggravation is no substitute for copulation. From time to time he tried reading Rilke but it was impossible to concentrate. He couldn't get past the first lines of the first Duino Elegy. 'Who, if I shouted, among the hierarchy of angels would hear me?'

Too right. Who indeed? Literature clashed with the surrounding frivolity. He abandoned himself to the visual stimuli. He painted with his eyes and rearranged the idealized components. The jagged mountain peaks became a sales graph. He thought about market penetration. But the

*altitude or the ozone or whatever switched on his flippant
mood.*

*Penetration is a sacrament. How many bottom lines
have you penetrated this month? This being the second
Sunday after Penetration, say three Our Fathers and six
Hail Marys. For six days shalt thou labour and the seventh
penetrate.*

*It was only fifteen hundred meters high but the air made
him light-headed. Sensuality pervaded the location.
Licentiousness was never far away in a ski resort. His
crotch was tight and for no apparent reason he felt a tumes-
cence. How extraordinarly deprived I am, he thought. How
deplorably physical. It had all gone on too bloody long.
Intellectual wrangling; intercultural competition. Too cerebral. Too bloody polite; too civilized. But an underlying
resentment. A never-ending state of conflict. Sensual star-
vation. No action. That day he would have jumped off the
mountain without skis or a hang-glider for a fast fix of
danger.*

*Good looking people in vivid ski-suits were all around.
A teenage waitress all in black with clinging tights molding
her little derrière under a short smock moved like a
medieval pageboy in her cowboy boots. He drew her as she
moved amongst the tables and reclining chairs. Two Danish
dairymaids and their excited husbands kept up a commen-
tary on what they would later boast about back in Viborg
and Randers. Occasionally, a burst of Swiss-German like a
saw cutting rusty metal rent the air. A few refugees from
Baghdad and Kuwait and the Greek shipowners huddled
together under their mink tents and jangled their jewelery.
The serious skiiers were all at Courchevel and the heavy
thinkers in Château d'Oex. The money and the movie stars
and the confidence tricksters were in Gstaad and intellectual baggage was checked in at the railway station above
Lac Léman in Montreux.*

*The restaurant was filling up for lunch and Giles
Pollock, an account executive who gave style to the advertising agency in Berkeley Square, sat down at his table. He
was not alone. He had a new girl with him.*

"This is Nana the Troll," Pollock said. "The Swedish troll. She's here with Rupert. Lives in London. Talk to her while I look for Caroline."

Dermot McManus went into shock.

Their eyes met and the world around disappeared. They looked. She blushed. They trembled. Surprise, wonder, certainty.

He whispered, "I shouted, and you among the hierarchy of angels heard me."

She laughed. And her eyes said, "Yes!"

Life had been a rehearsal for this.

He thought, I wanted danger. Here it was, in spades.

"Let's go to Greece," he said.

The first words he uttered to her. Why Greece? He didn't know. Gods, islands, isolation, naked bodies, get her away from the rest. Time to consolidate.

"I can't," she said, as if it was the most natural question in the world. "I can't just go away and leave Rupert."

That was the last time she said no to anything he suggested.

She said , "I can meet you in London next week. Giles has my number."

"Next week will never come."

The Pollocks came back with Rupert Higham. He knew him slightly and grew a sudden dislike of him. He was one of those strutting hussar types, podgy and full of his own unimportance. The Pollocks were animated, studying the menu. Higham sat tight-lipped and embarrassed and you could sense his frustration. He knew something had happened. It was not right. He was, after all, a managing director. He hadn't been getting anywhere with her and he had been so diplomatic and considerate. So generous.

Dermot watched them leave. She had the lines of a racing yacht of yesterday. Did Hemingway say that once? No matter. Spare and narrow-beam and with a fine entry. Racy, a Dragon or a Twelve built for speed. Balanced overhangs and small buttocks, the lines drawn on the body plan gave you a promise of buoyancy and lateral stability when heeled.

The metaphor pleased him.

He wanted to knife through the waves with her; to surf down the untameable seas. He wanted her gunnels under water and to hear the shriek of her rigging. To sink into the foam. To fuck up a storm. Lightly built though she was you could drive her hard and she would revel in it. A stayer. She was a vessel for fucking off the wind or in a calm and she would take you where you had never been before, to the secret places which as Melville said are not shown on any chart. She turned to smile 'a bientôt.'

He followed her slender figure until it was lost in the crowds and they turned the corner towards the tele-cabins. Giles came back with his wife, Caroline.

He said "Hello. What's this?"

He picked up a scarf from the seat where Troll had been sitting. She had left it for him. It couldn't have been accidental.

Dermot said "I'll take it".

Caroline said "Ho, ho."

He still had the scarf. It was almost time to get rid of it. Perhaps he would tie it around his neck the way the Kamikaze pilots used to before going to join their ancestors. It offered the same sort of end. And it delivered.

The phone call out of the blue, after their first meeting in London.

"I've decided I want to be your mistress."

And the excitement of it. The wild, acrobatic, unrestricted danger of it. The God-given antidote; the edge of chaos; the awakening. And, inevitably, the beginnings of apprehension. Her two children. Both wards of court. Her need to be seen by the judge to be 'respectable.'

Then, within a year, the unwanted phone call.

"I've decided I want to get married".

And his cowardly response. "I hope you have someone in mind"

Fury. Within a month, she was married to Alsen. And he was married to Laure. The accidental meeting after

Penelope's death and Laure's affair and years of sexual
deprivation. A quiet dinner in Lausanne. His polite peck on
her cheek as he left her. The phone call as he was lying there
at midnight, wanting her.

"I'll come away with you if you like."

The addiction. No remission for bad behavior. The
pendulum always swinging from mind to penis, from intel-
lectual Laure to wanton Nana. The empty mind hungering
for intelligent conversation when he was with Nana and the
tumescent prick fantasizing about Nana when he was with
ungiving Laure.

I paint with my prick, said Renoir.

You must write with an erection, said Flaubert.

It's the only part of me that works, said Dermot.

14. Laure in the Lion's Den

LAURE WALKED UP the hill from the cemetery. She was
desperate to see André. The liberator. The exorcist. The
sensual drug that banished thoughts and memories. She was
practically jogging. She was tense with the love for him. He
was there, in the Place, sitting by the fountain. They barely
had time to kiss before Monsieur Grégoire came by. He
stopped. He looked at her.

He said, "You're Laure?"

She answered, "Yes, Monsieur Grégoire."

She introduced André. The old man was well over
eighty. She thought he must now be the Elder of the Village.
Had been *maire* a number of times. He remembered her and
the incident in the wood. He sat down heavily.

He said, "Your aunt was a fine lady. The best of the
bunch."

"You didn't much care for the rest?"

"No, I didn't. But it's all in the past. We were on
different sides. They don't seem to learn. You know my
brother was executed. He was a member of the communist

110

cell in Pernes. Someone betrayed him. We've always had our suspicions. But it's all a long time ago now."

He looked long and hard at André.

He said, "A lot of us paid for Monsieur de Montriveau's writing. *N'est -ce pas, monsieur?*"

André hesitated and said, "Yes. I suppose so."

They exchanged some banalities and he got up and painfully worked his way down the main street. Monsieur Grégoire had been a farmer and a communist.

He had told her his granddaughter, Christiane, went to l'ENA. She now works in the Senate. The Palais du Luxembourg was just up the road from where Laure lived when she was in Paris. She reminded herself to look her up when she went back there. They could have lunch at the bar on the Rue de Tournon. The Café de Tournon, hard by the Palace. Appropriately enough, it was where Joseph Roth used to drink and write. He lived above it. Another Jew who fled fascism but never forgot his Austro-Hungarian homeland. He died in penury, in deprivation of his proper roots, an alcoholic genius. Christiane Grégoire could fill in some gaps.

Laure said, "I have to go to the house. Will you wait for me? You can go to Pernes for lunch. Drive me to the cemetery. It's on the way."

In the car, irresistible impulse. Touching. Pulled away from him as they reached the gates.

The family had gone. There was no sign of life except for an abandoned bulldozer by the side of the road. She pushed André down onto the iron seat outside the gate. She walked away just up the road a bit. To try to muster a modicum of holiness and respect. At the corner she climbed the bank and looked at the landscape. Still a windless day, pale sun, weak, lifeless. Uncertain. Held in suspension, like her memories. It's a stunted valley, a sort of afterthought scooped out between Mont Ventoux and the Plateau de Vaucluse. Vaucluse, meaning 'the closed valley.'

Oh, certainly, closed. Minds slammed shut. The world locked out. The cemetery of Montdidier-les-Murs. A kilometer to the house, La Fontanelle; five to Pernes-les-Fontaines. Not much further to Sorgues, from where the last cattle-wagons of Jews were taken away to the camps. The village high above, white houses staggered against the cliffs. A typical Provençal hill village. And an empty, dead valley. The valley of the dead.

Her father's dead are in the north. In Colonfay. And one in Paris. Penelope.

The hope of the world. The faithful Penelope. Always waiting for Dermot. The glue of the marriage.

She thought, 'When my turn comes I'll be burned and my ashes scattered, partly, from the Pont des Arts. When no one's looking. The rest near Urbino, in sight of the Palazzo Ducale. Where I have been happy. Where no memories of war intrude. She thought of the untold thousands sent to the camps with the approval of her beloved grandfather. André's family? She walked slowly back.

André asked, "Can I see the grave of your ancestors?"

"My maternal ancestors."

She lifted the latch and led him into the cemetery. Even in the small churchyard, the family lay proud. Two large plots, tucked away in a corner under the shade of the platane, facing up to the village. The white village backed by the cliffs, the simple houses stacked below the crest. *Our* village, they still thought, repopulated by their grandfather with grateful *Banat-ais*, refugees from Transylvania when the place was dying after the war. Well, grateful for a limited time. She pointed out the family grave.

He asked, in a funny voice, "Montriveau. Is that the name of your family?"

She said, "Yes. Have you heard of them?"

"It strikes a chord. Rings a bell somewhere. Like a funeral knell."

She said, "I never see any of the family. Only my brother, Patrick. I suppose I share their cultural conceit. There must be something in this genetic business."

He said, "I hope that's all you inherited."

She said, "Yes. I'm opposed to everything they stand for."

112

He said, "Good."

She was remembering the escape from them. Going to Greece. Sleeping out to see the sun come up at Delphi. Of course, that was before droves of tourists went there. Crete too, and then staying in the Villa Medici in Rome.

Alone. Always alone. While the others were going to Hydra or St. Tropez. With boys. Having affairs. Fun. The gnawing ache of apartness. Until Dermot.

PAX. She walked on the grave and traced the word with her finger. She pointed to the names, one after the other. She explained the members of the family who are buried there. She told him that later they will add her aunt's name to the gravestone, probably tomorrow. Marie Falconnet.

There's space for her in the grave. Below that of her husband, Jean. All they buried of him was his missal. His friend brought it back from Germany after the war, bloodstained, as the script demanded. He was demolished by a bomb in the prisoner of war camp just before the war ended. An RAF bomb. It would have to be, to suit the preconceptions of this company. *The litany. Agincourt, Fashoda, Mers el Kebir, Jean Falconnet.*

Pax indeed, but not for the English. Not this week. She told him she felt no emotion. No sadness, no solemnity. How she remembered her mother saying the only Englishman she admired was Macmillan because he had style. As he lay wounded in no-man's-land in the Great War, he read his Horace. Whenever a bullet is deflected, it is deflected miraculously by a bible or a holy medal. Or a Latin poet. Uncle Jean's missal was not good enough to deflect a British thousand-pound bomb.

She told André the last time she had been in this cemetery was when they buried Great-Uncle Pierre. Her grandfather had been smuggled out to Geneva and Pierre was left in La Fontanelle. He was safe. Another professor, at Aix, all he was guilty of was writing a book to prove Dreyfus was guilty.

André said "Well, well. Another liberal type."

She said "He wasn't the worst. He had a certain highhandedness with the tenants. One in particular had it in for him. He had dared to suggest that both farms should be sold to the tenants for a nominal sum. Pay had told him to leave. They were good to their tenants but they didn't realise how much times had changed. The communists had appropriated *la Résistance* for themselves, and all the Montriveau and their ilk were tarred with the same brush".

His name was just above that of her grandfather on the tombstone. She told him the story of the execution.

"What about your father's family?" he asked.

"You really want to know?"

So she told him a bit.

"I'm Laure de Coucy. De Coucy, it's a good northern name. Old name. Money from mills, mines, railways, local banking. Equally reactionary but not quite so distinguished intellectually. You want a memory of what happened during the war?

One time we were at Monbonnot, near Grenoble. For once I was with my mother and brother. My father stayed in Paris with occasional visits to the farm and the woods at Colonfay. He had permission to use his wing of the house and even was invited to dine with the German general and senior officers. But now, at the end of the war, everything was chaotic. We had been sent away to Grenoble. I didn't realize the significance of it at the time. Grenoble. That was the worst stage. Until the next worst. La Fontanelle. Then Colonfay. My father had arranged for us to go to Grenoble and stay with my uncle, my mother's other brother, when it looked as though Paris might become too dangerous. Because of his job, which they didn't talk about very often, he could get *laissez-passers* to visit us. They're always on about childhood trauma these days. But I'll never forget the anxiety the day he didn't arrive from Paris. The German patrols everywhere. Just south in the mountains of le Vercors thousands of Maquisards being prepared for the slaughter by the Germans. The most dangerous place in France at that time. The shortage of food. The illness of my grandfather. How Aunt Marie smuggled him out of the house in Vaucluse, hidden under a load of tomatoes, after

114

the avengers had come to get him three times and three times had accepted my aunt's assurance that he wasn't there. How she had brought him to Geneva, still hidden under the tomatoes as they crossed the border, and then back to Grenoble when they thought it safe. Grenoble. We were waiting for my father to come. He was bringing us some food that he said he had saved. Although we were protected by the fact that we were living with a well-regarded local surgeon, a friend of my uncle, who gave us a small house on his land, there was a desperate shortage of food. I wanted to see Papa. I remember how my missing father had knocked on the door in Grenoble in the middle of the night. How he told the story. The execution on the station of Saint-André le Gaz. How his only recollection of it was the catching of his first butterflies of a certain type. No remorse over the two victims. How Dermot had reminded him of the fact that he was wise to have chosen a gentile father and to have escaped by the skin of his penis.

André said, "Sounds amusing, your husband. Where is the Irish Dermot?"

"Supposed to be in Mexico. But more likely to be in Scandinavia. I think he has a Danish or Swedish mistress. Come here."

André moved onto the grave. Tentatively.

He said, nervously, "It's not true that Kierkegaard peed on his father's grave."

She reached out for him. He hesitated. She pulled him to her. He kissed her. A heaving up wave of intensity. Flood tide meeting ebb tide. The word *PAX* in the small of her back.

But she knew there would be no enduring peace this way.

She walked through the wood towards the house. André stayed with her. La Fontanelle, built on the grave of another Montriveau. *Mort pour la patrie* at Waterloo. It's not the House of Mirth. Truly, she thought, the House of Shame. Not an old bastide in the tradition of the country but a sort of Taj Mahal of a place. A strange abberation, this lapse of taste. Built around a central hall, it is resembles a bit the villa *La Rotonda*. Perhaps they had Palladio in mind. It's called a 'château' on the map. An important house. Hidden behind the tall pines. Last bastion of the family fiefdom. A faded citadel. They came to the orchard of apricot trees and cherries. Sat on the bench outside the main gate.

She said, "You can't come any further. I'll see you back in the village."

But she clung to him. There was time. She was apprehensive. Like going before the examiners for the oral discussion on the thesis. She remembered walking through the wood every Sunday. She was talking nervously, feeling a need to explain to André her apprehension, her fear of the place. She remembered 1944. The burial of the peasant and the warning for her grandfather.

The first signs of local animosity were evident. She was too young to understand what was happening. But she felt something. She went with her grandfather and Aunt Marie to the funeral of Henri Ripert, the peasant on the farm. He had been shot by the Germans. One of eight hostages. Their presence was unwelcome. The villagers looked at them and muttered. They were isolated not just by position but by presumed alliances. The locals thought her grandfather was working with the Germans. He was not. He hated the occupiers. But he hated the English too. The Bolsheviks most of all. And, of course, the Jews. He had written too that a German victory was to be desired because it was that or communism. Yet he had nothing to do with the Germans. He enjoyed protection and that was enough to damn him. The signals were easy to read. Grandfather refused to admit them. Who were they to question his actions? He continued to write, right up to the end. Drieu visited with his new mistress, the wife of Louis Renault. His friends were all men of letters, poets, above the common herd, beyond the reach of the law. Aunt Marie had pleaded with him to stop writing after the Vélodrome d'Hiver incident, the round-up of Jews in Paris and their shipment to the camps. Arrogantly, he

116

had refused. Then, when the Americans had landed in the south and it was all over bar the shouting, they came for him the first time. He hid behind the shutters upstairs. Marie, her daughter Martine in her arms, stood at the door and told them he wasn't at home. They respected her. They knew about her husband, a real soldier of France. They knew he had been offered his freedom in exchange for working for the Germans and that he had refused. They knew she cycled every day, rain or shine, to Carpentras, to teach their children. They came back three times, more insistent every time. Finally, René fixed it for a man with a small van to smuggle him away. They went down to a small road and waited. Aunt Marie and Laure. The van, an old Citroën filled with tomatoes, arrived late. Her Grandfather climbed into the back and prepared to cover himself with tomatoes. Aunt Marie sat in front with Laure on her knee. It was a big adventure. How big she didn't realize. They managed to cross into Switzerland, to Geneva. His brother, Great-Uncle Jacques, gave him a house outside Geneva. Later, her Grandfather went back to Grenoble.

Laure thought, 'Hubert de Montriveau. 5 Juillet 1876—25 Avril 1957. Grandfather. Patriarch. Beloved tyrant. Her hero with feet of clay. Polytechnicien. Author. Explorer. Went to China with his brother, Great-Uncle Jacques, and wrote a book, *To the Gobi Desert before Younghusband.* Spent his honeymoon in India. A year's honeymoon. Wrote a biography *MacMahon of Sedan.* And *1789: More than a Crime, an Error.* Translated Stevenson. He became political editor of *l'Action Française* in 1937. Laure had the page of the paper with his picture and his travels and his literary eminence. She didn't know this until recently. It's one of the exhibits found among her mother's belongings. She didn't know until she read (with shock and horror at *Sciences-Po*) about fascism in France that he was a friend of Léon Daudet, Drieu la Rochelle, Maurras, Brasillach. All the fascists, the anti-Semites. Didn't know that one day he would have an entry in *The Vichyists.* She had a vague recollection of important people coming to visit him and of being told to keep quiet. The library out of bounds for the afternoon. She knew that he had certain old-fashioned manners. Before the war he sent his shirts to London to be laundered. Only place where they knew how to starch a collar properly. Made his wife wear his new nightshirts at the beginning, to get the roughness worn away. Family jokes. This she told to André. She knew her love would overcome his aversion to her family's criminal behavior.

The priest's 2CV came rumbling through the gates. He stopped briefly. He looked at them and frowned. Then went on.

She said, "I'd better go in. It's time for lunch. I'll meet you in the village at three."

She was amazed at her new boldness. She had strength. She walked slowly up the drive. It was only 12:45. She went and sat by the fountain, waiting for the bell. Not at all looking forward to sitting around a table with the family. All strangers, including her Uncle René. He had inherited all his father's dictatorial habits, but few of his virtues. She remembered that the cardinal rule was to be prompt for meals. God help her grandmother if lunch wasn't on the table at precisely one o'clock. Still, Grandfather indulged her. She had been welcome to come into his study at any time, except when he was writing his column for *l'Action Française*. She well remembered the row one day when they wanted to erect a memorial in his woods. They had two farms attached to the property. One day a year the villagers were invited to shoot wild boar over the land. During the shoot someone 'accidentally' shot dead the communist *maire* of the village. The local party wanted to put a stone at the spot.

"How dare you!" he shouted at the man. "A memorial to a communist on my land. Never!"

He was choleric for days. But the peasants have long memories. And at the end of the war they were trying to take power. They still insist that the *Résistance* was mostly communist. What they don't tell you is that they didn't hesitate to betray all the rightist agents to the Gestapo.

Her grandfather used to push books at her. She was already—how do you say it?—a bookworm. And he would help her understand some of his translated works in their original English. She had been made serious, had already lost her childhood and her sense of fun. Her Uncle René had been less forthcoming. He was the master now, by God. And he disapproved of her. He disapproved of almost everybody. Except those who were working at Greek. He particularly disliked her father, who had encouraged her mother to sue for her part of the inheritance when her grandfather had tried to push most of it onto Uncle René.

Still, apart from the tension, and her sense of abandonment, life had been good at La Fontanelle. They always had enough to eat there. Lamb. The famous melons, strawberries, artichokes, big salads. Fruit from the trees in the orchard, cherries, almonds, apricots, figs. The best asparagus. Goat cheese, honey. The scent of lavender, rosemary, thyme. The wisteria over the pergola. The constant cooing of the doves. By comparison with the wartime restrictions and the shortages in Paris, it was a sort of Arcadia. With the serpent of war always trying to wriggle into the house.

She had spent most of her time at this fountain in front of her grandfather's study. There's a fabulous view north to the Dentelles de Montmirail. Two dogs, *Bergers des Pyrénées*, always playing. And Minos, the big grey cat lying in the sun. The skies were certainly bluer and the grass greener, or so it seemed. The Mistral blew away all the dirt. The cypresses bent in it, the platanes talked. It was a childhood that should have been unblemished but was tortured by loneliness. That was when she turned in on herself, lost contact with humanity. Her father was in Paris, or Vichy, and her aunts looked permanently worried. There were frequent huddled meetings, whispered news, an air of danger and conspiracy. Children pick up these things. Their antennas are more finely tuned to adult moods. It was, after all, the end of the war and they were on the losing side. There was talk of '*Le Maréchal*' and what would happen to him. There were messages from Paris about various friends who had been killed. There was the awful shock when Aunt Marie got the news about her husband. She remembered the day well.

Aunt Marie had been so looking forward to his return. Her younger daughter, Martine, had never seen her father. He had been a nice man. When he was taken prisoner by the Germans in 1940, they offered to release him if he would work for them. He was a librarian. He refused. Odd man out in that family, she was beginning to realize.

Great-Uncle Jacques came over from Geneva from time to time, bringing things that were scarce in France. Chocolates! Sugar! Coffee! He was a Swiss resident. He put up her grandfather when he fled in 1945. He had packed up and left France when Blum and the *Front Populaire* came to power in 1936. He's in his grave by Lac Léman, having shaken the dust of France off his feet and saved his fortune for his son, Jean, who was now spending it on a sailor from Nice and whose only job was to be for a limited time a *habilleur* at the Folies Bergères. 'Jean has certain little eccentricities,' is all they would say about him. She liked him. He used to play games with her, dressing up and so on. He was fun. He, more than the treatment, snapped her out of her withdrawal breakdown when she was in a clinic in Switzerland. She supposed he was still fun if he hadn't succumbed to the dreaded virus. Last she heard he was still alive, still in his *hotel particulier* in Geneva and spending his summers on Cap Ferrat. He gave her some valuable books that had belonged to her great-grandfather and some jewelery he thought should stay in the family. After all, he could have given them to the little *matelot*.

The beginning was the past and the past was made present. It's always there. Seared in the memory. The *épuration*, they called it. A cleansing. An excuse to settle scores. Everyone she liked was killed in 1944 or 1945.

According to Adrien Tixier, who was the post-war minister of justice, over 100,000 summary executions were carried out between June 1944 and February 1945. More conservative, and perhaps more reliable, estimates later put the figure at about ten thousand. Right where she lived when she was in Provence, in the next village, Lourmarin, they shot the clergyman and his wife because the wife denounced their brutality, their cowardice and their dishonest opportunism.

People said the Germans were 'correct' but the so-called *'résistance'* was often made up of thugs.

She missed the bell. She was late for the funerary lunch. Unforgiveable. But Uncle René sat her on his right, which was something. Something unwelcome. There was a fearful silence at the table. You do not speak unless spoken to. He treated them them all as if they were students in his Greek class at Aix.

"Ah, the late Madame McManus! Never on time."

"Yes, sorry, *mon oncle*. I went up to the village. I met old Monsieur Grégoire."

"And what did the old bolshevik have to say for himself?"

"Just the usual banalities. He liked Tante Marie. Don't you think it's time to stop worrying about the communists?"

"Perhaps. Have you still got your tame Jew? The picture expert."

"Marcel? Yes, he's still a friend. But I do know quite a lot of other Jewish people."

"Yes, I suppose so. Your business is rather tribal."

"Oh, well, so is yours. The Greek academics around the world speak only to other academics. I always thought it a rather incestuous calling. And the old gang seems to be functioning well."

"What does that mean exactly?"

"I was thinking of Touvier being protected for forty years. And Bousquet at large and having dinner with Mitterand. An embarrassment if he lives to be tried and names names. I gather both the right and the left want him out of the way. Leguay's trial has taken nearly ten years to prepare. De Gaulle had him sent to New York after the war for l'Oréal, owned by the leading fascist, so there'd be no recriminations. And Papon still free and unlikely to be allowed to spill the beans, as the English say. All the old fascists retiring from lucrative positions. The boys look after their own."

"We were never, as you put it, members of 'the old gang.' It seems to me that Mitterand has strange bedfellows. Of course, both Mitterand and his great friend Grosrouvre were on the far right until 1943. Followers of *l'Action Française*, even. Decorated by Pétain, your left-wing socialist. Members, both of them, old members of Vichy's *Service d'Ordre Légionnaire* which became the Milice. They saw which way the wind was blowing and entered the *maquis*. You do realise, my dear, that General Leclerc was a member of *l'Action Française*? That Dewavrin, Colonel Passy, was a Cagoulard? That de Gaulle had innumerable royalists with him? Colonel Rémy, for instance. We were never turncoats, my dear. Never dishonest moneymakers like your ministers. Never vulgarians."

"No? Grandfather didn't write vulgar things in *l'Action Française*? He didn't write nasty things about the Jews? Even after they were shipped away to the camps? He wasn't as guilty as Drieu, Léon Daudet, Maurras, Brasillach? Seems to me Boulin, Giscard's employment minister, was helped to commit suicide."

"You really have it in for us. My dear Laure. They were all great writers. Céline too. Judge the work. Read Drieu's *Les Chiens de paille*. Straw-dogs, they call it in English."

"Yes, Grandfather too was quite a writer. I gather his letters were worth reading."

He looked at her suspiciously. Tried to change the subject.

"When I consider how you could have gone to l'ENA, and how much my son, Jacques, wanted to and failed both tries. You were head of Chevalier's law practice in no time. Walked out in a huff, I understand. You could have been in a ministry. Or the Quai d'Orsay. Anything. Where did you come in *Sciences-Po*? First out of three hundred wasn't it? Your doctoral thesis on the Cyprus question published. With commendations."

"God forbid that I should have joined all those petrified functionaries, even in the Academy. What's Jacques doing now?"

She looked across at her cousin, who smiled conceitedly but left it to his father to answer for him.

"He's *chef de cabinet* of the minister of industry. How's it going, Jacques?"

"Very amusing. The other day we had to take the ambassador of an arab nation out to Chantilly to see some racehorses run. The king wanted one as a present. He chose it. Then a few days later the ambassador called and said he'd changed his mind. He wanted a woman instead."

"For the night, or longer?" Laure asked.

"For good. A present."

"How did you manage that?"

"Well, I refused to have anything to do with it but they enlisted the PR man of an armaments company and he said no problem, so I guess he got his present."

Laure said, "Sounds entertaining. Women as chattels still."

"Well, you know how they are in those countries."

"No, actually. The ones I've met in the art business seem more interested in blond boys. Catamites. I gather a certain monarch has a man in Paris as a sort of recruitment officer."

Her Uncle René asked, "Where's your Irish husband today, Laure? Michel, isn't it?"

"Dermot. Last heard of in Mexico. He travels a lot."

"I hope you're both behaving yourselves."

"Perhaps rather better than Grandfather. I understand the house in Les Barroux is no longer in the family?"

He looked at her in surprise and anger.

"What do you know about that? That's something we do not discuss."

The rest of the family were now listening intently. Uncle René glared at them.

Laure said, "No. We only talk about the things that glorify the family."

"I presume your father has been talking too much again."

"No. I heard it years ago. Apparently Grandfather was, as the English say, having it off with Madame Schidlovsky, the concert pianist."

"Laure, I forbid you!"

She went on, "When her husband died she was financially embarrassed. He bought the house and let her live there rent free. When he died she sent copies of his letters to you and Pay and said that if you didn't agree to sell her the house for ten thousand francs she would send the originals to Grandmother.

"Really, Laure, how dare you!"

"That would really have put the cat among the pigeons, as Grandmother had always boasted about her 'best friend,' Madame Schidlovsky, the famous concert pianist. Little did she know the lady was playing concertos in bed with Grandfather's piccolo."

"There's no need to be vulgar, Laure."

"Well, children, your uncles had little option but to agree to the demand. And your grandmother went to her grave believing in her husband's rectitude and still boasting of her friendship with the beautiful and talented pianist. Let us not forget the skeletons in the Montriveau closet. True, *mon oncle*?"

There was a long silence. He looked at her.

He murmured, "Let those of you who are without sin cast the first stone."

Laure laughed, "Ah, well, a little fornication is less reprehensible than the scurrilous things he wrote about Jews. Tell me, is Cousin Jean still living with his little sailor in Geneva, Uncle?"

"I think, unless you would prefer to leave, we will discontinue this conversation, Laure."

She was merciless. It had taken a long time to reach this state of independence.

"Then there was Great-Uncle Henri. He had an affair with the friend of his mother. She had his baby. It was adopted by another friend of the family. Everyone happy.

Quite a performance. So what's new? Would you like me to tell you about Uncle Didier? The Milicien. The paedophile. Who abused me when I was a little girl? No? I thought not."

There was an embarrassed silence. Finally broken by Uncle René. He struggled gamely to keep his cool.

"Do you remember this house?"

"Yes. I spent some interesting days here."

"Fortunately, you were too young to understand."

"Not altogether, Uncle. Remember, I was here when Grand-Uncle Pierre was shot. And when we took Grandfather to Geneva. I gather they had been on the wrong side."

"No. They were for France."

"*La vieille France.* What a joke."

"Oh, Laure. Joke, no. Our France."

"Not mine."

"Is yours better?" her uncle demanded, "drugs, crime, arabs, blacks everywhere. Corruption in every political party. Ministers in jail, power-mad vulgarians in the prefecture of Vaucluse, all the *maires* on the take. The fabric of society disintegrating. You can't walk in Avignon these days without getting robbed. Football hooligans in the assembly. Vulgarity everywhere. The oil company Elf set up to provide a spy base and supply money to the politicians. Mitterand, decorated by the Marshal and then a turncoat at the last minute. A Socialist for power. Dumas. Minister of foreign affairs. The most unscrupulous bunch ever. Avignon is the crime centre of France."

"Well, Avignon was like that in the days of the popes. A sanctuary for criminals. The law of the land ended outside the walls. What's different? And I seem to remember that it was a right-wing president who took diamonds from an African dictator. And right-wing scandals about property."

"Laure, you should remember something. We had a France that was decadent. The Marshal said, 'I summon you to an intellectual redressing!' What else could we do? We had a choice between communism, which very nearly took over here, and capitalism, American capitalism controlled by Jews and pretending to be democracy. Or totalitarianism. That was represented by National Socialism. We hated the

Germans, perhaps not so much as the English, again a Jewish-led society of bankers and Freemasons, but not so much as the Americans. We monarchists."

"You're not still playing that intellectual game, surely?"

"Go on, sneer. We always believed that it was monarchy which gave France its staple base for centuries. The Revolution and Napoleon destroyed our ancient society. What has it achieved? Look at the socialist dictator in the Elysée. All his friends shooting themselves. Let's drop it. Your views are too superficial. Too biased by your associates." He changed the subject. "How's your father? Still chasing butterflies?"

"He was until he had an accident. I gather he's laid up."

"Haven't you seen him?"

"Not for some time. He disapproves of my lifestyle. And I of his views."

"Why, Laure? Why?"

"Why what?"

"Why are you against everything? You must be very unhappy."

"No, not any longer. A Jewish psychiatrist saved my sanity and a Jewish art publisher gave me my direction."

"What a sad comment."

"In any case, I'm not so unhappy as my mother. She spent her life being a slave to my father. Terribly unhappy. No life of her own at all. Fighting her brother in the courts. Dominated by her fascist sister. Misguided, biased, racist."

"Well, it's a good job she didn't meet your friends. I never got along with my sister but Oriane did her duty. And she had her religion. She was made unhappy by the desertion of your brother. He didn't remember his duty."

"Duty! Patrick's concept of duty was different from Mother's. Her duty was to the ideals of her father. A blind duty. All wrong. His was the Free French. The truly free."

"That's your opinion, my niece."

"I have a few questions. May I ask them?"

"What are they about?"

"The war."

"Come into my study. The others will excuse us."

126

As they went through the hall, the telephone rang. He excused himself and took the call. He went white and staggered. He sat down heavily on the chair by the telephone table.

He said only, "Yes, I understand. Thank you."

She went over and touched him. He was very distressed. He shook her off, and marched back into the dining-room. Standing in the doorway, he rapped with his stick on the floor.

He said, "The gravestone has been broken. The grave desecrated. Our family disturbed. They have painted disgusting things. The *gendarmes* say they had a call to tell us 'Happy Anniversary.' I wish you farewell, Laure."

And he turned and went slowly up the stairs, his son Jacques holding his left elbow. His other son, René, came to her side.

He offered, "I'll drive you back to Maurepas."

She answered, "No. I've got someone waiting for me in the village. I'll walk back there."

Wednesday

15. Armand and Days of Glory

A NEWSREEL PASSED in front of Armand's eyes. FADE IN: Himself as a young man, an Olympic hurdler. CUT TO: *Sciences-Po*, doing the usual course for a degree in political science. He took a law degree concurrently and later took the '*agrégation*,' the top examination and the most difficult. He passed out number three. DISSOLVE TO: Him as an *inspecteur des Finances*, one of the twenty thousand top functionaries who run France and speak only to God or the President, roles which in France the latter often confuses with the former. FAST CUTS: At the Cavalry School at Saumur for his military service; as an officer when the war started; leading his men south on a reciprocal course to the fighting; demobilized in Toulouse in 1940, without hearing a shot fired. Armand, a pacific man, was not against the Armistice. He had little confidence that his sword, carried with style in his right hand and resting on his shoulder, would strike fear into the hearts of Hitler's Waffen SS.

He was probably right.

Dermot said "Had it been me, I would have put the trusty steed into a horse box and towed it behind a Ferrari to Bordeaux, leaving the stricken field to the foe."
Armand asked "What's a Ferrari?"

He joined the government of Vichy. He had very little choice. As a senior functionary he was at the call of the legitimate government and that was embodied in Marshal Pétain, an octogenarian who in the eyes of the French could do no wrong, being given to illicit copulation at the age of eighty-four, convincing proof of virility and fitness for leadership of the French nation in time of stress.

Armand was sent to Paris to negotiate quotas of labor to be exported (rather forcibly) to Germany. This job, which he fulfilled with apparent diligence, did not meet with universal approval after the war. It had put him in some very bad company indeed.

A series of visions. Blurred visions. Sunday afternoons in the apartment on the Rue Freycinet in Paris.

July 1942. The Great Raid of July 16/17 when the Jews were rounded up.

"President Laval has proposed in the case of deporting Jewish families from the non-occupied zone, to include as well children under sixteen years of age. The question of Jewish children in the occupied zone is of no interest to him."

He saw his brother-in-law laughing as he read his father's—Armand's father-in-law's—column in *l'Action Française*.

Bousquet, *Secrétaire Général* for the Police Nationale, sleek, distinguished, full of charm, smiling at Laval's statement. He remembered the conceit of Leguay, Bousquet's representative, who arranged the shipments of bodies, pleased to report the productivity and the non-assistance of the Germans.

Leguay boasting, "15,000 in one day! All our own work! And we gave them French Jews as well as the foreign Jews! And children, even though they didn't want them! A bonus!"

Brasillach, the talented writer, dumpy, bookish and disagreeably surprised at the number of yellow stars and the number of Jews he had been living amongst. Proud of his editorial in *Je Suis Partout*. Passing it around in the de Coucy apartment, drinking, licking his lips at the foie gras.

Saying, after a trip to Germany *"I had a love affair with Germany."*

Drieu la Rochelle, author and editor, rabid anti-Semite, bedding the wife of Louis Renault.

Drieu said *"I see no alternative to the genius of Hitler."*

The writers and the artists. All brilliant. The so-called independents. Armand saw them passing through the doors. The thought leaders. The intellectual elite.

Cardinal Baudrillart
Montherlant
Abel Bonnard

Cocteau
Daudet
Léautaud
Giraudoux
Braque
Derain
Vlaminck
Maillol

All pro-German, if not collaborators. And the comfort
ladies, the soldiers' friends:

Coco Chanel
Arletty (My heart is French but my ass is international)
Louise de Villemorin (It's more chic to be a collaborator!)
Princess Murat
Daisy Fellowes and Daughters

All happy to mingle with the likes of Ernst Jünger, with
all the homosexuals in love with Karl-Heinz Bremer at the
Deutsche Institut, blond and handsome and inspiring
Brasillach to write, '*You will always arise for us like a
young Siegfried conquering evil spells.*'
Children too, for some of the collaborators. Brought in
at night and taken to the bedrooms. Girls and boys. Mostly
the latter. The sickness. But in a world that was so diseased
anything was normal. Even pedophilia. Armand was
shocked, embarrassed. Then, again in denial of unpleasant
affairs, dismissed it and refused to acknowledge its occurrence.
Max Farber, downstairs in Paris, just before they took
him away. The Vélodrome d'Hiver, grandstands, packed
with 15,000 people. Children. Mothers pleading. Max and
Karen Farber pushed around. Laughed at. Spat upon.
Trains. Filth. Incomprehension.

Dermot: What were the Germans really like?
Armand: They were correct.

Dermot: And efficient.

Armand: Oh, very efficient.

Dermot: Keen on the old productivity.

Armand: You could say that.

Dermot: Yes. You could. In three months in 1944, 437,000 Jews were gassed to death in Auschwitz.

Armand: *Ce n'est pas vrai!*

Dermot: Yes, indeed. Great organizers. Of course, they had some help. 30,000 French Milice. 100,000 French in German uniforms by 1943.

Armand: *Mais non!*

Dermot: 'Fraid so, *mon vieux*. How many did you deport?

Armand: I suppose about 200,000. A lot were volunteers.

Dermot: Volunteers for the camps?

Armand: No, the labor for German industry.

Dermot: Some communists too.

Armand: Oh, yes. Marchais, head of the Party, volunteered twice for the Messerschmitt factory.

Dermot: No wonder the ME109 fighter wasn't up to the Spitfire.

Armand: Listen, Dermot. If I hadn't argued every day with my German counterpart, they'd have taken twice as many French people to Germany.

Dermot: I believe you. Begod, they should have given you a medal. I mean, Pétain decorated Mitterrand.

Armand: Me too!

Dermot: Attaboy, *mon beau-père!*

Armand married a saint. A woman of unrelenting religiosity and unbending principles. Full of Christian charity, within the limits of the family code on race. Oriane de Montriveau of La Fontanelle near Montdidier-les-Murs in the Vaucluse of Provence.

Her father, Hubert de Montriveau, *député* and *maire* of Montdidier, political correspondent of *l'Action Française*, the extreme right-wing, Catholic, anti-Semitic, monarchist paper of Charles Maurras. Partner of Armand's father in the Lille mine and sundry other activities. A natural match.

Oriane. And her sister, Bernadette, a Catholic funda-
mentalist and watchdog of the family morals, a racist who
lived with them during the war.

But La Fontanelle is the South Pole to Colonfay, the
North Pole. The 45th parallel, halfway between the true
North Pole and the equator, passes through Valence, not far
to the north of Montdidier-les-Murs. There has always been
a sort of tug-of-war between Colonfay and the de Coucys
and La Fontanelle and the Montriveau.

Oriane, dominated by her sister, never really lost her
family ties. In the fullness of time three children were born.
In 1940 Laure was shipped down to La Fontanelle for safe-
keeping. With terrible consequences.

16. Mouse back to Erin

ME BACK TO Ireland. My house now. Dermot's house
before. A millstone round my neck but I can't bear to part
with it. Near Piltown, County Kilkenny. Grove House used
to be 'the Dower House' of Bessborough House, that great
Palladian pile. The Dower House was Dermot's birthplace
and childhood home. For him it was not the House of Mirth.
His prison, he calls it.

Not like that for me. Coming every summer from
England, all school uniforms and hockey sticks and rules
and regulations and little goody-two-shoes girls, Ireland
was a place of fun and freedom. The skies were always
bluer and the grass greener and every day there were new
antics of the locals to laugh about. It was, as Uncle Mike put
it, 'worth a guinea a minute.' I was always 'one of the
boys.' Three up on a bucking donkey, chasing the pony
around the field. Swimming in the river and exploring each
other's nether regions in the small cabin of the cutter.
Weekly expedition to Tramore in the old Fiat. Salmon
leaping, the woods and the beeches sighing. The old steam
threshing machine, straw in the hair and the dust in the eyes

and the billycan of tea with the soda bread and the apple tart with the juice running out of the top. Pitchforks and honest sweat.

Dermot, an outsider. A silent dreamer. Always off by himself, refusing to join the other children at play. Being older, I was a sort of gang leader. I understood him. He was alienated from the rest.

I liked Uncle Mike, but Dermot disagreed with his father.

'The Boss,' as we called him, was an old soldier, what he called 'an Irish loyalist.' Ridiculous loyalty. Clinging to the wreckage. Pretty silly way of being agin the government in Ireland in the Thirties. A disciplinarian, Victorian, trying to force Dermot into a pattern for which he was unsuited. Trying, with the best intentions, to mold him into a different adult to himself. Laughing at Dermot's republican instincts, angry at his beliefs. Making him an outcast amongst his fellows. The road to hell is paved with the good intentions of Irish fathers.

There were various outbuildings at the Dower House. A boat-house, where the rowing boats and a small gaff cutter were kept, before being taken down to the jetty near the bridge on the River Suir in the spring. The signal for fun and games.

One game too many for Dermot.

He was always in a state of conflict with his father but fishing the old man out of the river was traumatic.

I was there that day. He became a changed boy. Angry. Older than his years and full of hate for the murderers. He was determined never to live in Ireland again. He made the one visit and that was that. But what he learned that day from Paddy Kennington added a handicap that he found impossible to shake off.

When I think of all the things that went into the making of Dermot versus the things that went into Laure, I wonder they could even talk to each other at all. There she was at her Horace or learning Greek, when she was his age, and there he was a physical Irish lad.

*Ready about! How well I remember the old gaff cutter.
There we came, sailing up the river, the flood tide giving the
boat a lift of three knots and the breeze off the Comeraghs
helping with a broad reach. A last short tack, from the
Waterford side to the Kilkenny side of the wide River Suir.
Dermot, eleven, at the tiller; his father, Uncle Mike,
handling the sheets and pumping the bilge and handing the
sails. 'Let's tame the flogging canvas, boy!' Lifting up the
centerboard, running up into the reeds just below Fiddown
Bridge. Dropping the gaff, lowering the burgee, the Royal
Cork, red with a gold harp and 1720, sitting in the cockpit,
Mike having a shot of brandy, already three sheets to the
wind; Dermot and me with lemonade, both of us bored with
the whole business. Dermot muttering a salty aside. 'She's
making too much water. There's rot in the garboards.' 'My
son, all good vessels have a bit of rot in them.' The penta-
gram that encompassed his childhood. The Valley, the River,
the Boat, the Bridge, and in the distance, Slievenamon, the
faeries' mountain, heaving up there like a hog's back on an
empty plain. Our bucolic gopher hole, Dermot called it.
Smell of mud and vague putrescence. Now, the Angelus bell.
Then, a faint faint whistle in the distance, silence but for the
water rushing by, then a long, lingering whistle, echoing off
the hills, and the train, the Rosslare Express, thundering
through the station at Fiddown. The inevitable comment:
'She's on time tonight.' Dermot looking at me and saying,
'Not again! Who cares?' Waiting for Seamus MacMahon,
the bridge keeper, to come and help haul the yacht into the
reeds past the high-water limit. Then the pony and trap up
to Grove House. Up the Long Drive, evening clouds
billowing, beeches sighing, smell of lilac, gravel crunching
under the wheels. Another time. I remember our fumbling
education. Dermot and me in the boat. 'It's dark in here.'
'Did anyone see us?' 'No. Close the hatch.' 'Get up on the
bunk.' 'What are you doing?' 'I heard Father talking about
showing a woman the golden rivet. Here, hold it.' 'You're
bad. It's big.' 'Open your legs a little.' 'You musn't.' 'No,*

just the finger.' 'Oh, careful! Do you want me to pull your thing?' 'Oh, yes. Squeeze as you pull it. Like this. Milking a cow.' Guiding her hand. 'Doesn't it hurt now? 'No.' 'Oh, Jaysus! It's all over me. I'm all sticky.' Pooh. Boys. No wonder I came to like girls better. And Aunt Mary that time she told Uncle Mike about finding his private diary. His first scribbles, highly unorthodox and already agin the government. 'Your son has a literary bent.''Naturally. It's in the genes. Isn't his father a poet?' 'It manifests itself in a strange way. Irreligious. Listen. In his diary. His prayer. 'Our Fin Varra who art in Tir-na-n'Og, hallowed be thy name.' What's all that about?' 'Fin Varra is supposed to be the King of the Faeries. Tir-na-n'Og, the land of the ever young. Under the water, where some of the fairies live. "'And instead of the Holy Trinity what do you think he's written in?' 'Go on.' 'The Fin Varra, the Leprachaun and the Banshee.' 'I like the Banshee for the Holy Ghost.' 'He talks about the Cluricauns.' 'Munster sprites.' 'The four evangalists. Cob, Paralda, Djin and Hicks. Nothing so traditional as Matthew, Mark, Luke and John.' 'Begod, he has a powerful imagination. Earth, air, fire and water spirits. Wait till he gets to the Virgin Mary.' 'He has. She's The Queen of the Faeries. 'Let us profoundly hope Father Aloysius doesn't hear that one. There's a certain ambiguity about it, and he teaches in an English public school where there may well be another queen of the fairies.' 'Is that Jesuit coming again?' 'Next week, God help us.' 'Jaysus. You're sure?' 'Sure as God made little apples in the Golden Vale.' Crottin de Cheval. 1937. Boxing Day. Me on my holidays for Christmas. The Meet. Hunters snorting at the Main Gates of Bessborough. Near the fallen tree where Seamus Malone got his back broken. They shouted contradictory instructions and he ran the wrong way. Pat looks at it, the murderous trunk. Seamus used to come to Grove House to play bridge every Wednesday and he'd always slip Dermot and me a half-a-crown as he left. He would hoist us up on the rick when they were threshing. The old stream engine driving the threshing machine through the figure-of-eight long belt. Straw, dust, tea that tasted ten times better out of a billycan sitting with the men. Seamus, who took Dermot out shooting woodcock and let him fire once. We look at Lady MacConnell sitting there sidesaddle in her black riding habit and top hat and a glass in her hand and her laughter louder than the baying of the hounds. The two of us on on our ponies, hands frozen, the road rutted and the tracks covered in thin ice. The beeches moaning in sympathy. Unenthusiastic. If it's true that the Irish love a lord they worship a lady. Especially if she has a good seat on a horse and can hold her whiskey. She was something, that one. Dermot watches her, fascinated, before she mounts. He doesn't understand why his father avoids her and she studiously ignores him. He thinks they must hate each other. She sits there with her shooting stick disappearing up her backside, near the back end of the Rolls with the trunk open and a bar in it. And the big chestnut backs round and lifts his tail with its little red ribbon and snorts disdainfully and gives her a baleful look as the message drops out. Plop, plop, plop. Three, then one for the pot. Plop! It splatters her shining boots and her immaculate habit and leaves a steaming pile in front of the local dignitaries. So they give her a leg up and hand her up the glass and she laughs as she knocks it back. 'Crottin de Cheval'. Horseshit. The national perfume of Ireland. They should bottle it. Dermot falls behind and walks the pony to the Harrington farmhouse at The Paddock. I trot home.

17. Dermot & Patrick

THEY'RE SITTING IN the Café de la Mairie in the Place Saint-Sulpice in Paris talking of Colonfay and of wars and rumors of wars.

Patrick, nursing a pastis, unremarkable, thinking of his half-written story about—what else?—an invisible man. He would spend the day alone, writing, listening to *Radio*

Classique. Solitary, self-effacing, and looking at the world through his one good but slightly jaundiced eye. Anyone looking less subversive than Laure's brother, Patrick de Coucy, would be hard to find. Short, rotund, myopic, he would make John le Carré's George Smiley look like Superman. It didn't surprise Dermot that his work in progress was a story about an invisible man.

Yet Patrick got up to some fine capers thirty years ago. Laure hardly knew him. She was a baby when he left home and after the war he refused to see any of the family except Laure. When their mother died he was obliged to go to a meeting at the *notaire's* because he inherited some of her part of the fortune. He wanted to give it all to Laure, but was persuaded to keep his share for various technical and taxation reasons.

From time to time Laure or Dermot had met him for lunch, but he was nearly always abroad. Now he had retired and was in ill health. He lived in a nondescript building in the fifth arrondissement. He had no pretensions, no ambitions, few illusions. His attitude towards his father reinforced Laure's antagonism towards Armand. His wartime experiences served to harden his resolve never to have anything to do with him again. She concurred.

He had never talked about the war years. Until now.

This time Dermot was there to find out about the antagonisms which existed between Armand and his children. He simply couldn't figure out why Laure especially was so anti her father. Why she so virulently rejected him. Patrick's story explained half, but not the important part, of the rejection.

They walked through the Luxembourg Garden and Patrick talked.

In September 1939, at the beginning of the war, I was in Aix en Provence. I volunteered for the army. They took one look at my unsoldierly figure and near blindness in one eye and said no thanks. The idea of me drilling in a squad or charging the enemy must have seemed immediately preposterous.

France fell. I was shocked and disgusted. I felt impotent. I had to do something. I was staying with my grandfather and my uncle René and I couldn't listen to their adulation of the doddering old Pétain.

There was a Jew at the Lycée Mignet, Professor Hallwachs. He knew Frenay in Lyon who was the founder of the Résistance *group 'Combat,' and the printer of the journal of that name. I volunteered to distribute the paper. I was given first the department of Bouches du Rhône, and subsequently the entire southern region as my responsibility. At the beginning, I used to cycle around the territory, sometimes as far from Aix as Arles. This was no job for the timid. It demanded stamina and, I suppose, a certain amount of courage. Or folly. Who knows?*

Then I met a Dominican at St. Maximin, the famous Dom Bruckberger. He gave me the job of distributing books from a 'Bibliobus de Provence.' A travelling library. I was paid ten francs a day, to cover all my living expenses. The acetylene-powered bibliobus served as a useful distribution system for passing out Combat. *Unfortunately, this dangerous contraption burnt out in Cassis, complete with the books, nearly immolating the inept driver. It was not replaced.*

One of my drops was a newspaper kiosk in Aix. The man who operated it was an idiot. He used to mix up 'Combat' and the local papers, with the consequence that people buying 'Le Petit Marseillais' would find themselves with the banned paper as well. The chap who had the kiosk was arrested one day. Not because the authorities found out about 'Combat' but because he was selling tobacco illegally. He grew it in his garden. However, they found 'Combat.' He tried to get off the hook. He said it was given to him by 'Arthur'.

'Arthur' was my code name in the Résistance.

They arrested us both. The kiosk man shared a cell with another member of the Résistance. *He was instructed to tell the kiosk chap that if he identified me as the person who distributed* Combat, *he would be killed. This put the fear of*

141

God into him. The juge d'instruction *called us before him. He asked the kiosk man formally to identify me as the source of the subversive literature. He said he could not. Definitely it was not me. But he was obviously frightened and the judge certainly knew that he was lying.*

I was granted provisional liberty until the proper case came up. I could have no contact with my friends in the Résistance. *That was an absolute rule.*

Nothing that happened afterwards affected me as much as that experience in the jail in Aix. Being shaved in public from head to toe. Sharing a cell with a blind man. He said the prison orderly had blinded him by treating his eyes with the wrong stuff.

Obscene graffiti on the filthy walls. Nests of bugs on the ceiling that fell on you at night. The bucket toilet. The stink. The sadism.

I saw a guard stomping on a prisoner's face in the courtyard. Kicking the life out of him. He could have been a guard in Belsen. Given the conditions, some men become animals. As the French army did in Algeria. Or the CRS, the compagnies républicaines de sécurité, *the state security police, have been known to do on certain occasions.*

Just when I was let out of the prison in Aix the Germans occupied southern France. It became very unhealthy. I decided not to await the verdict of the court case. A doctor in Aix gave me a paper to say that I needed to go to the Pyrénées for my health. This got me a laissez passer.

Three of us left Aix on a train. One was a young aristocrat, de Lanversin. It was tense. We detrained at Mont Louis. Walked to the village of Bolquere. Waited for a man to guide us to the Spanish side. We stayed in the little auberge for two days. We paid 100 francs each to the guide. We climbed in snow, slept in an animal shelter. It took one whole day, a night, and another half day, but we walked only by night.

This was November 1942. It was a survival course. I didn't think I'd make it. But I managed to keep up with the rest. The guide abandoned us on the frontier and pointed the way towards Barcelona. We managed to get far enough inside the frontier so that when we were picked up by the Guardia Civil, *we were not immediately returned to France but were taken to the village of Camprodon, fifteen kilometers inside Spain, where we were kept in the school. There were others there already.*

It was not good for an escaper to be French. The French Embassy was Pétainist and would have demanded my return to France. Then, the penalty would have been severe. So, using the broken English and local knowledge acquired during a year I spent in Kent, I claimed British nationality and assumed the name 'Jack Howat.'

In the temporary jail was a Jewish banker who spoke perfect English and recognized that I was not English. Naturally he kept quiet about it.

We moved to Gerona for a week, and then Figueras for a month.

While we were being marched to the station in Gerona, roped together, twenty of us in file like convicts on Devil Island, a Spanish policeman said to me, "See that man over there? He's the British Consul."

I took the hint and beckoned the man over. I told him I was English. The Consul asked my name and said, "Don't worry. I'll remember you."

The prison in Figueras was indescribably squalid. There were twelve in a cell 'être au secret', meaning we were never allowed to leave it.

Sometimes you had to sleep with your head under the WC, with people shitting in it perched above you. I have always been too cerebral and fastidious. Constant bowel movements are not Beethoven sonatas. Someone said God couldn't have made humans: He wouldn't have made them shit.

The Spanish jailers were not deliberately cruel, merely indifferent.

When we were due to leave Figueras, we were told to be ready to move the next morning The Jewish banker—his name was Weinstein, I think, and he too had escaped over the mountain with the Gestapo on his heels—extracted a wad of notes from his shoe and gave every man a hundred pesetas. This was a useful gift. I wish I knew who he was. He did not leave with us and I never saw him again.

We were taken by train, a hundred of us crowded into horse wagons, for the forty-eight hour journey. There was a stop every eight hours for ten minutes to let us pee. We arrived at the concentration camp of Miranda de Ebro on Christmas night. I stayed there until the end of April, 1943.

This concentration camp had a long-term population of various nationalities, mostly from the International Brigade of the Civil War. A sizeable percentage were Poles. They resented the newcomers. It disturbed their established routine of bribery of guards and appropriation of the meager rations. They were inhuman. When the food arrived, on one big platter, they would sometimes knock it over.

I saw one man, hungry, fall to his knees and try to eat off the floor. The Poles battered him on the head with a plank.

Survival was a battle. Your unsoldierly brother- in-law won through.

In the camp, every morning, the colors were raised and the band played the Spanish national anthem. The Spanish soldiers, a ragged and undisciplined bunch, showed little respect for the ceremony but the prisoners were obliged to give the fascist salute.

There was a Jew from Vienna in the band. He played the clarinet. Afterwards, he whistled a Beethoven sonata. I finished it. We became friends. He had been imprisoned in a camp in Austria but escaped. I was bemused by the fact that he said he wanted to escape from his wife as much as from the Nazis.

During my time in the camp, I, being 'English,' received packages of cigarettes and chocolate from the British Embassy in Madrid, and in April was one of the first to be liberated. I was sprung by the Military Attaché and taken to a hotel in Madrid.

I couldn't sleep. The luxury of sheets and a proper bed was too unfamiliar an experience. Next morning, I took a train to La Linea, near Gibraltar, and crossed in a small boat with a British Ensign to the fortress.

There the collected French were paraded. We were asked to fall in according to whether we wanted to join de Gaulle in England or Giraud in Algeria. Twice as many opted for Giraud as for de Gaulle. About eighty versus forty. This tells you quite a lot about de Gaulle's standing at that time. Giraud was always a questionable commodity. Brave enough and an escaper from a German camp, perhaps with the connivance of Vichy and his captors, to undermine the authority of the 'traitor,' de Gaulle, he was an ego-maniac and a wavering Pétainist. But he was seen to be a more legitimate army commander than de Gaulle and he was backed by Roosevelt. The groups divided and never met after that parade.

I went aboard the American ship, the 'Santa Rosa,' and we remained in harbor for some time waiting for a convoy to assemble. We sailed for the Clyde with an escort of warships. I didn't like being in the bowels of the ship so, using my head instead of my muscles, I volunteered to help man a gun. I escaped to the superstructure.

We landed at Greenock. I was taken under escort to London. We were billeted first in a miserable old peoples' home in a tawdry suburb, before going to the 'Patriotic School,' this in a sumptuous castle.

English intelligence officers interviewed me three or four times a day to see whether I was a kosher patriot or just an infiltrated spy. One of the intelligence officers asked if I would be prepared to be dropped by parachute into France, somewhere near Grenoble. Being an odd shape to be dropped out of an aircraft, I thought this was a trifle too precarious but, after all, why not? I asked for a few days to think it over.

I went to La Maison d'Accueil, *where a certain Colonel Corniglion-Molinier, a friend of Malraux, kept me in luxury in the mansion for three days.*

The famous Résistance *leader, Colonel Rémy (Gilbert Renault) came to get me.*

I told him about the English proposal. Rémy blew up.

He said, " Absolutely not! I need you to work with me."

He took me to the small studio he inhabited and I slept there for a week before being ejected to find quarters for myself.

No more talking.

I spent the war in London working on intelligence. Sorting out reports that were picked up every night by Lysander or brought to England in fishing boats. There was nothing heroic about the job.

All my friends from Aix died in camps.

That's why I have no stomach for La Fontanelle or Colonfay. It's why I can do without contact with my father. But he did help us once.

I hope all the Vichyists rot in hell.

Patrick continued, "It's nothing to shout about but at least one of us was on the right side. As for the family, they got what they deserved."

Dermot said, "The family acted as most people would have acted at that time. Your father could not have gone to England as you did. He had dependants. There's no great merit in going off if you're single with no responsibilities. His job was to send labor forces to Germany. He fought every day with his German counterpart. Who knows how many lives he saved?"

"But how many did he kill by shipping them away to Germany?"

"The lesser of two evils, Patrick. He told me once that he managed to give them half of what they wanted. Give him the benefit of the doubt. I do."

"You don't have to live with the family's sick affiliations. You have no idea how reactionary they were before the war. And now."

"Oh, look, Patrick, you know that half the collaborators were rewarded after the war with safe jobs. Some have the

Medal of the *Résistance*. Thus are the just punished and the guilty let go free."

"Dermot, you're you and I'm me. Maybe in the fullness of time I'll be reconciled with him but not yet. Until he admits my Jewish friends to the house, I'll stay out."

"And maybe when you go in it will be too late."

"It's always too late, Dermot."

"Yes, the clock's ticking. The bell tolls."

18. Dermot & Nana the Troll

DERMOT WALKING ALONG the beach to Nana's house. He saw her in the distance. Walking towards him. Swinging her hips, the peasant skirt swirling. Nana. The Swedish Troll. The consolation. The drug. The sexual narcosis. She ran the last few yards. He opened his arms and caught her. Instantaneous erection. They came together in a sudden frenzy. Like always. They devoured each other. His hands ran up her thighs. She fumbled for his fly. They stumbled over the high dune and collapsed in a hollow. All sand and sex. Afterwards, the let-down.

Later, in the house Nana interrupted his musing.

She said, "You're very quiet. What are you thinking?"

"How nice it is to be free."

"But you're not free. You're married."

"It's all over bar the shouting."

"I've heard that before."

"Yes. But this time it's final."

"Where will you live? In Paris? I hate the French."

"Probably it's reciprocated. I don't know yet. It's all so sudden."

"Why don't you go back to Ireland?"

"No shrimps there. No Troll."

They're eating shrimps on bread. Those small pink shrimps you get in Denmark. She's buttering the bread and heaping them up. Holding them to him. He takes a bite; then she follows. Big mouth, evident enjoyment. Oral, voracious.

He loves watching her eating. She understands why. She looks at him. It's a sex act. Often they play. Eating off each other. Laughing.

There are pictures everywhere. The drawing of her as a little girl. Done when they were living up at Arild in Skane. Her father had not yet joined the family ship-building business in Malmö. He was pretending to be an artist. Had talent. Her portrait in oils as a baby. With her mother, Lisa. Expressionist. Photographs. At seven on her grandfather's yacht at Marstrand. At seventeen, on Capri. Stunning. Skiing at Zermatt. With Harry, her son, when he was at Le Rosey. Of her daughter. His favorite picture. A photograph of Nana, coming out of the sea at Arild, in a miniscule bikini. 1965. All red-gold, Rusty they called her in swinging London, in Annabel's, all six-foot-two, freckled thighs, flat stomach and firm breasts. Provocative look. Every move an invitation. Green eyes. Wild, natural hair. Not by any means conventionally beautiful. Slightly crooked nose and twisted mouth, but bold, exuding sexuality.

Shameless. Wanton. An original. Everything about her was alive, challenging, full-blooded. Everyone looking at her. Every man envying him. Isn't that what it's about? Now, lying there with a light wrap exposing everything, she didn't look any different from what she was like in 1964. He remembered taking the picture. And kissing her on the beach after. Sand all over her tummy and in her spun-gold pubic hair. Always laughing. Pretending shy.

"Don't! People will see us!"

"Do you care?"

"No."

Nana, nude on the dune at Skagen, cut to show only the long thighs and the line of the pubic bone. Abstract. A brown, speckled composition with three lines breaking it into equal horizontal sections and so over-exposed as to be almost monotone and unreadable. He took it, but no-one knows that. Or about the others, less abstract, which, together with an envelope of gold hair, he keeps locked away in Paris. The impressionist painting of her mother, Lisa, must have been when she was twenty and just before Nana was born. Nana, daughter of Lisa. Like mother, like daughter. Lisa. A delicate beauty. Too delicate to survive.

Nana, the Troll, pregnant at seventeen. Her son, Harry, born in the Hotel Beau Rivage at Ouchy, Lausanne, where all the smart girls went into hidden confinement. Living in a chalet at Gstaad, both husband and young wife unfaithful, she with a Greek shipping heir, and a one-eyed Spanish sherry type. Then, in company with other Scandinavian beauties, in Paris. Picked up on the Champs Elysées by a rich French industrialist. On his yacht to Greece, St. Tropez. Weekends in his house at Grasse when his wife was in Paris. Little trinkets, diamonds and suchlike, collected every weekend and stored in her safety-deposit box at Harrods in London. A squirrel hiding her nuts away against the winter ahead. The family business bankrupt. The trust limited and held for her children. In London, a brief fling, but long enough to produce another baby with guaranteed maintenance from a rich meat importer, grocer on a big scale, peer of the realm with his own motor yacht. Then, free and rich enough, ready to fall, non-conniving, without doing a Dun and Bradstreet on him, into the arms of Dermot McManus.

After, married to Alsen. Finding Hamburg insufferable. A house in La Napoule, a summer house in Gilleleje, an apartment in London.

Suddenly he became restive. Impatient to be away. It came to him in a flash. He had no grip. Ireland. Mouse was right. Of course she was. Why not? Maybe it's time to go back to his roots. He had avoided the demons long enough. Just one fast trip some years ago.

He said, "Ireland's a thought."

Nana said, "Ireland? Oh, I'd love to go there!"

"Yes, well. It may be traumatic but I need to find my origins. I don't think you'd like it."

He knew she'd find it socially inadequate. A poor Irish cottage on a lonely hill with old Paddy cutting turf was no

149

substitute for the King's Bar at Porto Ercole with all those smart Roman playboys ogling her. She often protested that all she wanted was a cottage with roses round the door but the reality was to be an English country lady with a manor in Maidenhead.

"I see. You want to go alone. Well, go! Besides, you've been here a whole night and half a day. I don't mind. I have to go to a party on Fyn tomorrow. With my husband. He's coming up from Hamburg for it."

Suddenly he was afraid of losing her. Then there would be nothing.

"*Merde.* A week at the most."

"I may not be here when you come back."

The mood swings again.

She stood and went into the bedroom, slamming the door after her. Well, you can understand it. He followed her into the bedroom and she was on the phone. She was speaking German so he didn't know who she was calling. But she looked up at him in a dismissive way. It was gone. Again. It's always like this. Post-coital anger. Normally, a few days later, the call. 'I miss you.' And the telephonic orgasm. But there was a limit. Let it not be reached this time, please. Please don't take my comforter away, mummy. He didn't like her. There were times when her selfishness and callous treatment made him hate her. He was constantly aware of how immoral she was. But he was addicted. Like to brandy in the old days. He hated it but he couldn't leave it alone. Who was it said the best sex is with someone you hate? It was true. That was exactly it.

She drove him to Kastrup airport at Copenhagen. She accelerated away as soon as he took his small case out of the car.

He got a ticket to Paris. There was a half-hour to wait for the connection. Just before boarding he telephoned her. He had this need. To have someone. Not to be alone.

"Meet me in Paris?"

"*What?*"

"Yes. You can get a flight tomorrow morning. I'll pick you up at Roissy. We'll get the ferry from Le Havre

Wednesday night and be in Ireland Thursday morning. But you have to move!"

"You're mad."

"Yes. Mad for you."

But he knew this was the kind of thing she couldn't resist. She'd find some excuse. She had a friend living in west Cork. She had friends everywhere. Convenient alibis. Kirstin is sick; I have to go to her. Josephine's daughter has bulimia; I must go and help her. Nina's boy-friend has left her; she's in a mess.

"You may have to keep me if I come."

"Fine."

But it wouldn't be fine at all. She was always trying it on. Wanting him to be prepared to give up everything for her. Not that she wanted to lose her millionaire husband.

He watched the runway slip past, the breakwater, the whitecaps under the wings as they banked over the island of Anholm, the Swedish coast and the white sails of yachts beating up the Sound. The flats and the islands. They were flying low, just under the overcast. He read the coast at Rogbyhavn and the line of the bridge at Fordingborg. The bridge. The image slips again. The river, the body. The past is always with us. Fuck it.

Thursday

19. Armand Clings On

MAÎTRE ALAIN DE MALHERBE was in Aix at the Tribunal when he heard about the accident. He flew from Marseille airport at Marignane and arrived in Paris late on Wednesday. He drove up to Colonfay and was there by ten on Thursday morning.

He found Armand on the dining-room table, strapped down with his head held in place by sandbags. There was a woman doctor there and the housekeeper. It was obvious that his back and probably some ribs were broken and they were trying to persuade him to go where he could have proper X-rays and treatment. The doctor had given him an injection and he was not in pain. All his principal functions appeared to be in order, pulse slow but blood pressure, heart, etc. working.

"He won't go until he sees you," the doctor said. "I hope you can impress upon him the urgent need for hospital treatment."

"I'll try. Armand. Can you hear me?"

"*Oui*, Alain. You must listen to me. Get Dermot. Get Laure."

He called the Paris number. No reply. He could do nothing until he tracked down Laure or Dermot.

He went out and sat under the cedar of Lebanon. The cracked branch was still hanging down and the ladder lying under it.

The killing tree.

He went back to the house. He called his secretary. He asked her to try and find out where Dermot was working. He knew he had an assignment in Cologne, with a tobacco company because Alain had looked over the contract for him. They would know his whereabouts.

Alain then called another friend in Paris, Hervé, a surgeon, who was a butterfly collector and a great admirer of Armand. He had operated on him when Armand broke the vertebrae a few years ago. He said he'd be up there as fast as his car could carry him. And he would probably get him taken to hospital or even to his clinic in Paris regardless of his obstinacy. He asked to talk to the doctor on the spot and gave certain instructions, saying he'd be there within three hours.

His assistant called back to say Dermot was on a photographic location job in Mexico and wasn't expected back for a week. The last they heard from him was from the Hotel Villa Montana in Morelia and his assistant was one Madame Grover. Should he attempt to make contact with her there?

"No. Find the number and call me back."

"I have it."

He read it out while Alain took it down. It was only four o'clock in the morning in Morelia, but he decided to telephone.

Then he had an idea. He remembered that Laure had a habit of walking to the village of Lourmarin and having a coffee and tartine outside the Café de l'Ormeau. He telephoned and asked the patron whether Madame McManus was outside. He said yes and went to get her.

Alain was shocked when she vehemently refused to come up to see her dying father. He was still shocked when he called the Villa Montana in Morelia.

After an age, the hotel answered, and very reluctantly put him through to Mouse Glover. They said Mr. McManus had checked out and didn't leave a forwarding address.

20. Mouse to the Rescue

I WAS IN BED. Exhausted. Due to fly out at the crack of a sparrow's fart. That was not yet.

I answered. "Yes, what bloody insomniac is this?"

"Alain de Malherbe. I'm a lawyer in Paris. I need to speak to Dermot McManus urgently."

"So do I. So does his client. But none of us is likely to reach him. The bugger's in Denmark. Or was yesterday."

"Do you know where?"

156

"No, I don't. Up a fjord of sorts. Ho, ho. But I do know he's going on to Ireland. The only chance is if he calls me or if he calls his answering machine."

"Will you tell him to call me if he calls you? His father-in-law has had an accident and may be dying. He wants to see Dermot and I'm sure Dermot would want to see him."

"Of course I will. I shouldn't be telling you this but there's a marital crisis and he's going off the rails."

"I knew things were pretty strained."

"Yes, *maître*. I don't know why people go in for it. Lampedusa got it right. Fire for one month and ashes for twenty years. Oil and water, the two of them. Fire and ice."

"Madame Grover, they would be lost without each other. They're really alike. Me, I've been married three times and I can tell you, as you say in English, it's better the devil you know than the devil you don't. *Et la nuit, tous les chats sont gris.*"

"Dermot's as male chauvinist as you, *maître*. But less refined. He says, you don't look at the mantelpiece when you're poking the fire."

"Madame, I hope we meet some time. Thank you for your help. I'm sorry to have disturbed your sleep."

"Goodbye, *maître*."

So I called his Paris answering machine and left the message. Well, that did it. I knew what was coming next. A request to process the ads and tell the client he got sick in Mexico. Jaundice or Montezuma's Revenge or some incapacitating disease. I needed Ireland myself. To get away from Cologne and Zurich and even Paris. To smell the river and the cowshit and talk to the real people and get a fast fix of humanity. I decided to go there first and let the photographer take the film to Paris.

21. Laure Rejects the Call

ANDRÉ LEFT EARLY and later Laure walked to the village of Lourmarin, down the field and through the wood. Aware of nature and her own awakened sexuality. Up by the château and to the Café de l'Ormeau. It was her ritual. An hour for coffee and a tartine and a chapter of whatever biography she happened to be reading. She ignored everyone, locals and tourists.

The mad woman looked down at her from her window in the flat above the *notaire's*. The Witch. She reads Tarot cards. The old crow in black walked up the street, stopping every few steps. She leant on her stick, looking intently at her. Wondered. What's she up to? Where's her husband? That Irishman? The little village policeman nodded respectfully to her as he went up to the *mairie*.

The patron came out and called her to the telephone. Puzzled, she went in and took the receiver. She didn't like telephones. The youths playing the pinball machine shouted, made animal noises. She could hardly hear.

She shouted, "Who? Alain? Yes. What? My father, an accident? No! No, I won't come. *Je ne peux pas. Je ne peux pas!* I can't. I can't. Call Dermot."

She replaced the instrument, walked out, put money on the table and left. She thought, is there no peace? Is there no escape from the tentacles of the family? Even when they die they blackmail you. 'You owe me this at least.' Tomorrow she must pay her debt to Tante Marie. Now she was expected to join the death watch for her father. She hated everything he stood for. She remembered every second of her lost childhood. No companions. An emptiness, deficiency. Isolation with the old fascists. False ideals. Racists.

Murderers. Leaving their stain on her. Indelible. Her life an endless penance for their acts.

She walked back down the rough track past the Renaissance château and sat on the little stone bridge over the stream, the Aigue Brun. Death and violence. And a heritage of guilt. The link between them. She thought of her grandfather, her great-uncle, her Uncle Didier. Her sore vagina. Her hatred of being touched there. Until André. And their victims. Especially Marcel.

Her first and only extra-marital affair. Non-sexual because it just didn't work after the first time. Marcel, misshapen, even ugly, introspective, but charming and with a brain. Met at Sciences-Po and accidentally again at a lecture at the Louvre.

Never a thought of anything physical at first. But his encyclopedic knowledge of the Mannerist artists and his dedication to her education, plus his gentle, almost fearful care for her eventually made her almost oblivious to his obvious physical defects. His friends the leading museum curators and art experts of the world. Flattering, flirting.

He wore her like a decoration, a sort of compensation for his homeliness. Proud to be seen with her, to have these august personages think she was his. Beauty and the Beast.

Marcel had been hidden by a family in the Dordogne during the war, literally in the back of a wardrobe. His entire family had been shipped off to Auschwitz and none came back. She lived in fear that he would discover the participation of her maternal grandfather in supporting that 'ethnic cleansing.' Foolishly, as a deliberate provocation or to establish her own affiliations, she had taken him to the family home, La Fontanelle, to meet her Uncle René. She had sworn it would be the last time she visited her mother's home.

It was soon after the death of her daughter, Penelope. Dermot was away a lot and she suspected he had started seeing Nana again. A wall of indifference had descended between them. Antagonism. He was finding excitement elsewhere. She was resentful. He was sailing in Scandinavia at this time. Out of touch.

She went with Marcel to see the Ingres in Aix. Her Uncle René had asked her advice about a picture they always said might be a Raphael. Marcel was an an expert on that period of Italian art. So she took him up to La Fontanelle. He was driving a BMW car.

Her uncle met them at the bottom of the steps. He looked at Marcel. He looked at the car.

His first words were, " Une vraie voiture de proxénète! " A pimp's car.

159

Secretly, she tended to agree with him. But he had already categorised Marcel. The name Ferdmann and Marcel's very Jewish face immediately switched on his antipathy. He made it obvious.

He turned aside when Marcel offered to shake hands. When Marcel said he thought it was not a Raphael but was of the period, Uncle René shrugged as if to say, What can you expect of a Jew? He would buy it for a pittance and sell it later as a Raphael, just like that type at the Louvre who had bought a painting for practically nothing and immediately attributed it to Poussin. They were forced by the court to return it to the family who sold it for the proper price.

He said, "Well, I suppose you have to make your profit. Business is business."

Not recognizing the fact that Marcel wasn't interested in buying or selling the picture for him. Then he had deliberately insulted Marcel by asking how they had made out during the war.

Marcel replied, "I spent it hidden in an armoire in Périgord. There were some decent French even in those days. Not in these parts, from what I hear."

It was not a success. Laure was furious. Ashamed. Never again. She tried to make love to him that night at the Auberge Provençale in Eygalières. It was a disaster. Dry and sore and closed up tight. She couldn't be touched in her secret place. Marcel wept.

It was the first time she had been mentally unfaithful to Dermot.

22. Dermot, Up the Creek, Dries Out

MEMORIES, INDELIBLE MEMORIES. Betrayal.

Valdemarsvik, a small port up a fjord in Sweden. Remote, unknown. The end of the world. The end of the season. A Saturday afternoon. The town deserted.

The crew already left in a hire car to Norrkoping. Dermot alone in his yawl, waiting for the yard to open on

Monday. To unship the masts and slip the boat. Haul her up into the shed for the winter.

The long Swedish winter. Already signs. Trees shedding leaves. Ducks on the vik looking cold. 'Vik' a fjord of the Vikings. The dying year. The islands deserted. Cabins closed. The skerries, the world's last unspoilt playground. 'Walking in the garden,' the Swedes called sailing among the rocks. Soon to be locked in ice. Cold, dark, friendless. Only the cries of the birds 'til the ice broke up in April, or often May. Lonely. Cries and whispers. The sadness of a Bergman film.

There's no place as lonely as an empty vessel. No more desolate feeling than to be alone in a cabin up a forgotten fjord, alone in a boat that cries out for—for what?

For Laure.

Who hated Scandinavia because it wasn't Latin.

Impoverished. Empty blondes. Frigidity. No art, no literature, no culture. Strindberg? Ugh. Ibsen? Ugh. No feeling for yachts, no interest in vessels. Immune to the beauty, the elegance, the craftsmanship, the protectiveness of his ship. The warm cabin, all oiled teak and golden mahogany and hand-woven fabrics from Gotland.

He needed Laure.

Up the road to the small hotel and made a call. She would be there on Saturday, listening to Beethoven, reading Stendhal. Sitting in a Louis Quinze fauteuil, the carved legs full of worm holes and half destroyed by the cats.

No reply. Maybe she was at the cinema. He had coffee. Tried again. And again. Suddenly knew. Emptiness. Desperation. An urgent need to be back in Paris. Left a note for the yard, got a taxi to Norrkoping. Called from the airport. No reply. A flight to Copenhagen and stayed at the SAS hotel until the first flight in the morning. Called all night. Every half-hour, sick with apprehension. Fear. Back to Paris, the taxi slow to the Rue Madame. Upstairs, heart beating wildly. Apartment empty. Bed made. Cats screaming for food. All night alone, dying.

Then the arrival on Monday morning. The anger, the

resentment at his questions, the careless, unapologetic manner.

"Yes, I spent the weekend with Marcel. Yes, I have every right. It's none of your business."

How near he came to falling off the wagon. Then remembered. 1957. A rough pheasant shoot in Hampshire. Him shaking. Carried the shotgun broken all morning. Settled his nerves with a few fast brandies at lunchtime. Shot the only cock pheasant in the afternoon. A good shot. But he couldn't pick it up. Nearly blew his foot off giving it the other barrel on the ground. Nerves shot too. Nearly drove them off the road going back to London. Stopped the car. He said to Mouse, "I want to go somewhere and die." Through a reformed drunk she got the name of Lincoln Williams and talked him into accepting Dermot without a prior interview. They went straight out to the Hall at Harrow Weald. He had absolutely no confidence in ever kicking the booze. Committed himself just to have a place to crawl into and die. Lincoln Williams got through to him. Because he was simple and human. No bullshit like the other shrinks. After all, Dermot had read all about Freud and psychology for his job of understanding perceptions and motives. Lincoln Williams told him a few dirty jokes. Let him see that he was worthwhile. Believed in building up his self-esteeem rather than reducing him to the clochard *level. Luxury. Chef, valet, civilized surroundings. Other patients of intelligence, importance. Sex. The doctor sent in various people to talk to him and make him feel at home amongst the inmates. One redhead from Munich proved most welcoming. Lincoln Williams came in unexpectedly and found her administering to him. With her voracious mouth. The doctor said, "Always looking for something to put in the mouth, Alexandra. Oral gratification, my dear. Carry on!" Mouse went to see him in the Hall after he had been through the mill. He said, "Mouse, nothing the Japs did was half as bad as this. They come in at the break of dawn. They give you a jab of something to make you sick. Then they force you to drink quarts of a warm saline solu-*

tion. They wheel you into a dark room. They bring up a trolley laden with every type of alcohol you can imagine. They also wheel in an oxygen cylinder in case you peg out. They make you sniff the various glasses of booze. By this time you're starting to vomit. They then make you sip one of each of the different drinks. You are now puking your guts up. They make you drink full glasses of gin, whisky, brandy and a variety of other drinks. You are now really sick, everywhere. They don't stop. They go on forcing it down your gullet. This goes on for what seems hours. You don't care whether you live or die. The booze tastes awful. Must be just like the way the Japs used to pour water down the prisoners' throats as a form of torture. Just when you think it's at an end they bring in glasses of warm beer. Ugh! The memory of it is too much."

This was an aversion treatment?

"No, nothing that simple. All the time the doctor is talking to you, implanting positive messages in your jellylike brain. What it is is a breaking down of your personality so that he can commence building it up again from scratch. It seemed to have worked."

23. Laure Exposes Herself

SHE WALKED BACK to the house. Into the courtyard. The black cat was looking up at the pigeons' nest. Another killer. She hadn't realized when she was a child that she would grow up to find the family's behavior sickening. That the day would come when she couldn't stomach them. Vichyistes. Anti-Semites. They stamped her with their name. It was like the number tattooed in a camp. But this one was the stamp of the murderer. Her grandfathers, especially her maternal grandfather, and her father. Criminals, all. She found out about them at the lectures on recent history when the names Montriveau and de Coucy came up in books on fascism, on Dreyfus, on *l'Action Française* before and during the war.

It destroyed the past. It was a betrayal of her childhood. It demolished her family base. By this time Marcel was well on his way to eminence in the world of art. His scholarship was recognized. He was an intermediary in the acquisition of old masters by all the museums of the world. She owed him a lot, not least the ownership of a small collection of old master drawings that he had steered her towards at various times.

She was lying on a chaise lounge by the pool. André was sitting in the lotus position at her feet. They were both nude. Unselfconscious. He was drawing. Her mons was enormous in the drawings, her head in the distance small. It suddenly occurred to her that his drawing was making a point.

She said, "You are moving the point of interest to the lower extremities."

André said, "Yes. The head doesn't work."

"Oh, I think it does. And the heart. I want a spiritual relationship with you."

He avoided the invitation.

He asked, "Tell me more about your father."

She said, "My father's family come from the north. They owned a mine and enough of the *Chemins de Fer du Nord* to have a station put on their land, and a fair slice of the *Chemins de Fer de l'Est*. The family house is at Colonfay in the Aisne. Northeners are different to southerners.

"De Gaulle had no time for the people from the Midi. He divided France into the coffee drinkers versus the wine drinkers. The serious versus the frivolous. A bit arbitrary but he was not a man who cared much for details. This family hated him. I liked him. When I worked in Chevalier's cabinet he invited me to a ball at Versailles.

"So I'm north and south. Two poles. Split in two. We had our eccentrics in my father's family too. *Le Vieux*. My great-grandfather. An exception to all the rules. He graduated first at the Polytechnique, with Joffre second. At seventeen. That's bright. Unusually bright academically for that industrial family".

"I only did it to please my mother," he said.

"There's a photograph of him looking like a real tramp. Big beard, Cézanne peasant's hat, clay pipe. He was surounded by cats. Bribed my father and my uncle to insult members of the Montriveau family when they hove in sight. Rewarded them with money. In between the Aisne and the Vaucluse is Paris. My Paris. I don't feel happy when I'm away from it for too long. Neither, despite his little adventures, does Dermot. I have no intention of ever seeing the house at Colonfay again. The memory bank is overloaded for me."

It was when they went back to Paris in 1945. Back to the building on the Rue Freycinet. Her Uncle Didier's friend, Claude, friend of Brasillach, Drieu. Another poet. Catholic, monarchist, anti-Bolshevik. He never went out. He played with her, read to her, Rimbaud, Valéry. No Baudelaire. She was told never to mention his presence in the house. One day they came to get him. Her mother was distressed. There was a row between her mother and father, coolness thereafter. Later she found Claude was executed with Brasillach, tried and shot. He left a long poem for her, written in the prison. Calvary Two.

Later still they went back to the château at Colonfay, the country home. Her mother stayed in Paris. Her embittered Aunt Bernadette went back to La Fontanelle. Her brother hadn't come back from wherever he was. They said he was in America.

She wondered. Although they never talked about him she knew that Patrick, her much older brother, had been with de Gaulle in England.

The house was a mess. It had been used as a German headquarters, fires built everywhere, railway tracks across the attic; it was an observation post up there. Windows broken, panelling stripped off, shutters rotten, slates off the long roof, the park a jungle. Thirty rooms and only five habitable. They had not invaded the family wing, the part they had agreed to leave alone. It was locked up. No heat. But the war over.

She ran down into the park. Through the high grass. The terrier leading. The trees were still standing, the variety of exotic trees planted by successive generations, dominated by the tall cedar of Lebanon. There was a beaten track to it. She wondered why as she skipped along. She found out why. The dog was barking, jumping excitedly. Sniffing. The body was lying there, hands tied behind his back. A sodden bundle. Her Uncle Didier, her mother's brother, in a Milice uniform. The execution tree. She was hysterical. She screamed. Her father rushed out. He saw the body. He said "They promised to take him away and try him". She remembered his words. They kept coming back, awake and in the nightmares. Later, she realized he knew about it before the event. He was responsible for the killing. Too late. Why hadn't he personally killed him long before? Horror scenes that lasted for years. Too dramatic? Too many scenes? You couldn't dramatize it. The reality was worse than any fiction.

A doctor came and gave her an injection. She became tranquil, almost comatose. She was taken to Switzerland. She stayed in a clinic for three months.

Her Uncle Jacques came to see her every week. His son, Jean, came in between. He made her laugh. He took her out with his friend. They went to Lausanne and even up to Gstaad one weekend. They went all the way to Zurich to see the paintings in the Kunsthalle.

There was a Claude Lorrain. *The Enchanted Castle.* On loan from London. She stood before it until they hauled her away. The golden light, the mystery. She went into the picture. Into the Golden Age. Back into innocence. A world without threat. It was a marvelous journey. She was lost in her substitute world where all terror is absent. She was reborn. It was the beginning of her art education. Her essential freedom from people. Nothing could intrude if she didn't want it to. The appreciation that makes all other endeavors inconsequential. It gave her a target. Everything important would be enclosed in this special world to which only she had the key.

André asked, "But didn't this keep out the good things as well?"

"Yes."

"And didn't it distort your emotional reactions to people around you?"

"Yes."

"Would it be the reason why your relationship with Dermot never actually got off the ground, so to speak?"

"Yes. Partly. But we are as different, as you say, as chalk and cheese. Dermot's an activist, I'm contemplative. Dermot's background is adventurous, mine's cultural, if that's not being conceited. We can't talk about a lot of things because he hasn't got the key. Besides, he likes dogs, I like cats. If you want to reduce it to important differences! He's a sensualist, I'm—"

"Acting like one too. But your classical underpinning resulted in a certain conceit?"

"Yes. I felt superior to everyone. Until now."

"You fucked with the mind instead of the body."

"Yes, if you want to put it that way."

"There's no other way."

André was still doing rapid sketches and tearing the sheets off and discarding them. She was now foreshortened to the point where the opening of her thighs was massive and the body diminished, exaggerated but readable. It was distorted almost to the abstract. A mix of Henry Moore in shape but Maillol in sensual femininity. All volume, no longer lines. Any likeness would soon disappear altogether and soon he would be entering her, abstracting out the vulva, like going into a flower painting by Georgia O'Keeffe. It was real art.

"You're a rose of Picardy," he said.

She reached over and picked up the pile of discarded drawings.

"More and more you have shifted the emphasis to my sex."

"Yes."

"Is that the only way you see me?"

"That's how I want to see you. I told you, I don't believe much in the mind and all that intellectual horseshit."

"You're getting very American. Dermot-like."

"Could be I'm reacting like him? I'm feeling earthy. Tell me more about your progress to today."

"Very well, Doctor Wiseman."

Laure in the clinic. She convinced them she was cured. This is an achievement in a Swiss clinic where expensive cures tend to be endless. She was over the trauma of losing her favorite people. Over the shock of learning that her father had betrayed her uncle and probably her great-uncle. As well, the young man they hid who was so nice to her and was taken away and executed.

She went back to Paris but never to Colonfay. Or La Fontanelle. Never. She hated her mother and her father but her less than him because she was guilty only of the sin of omission. She positively loathed the memory of her Aunt Bernadette.

Her father insisted on taking her to the Alps chasing butterflies. He was protective. Trying too hard. Not good enough to compensate for his negligence over Uncle Didier. Already, he was an authority. He became the pre-eminent entomologist in his field. 'The Moth Man.' Such is fame! They had no communication. She swore she'd escape completely.

She bided her time and she studied hard. She'd be the best. The very best. And no distractions. She was top of the class at Sainte-Marie de Passy, une école privée pour jeunes filles. *The same at thirteen when she left the Cours Hattemaire, the private school in the Rue de la Faisanderie. She got her Bac at sixteen, with two mentions, at the* Lycée Molière. *At seventeen, one year of* Hypokhâgne *at the* Lycée Jeanson *to prepare for the* Ecole Normale Supérieure. *At eighteen, she went to* Sciences-Po, *the* Institut d'Etudes Politiques de Paris.

*No entrance examination because she had the two
'mentions' at her Bac. At twenty-one she gained the*
Diplôme de Sciences-Po. *At the same time she was going to
the* Faculté de Droit *and at twenty-two got her Licence,
again with 'mentions.' At twenty-three,* Diplome d'Etudes
Supérieures de Droit Public *with* "Félicitations du Jury." *At
twenty-four, her thesis and her* Doctorat *in International
Law. Then, at twenty-six, her first job, in the law cabinet of
Chevalier. With her first salary, she bought her first print, a
Piranesi. Now she didn't need anyone. She never looked
back. Except once in a while. In anger. She was twenty-six
and never been kissed.*

André bent over her and kissed her, deeply. Then lower
down. Mechanically. With skill but not with love. She sat up
and swung off the chaise lounge.

She said, "No, not that. I want something more."

He said, "Sufficient unto the day is the evil thereof. I'm
fresh out of love and spirituality."

"So all you ever wanted was sex?"

"Sex is love. Did I ever promise anything else?"

"No. But I thought we had an emotional connection."

"My dear—"

"Not that, please."

"OK. Laure. After one marriage that turned out badly
I'm convinced that whoever said you should not mix breeds
was right. We inherit not only cultural habits and attitudes
but genetic aversions to other species."

"Racism. So de Gaulle was right when he said you were
the most élite race in the world."

"I don't know about that. But in the background would
always be the élitism of the Montriveau. We live in the
shadow of Auschwitz. It will never fade. Your people were
responsible for thousands of my people going to the gas
chambers."

"But that's so unfair. All my life I've been in opposition
to everything they stand for."

"Of course it's unfair. You're innocent. But who's
talking about fairness? I'm talking about subconscious

resentments. Ingrained beliefs. I don't believe your parents or your grandparents were inherently bad. They were misguided. By their cultural upbringing, their class, their religion. Catholics, monarchists, products of their time. Like the Brits killing Indians or Zulus. Kill the Jews."

"But I'm not of their time."

"No. It's a loose concept. But I'll bet it wouldn't be more than six months before you started to make condescending remarks about, say, Americans. Already I'm sure that you have an historical dislike of the English."

"The English, yes. With good reason."

"You see. Forgetting that they saved you in 1940. Or an added reason to distrust them because they didn't throw in the towel when you did."

"But we like Americans."

"Since when? Lafayette? Eisenhower? I'll bet you despise our culture. Sure all the young French are heading towards New York. They're not living on past glories. They want a slice of the cake of modernity. Of American culture."

"What culture?"

"You see? Again. An IBM computer ain't a Louis XVI fauteuil, *ma chère*."

"Well, you must admit it is a culture based mostly on money."

"The almighty dollar again."

"Dermot says if you want to know what the good Lord thinks about money you only have to look at those He gave it to."

"Look. We're a race of bastards. But like mongrels we're intelligent, and strong. America is the cultural mixmaster. You put in worn-out Russians, Germans, Irish, Italians, Spanish, English, Africans, Jews, Gentiles, Buddhists, the marginals, and the music goes round and round and what comes out is a retreaded, newly-blended American. Reborn. Rarin' to go. No limits. A genetic mix made possible by the geographical transplant. New beginnings. An American Jew can marry an American Gentile. It's still fraught but they see themselves as Americans first.

There's still ethnic pride and some ethnic sneers. Polacks, micks, wops, spics. But it doesn't count. Racial stress, yes. Imbalances. But not as inflexible as in Europe. Success measured, naturally, by commercial achievement. Start driving a cab and wind up with a fleet. Start growing peanuts and arrive in the White House."

"Not always with salutary consequences."

"No, you can't win them all. We're not as cunning as, say, Mitterand. Mistakes are made. Yardsticks are too venal. The TV medium is the message. Hollywood reigns. But as Brecht said in another quite different context, grub first, then ethics. I say, financial security first, then culture."

"You're certainly virile."

"A standing prick has no culture."

"Crude too."

"That's how you see us. A spade's a spade and no racial comment intended. You believe in the old-fashioned seduction scene. Music by Bizet or Ravel in the background, pictures by Fragonard or Delacroix overhanging, Balzac for a pillow and Chambolle-Musigny '91 decanted at room temperature in the glass, honeyed words, practiced and insincere as hell, in the shell-like ear. While we down a bottle of Budwesier—from the bottle—and whip it in, whip it out and wipe it. Slam, bam, thank you, ma'am. Is there a ballgame on television? The only race that went from barbarity to decadence with no civilizing period in between. I've heard that one too. The fact is, we have the best orchestras, the best ballet, the best opera, the most progressive museums, the most dynamic literature, the best contemporary art, Bacon excepted."

"The biggest and the best of everything!"

"Damn right, baby. We don't sit around admiring our decrepitude, watching the walls fall down. Knock 'em down and build!"

"That's why you're in France?"

"No, of course not. I'm here for the balance. To extract from the ancient and convert to the modern. Besides, I'm only one generation removed from the struggling Russian

Jewish masses yearning to be free. By way of France, incidentally. I'm here to paint without the distractions of telephones and faxes and 'let's take a meeting.' To lie fallow for six months. To recharge the batteries."

"Then?"

"Back to the west coast. Not to Los Angeles but San Francisco. The houseboat studio in Sausalito. The racing on the Bay. And a certain lady."

"You never mentioned her."

"You never asked. A friendly fuck is not a lifetime contract. I think with all his hangups, Dermot's your man. I don't believe he's afraid of sex. Only afraid of sex with you. Ask the Scandinavian broad. The Irish and the French are fairly compatible. Not if you castrate him, of course. Not if you look down upon him. Read some Irish poets. Where's your Seamus Heaney? Your Joyce? Your Beckett? And I think you should forgive your father and go up and see him before he dies. We are all trying to get by as best we can. I'm sure he regrets part of his past. There ain't many heroes around. There were some very bad Jews in the camps and outside them. Wait, Laure—"

She ran away into the house. He dived into the pool and swam a fast crawl to the shallow end. Picked up a towel, and walked slowly and with finality to the Pavilion to get dressed.

Friday

24. Dermot: The Wanderer Returns

THEY ARRIVED IN IRELAND—Dermot and Nana—when the grey dawn was breaking over Rosslare. The car ferry was late docking. Force 7 in the Irish Sea. Blowing hard. SW wind against ebb tide and the skyscraper superstructure making windage that was barely checked by the shallow draught. No grip. A drifter, like himself. Crabbing its way across. Rabbit-hutch cabin, athwartship bunk, smell of stale urine, vomit in the corridors, drunks in the lounge. Sleeplessness. Bile. And a certain irritability between them.

He had spent most of the night on deck. Alone. With the sea and things you cannot share. Another baptism. He stood in the waist of the ship, alone in the only part that was open to the weather. He faced to windward and the spray cut his face with a cold, invigorating sting. Sort of cleansing. He leant against the rail and hung on as the seas slapped against the hull and rose up almost to his deck level. The vessel staggered. He braced himself against the movement, and his muscles came alive. The wind shrieked in the super-structure. He relived a North Atlantic storm when he was swept from the starboard to the port side of the ship by a boarding sea and he was lucky to get caught up in a coil of ropes before being smashed against a pillar. He remem-bered a typhoon in the Pacific after he left the Arakan, wounded, and reverted to sea service, when it was forbidden to go on deck at all and the operations against Japan were postponed. That time when he was delivering the ketch from Adelaide to Sydney in a southwesterly gale, bare poles in the Bass Strait, pooped and petrified. Character-building, they say. It didn't seem to have worked too well. It was the only elemental experience left. Except one, and he was not in the mood for the small death right now. He went below reluctantly and only because he needed some sleep. As he climbed into the top berth she reached out and touched his leg but he ignored it.

That Friday the rain came down in buckets. It lashed the ferry terminal in sheets of solid water, horizontal under the overhang. The sky came down to the bleak harbor and everything was grey and unwelcoming.

It was an inauspicious return of the native.

Nana The Troll said, "God, that was awful! I hope Ireland is better."

Dermot, garrulous as they drove down the ramp, his garrulousness an attempt to conceal nervousness and to block conversation, declaimed in a nervous, nonstop way. He was facetious with an edge of bitterness. It all went above her head. Well, maybe she got the drift. Already he felt remote from her. It had been a mistake.

"When did it not rain in Holy Ireland? I remember reading somewhere that Tutunendo in Colombia is supposed to be the wettest place in the world but anyone who believes that hasn't been to Galway where it seems to rain 366 days of the year except leap years when it rains 367. An Irish year is like an Irish mile or an Irish fact; it's a flexible commodity. It seems a lot longer than it actually is. 'As long as a wet week' is an Irish saying. In Kerry of course you go around in a wet suit and a diving mask picking up the old cod off the street. Hence the saying, 'Ah, go on with you, you're only codding!'"

Nana laughed. "It doesn't matter, darling. Rain on the roof of an Irish cottage. It might be sexy!"

She reached over and attempted to squeeze his cock. He brushed her hand away, pretending he needed to concentrate on the disembarkation.

It was the sort of facile remark he least welcomed. There was something heavy and serious about this return to Ireland. Not a time for outsider's comment. Already he felt uncomfortable about bringing her with him. It was a kind of pilgrimage, a highly personal thing. And filled with dread.

Also, he was embarrassed. Not only would she be out of place in Piltown but what would Mouse say when she learned of his company? Nana would not be welcome in Grove House. Even in jeans she looked more like a client of the Eden Roc of Antibes than of an obscure Irish village.

The things he wanted to see, the fragments he wanted to collect, would have no meaning for her and he would be constantly aware of her disinterest and impatience.

Besides, gloom hung over him after the fast visit to Paris, the empty flat, to the Fifteenth arrondissement to get the car, back to Roissy, the fast drive to Le Havre to get the night ferry to Rosslare. His inability to respond to her sexual overtures.

He was angry with Nana and with himself. Irrational flashes. She was a supernumerary, excess baggage. She was there, he realized, just to provide warm flesh in bed and an anchorage for his lonely penis. Unforgivable.

He was on a dry drunk, completely off the bulkhead. The shock. The emptiness. The imbalance. The emotional vertigo. His awareness of his tenuous lease on Nana. And the limited needs she supplied. The abandonment by Laure was like a kick in the balls or an iron fist in the solar plexus. Only relieved by the sexual narcotic. Or maybe facing up to the demons of his childhood.

Mouse insisted that living in Ireland was better for screwed-up people than a Harley Street shrink. No matter that it screwed them up in the first place. Laughter and the sound of friends the cure-all. Why do today what you can put off 'till tomorrow? You're not allowed to be serious, she said. It's where the mad are truly sane, she said. Where your ribs ache with healthy laughter. And she'd burst into song with *'Come back to Erin, Mavourneen . . .'*

The customs officer was taking his time about checking them out. As the man said, there is no word with the same urgency as '*mañana*' in Irish. Dermot was glad to talk to him. He was a distraction from Nana. An opportunity to joke with someone who would play verbal ping-pong with him. Banish his childhood nightmares which were hovering there in the background. Black Gustave Doré caves with snakes and dragons. Interspersed bursts of inanity. No, insanity. A great gas, isn't that what they used to say?

"That's an interesting vehicle, you have there," he said, suspiciously.

177

"Yes, a vehicle that's a horseless carriage called a car, Orsifer. Voiture, machina, Wagen. Or an auto-*mo*-bile, as the Americans prefer. Internal combustion, isn't it, sahib? The pistons go up and down and the wheel goes round and round and the smoke comes out here."

"Ah, another madman we have here! Welcome back to the asylum. And let's have a look in the boot, if you don't mind."

"The trunk? By all means. There's only room for a toothbrush. Maybe two. And a box of french letters. Contraband in Holy Ireland. No? No contraceptives, no abortions, no divorce, no sex. Copulation no substitute for masturbation."

The official didn't bat an eyelid. Dermot knew that given half a chance he would keep him there for an hour to take him down a peg or two and to relieve the boredom. Six hours to wait before the next ferry-load of victims. Anything for 'the crack.'

"What's that number-plate? French?"

"No, Italian. Reggio Emilia."

"But I see you live in France. Why a car registered in Italy?"

"I like spaghetti better than foie gras. Me and the Pope of Rome who gave up Avignon a few weeks back. I'm an Irish peasant, like you. And I couldn't get it registered in Lichtenstein or the Cayman Islands. Where of course I wash the filthy lucre."

"Begod, you're a bright one, all right."

"That's because I fuck a lot, Father."

That was too much. Dermot could see his little Sacred Heart badge blushing redder.

It was a mistake to bait the customs man. Religion was a no-no subject for jokes. Dermot thought he was going to take the car apart for a while so he smiled and they decided to call it a draw. Just as he was about to close the lid of the boot/trunk the chap reached in and pulled a book out of the corner where it was lying in a box on top of other books. It was a book of abstract drawings facing poems, or 'word flashes' called *Footprints of the Soul*, by Jean Perret, a French artist, and Sean O Caoimh, a relatively unknown Irish poet. He opened it, looked at the art squiggles, and read out:

> *The water lily floats*
> *serene. But under the leaf*
> *swims angry eel.*

"Well, now, there's a nice thought."
Dermot asked, "You don't find it a trifle salacious?"
"Would you say your man intended a *double-entendre*?"
"Could be. Try the next."
So the officer read out:

> *The oyster half-shell.*
> *Someone has stolen the pearl.*
> *Ah, there is my hell.*

"Haikus, aren't they?" the man asked.
"Well, I didn't plan them that way but that's the way some of them came out."
"Is it yourself wrote them? Under a *nom de plume*?"
"Guilty, milord. I like some better than others. This is apt for today, wouldn't you say?" And Dermot quoted:

> *The madness of Munch*
> *Proved the blindness of sanity.*

The customs man pronounced, "Well, it may not be Yeats but you're not as frivolous as you seem."
Dermot said, "Yeats, he never put a word wrong." And he started:

> *Though I am old with wandering*
> *Through hollow lands and hilly lands,*
> *I will find out where she has gone,*
> *And kiss her lips and take her hands;*

And walk among long dappled grass
And pluck till time and times are done

The officer broke in and they finished it together:

The silver apples of the moon,
The golden apples of the sun.

Suddenly he was proud of his race. He thought it would be the frosty Friday before he caught a French customs official with Verlaine or an English one with Houseman.

The customs officer let him go reluctantly. He was a nice man. With depth. Bored. Dissatisfied in that peculiarly Irish way. In limbo. Keeping melancholia at bay. Had Dermot stayed they would have wound up in the local pub and he would have reached Piltown at Christmas. Besides, he's a reformed alcoholic. Nowadays he gets pissed as a newt on words and water.

But he wanted to stay. He desperately needed the companionship of a man like that, simple yet literate. To talk the troubles away.

They blasted off towards New Ross and Waterford.

He said, "It might not be a bad life to be a customs inspector with a loaf of bread beneath the shed, a flask of Paddy, a book of verse and Cathleen ni Houlihan. Better than getting the 0740 Lufthansa flight to Cologne to hear tired buzz words about market penetration and perceptual segmentation. *Goethe? Who he? Mehr Licht, Heinie.*"

"I don't think you'd like it," she said. "No suites in the Carlyle Hotel, no yachts, no models to play with."

"You mean you wouldn't join me?"

"No thanks. You'd have to find a nice red-haired Irish girl."

"They say convent girls are the best."

"Better than me?"

And she reached across.

"Ah, no."

The automatic unfelt response.

"Where are we going?"

"Into the Hole again. To see the view from the bridge. The valley of the Suir."

"That's nice."

"Not as nice as Vaucluse, the closed valley."

"That's because your wife's there."

"No."

But he didn't sound convincing.

"It's so peaceful."

"Yes, that's the word, all right. Peace comes dropping slow. Calm on the surface, turbulent underneath."

He was going to the village of Piltown in the County Kilkenny. The place where he was born. Where the genetic virus was injected. Back in the hole. But first he would stop at Fiddown. To test himself at the river. Could he take it?

He drove on and the ghosts crawled out of the bogs.

The towering figure was his father, The Boss, as they called him, ironically, copying his own mimicry of the local yahoos.

"Tell me about your father," she said. "Was he like you?"

"The Boss? Yes, now I think so. When he was alive he was the bane of my existence."

"Why?"

"Oh, he was too pacifist for the times. He had been badly wounded in France during the war and couldn't stand the so-called heroes of the Troubles. He let them see he didn't have much time for them. They got him in the end. But in the meantime I had to pay for his outspokenness. Let me try to remember."

He talked, as if to himself.

"Jesus wept—and well He might!" That was my father's usual comment on the antics of his Irish countrymen. It exploded out of him every time they did something he disagreed with. Every day. Everything.

"The tears of God flow, my dear, copious, keeping the Emerald Isle green. 'Sure 'tis a soft rain!' The stagey tourist saying. The old *plamas*, for which there is no accurate equivalent. Pronounced plaw-mawse, it's what the Irish-Americans like to call the 'Blarney.'"

"You have it, my darling. And a very soporific voice, especially on the telephone. You always talk me into things I don't want to do."

"I hadn't noticed any strong resistence. Bullshit is what it is. And soft rain was not how it seemed when I was sloshing through pools of liquid cow-dung bringing the dumb, lumbering beasts in for milking. *Arrah*, not to say *alannah*, and *sodom and begorrah*, and a *broth of a boy* drinking tea so strong *you could trot a mouse on it*. Funny little people with their shillelaghs and their shamrocks and Celtic twilight myths. *Come back to Erin, Mavourneen*, if you're on a round-trip ticket with a fixed return booking to Paris."

She said, "You can't leave it, can you? I never liked the French."

"The French? Well, Nana, there are those who say they're shits and that's certainly true, in a way. Because they're contrary. Utterly chauvinistic. But they're unboring shits. Although they drive me up the wall with their infernal conceit they suited me better than the amiable nincompoops I've worked with in some countries. You know the sort. Pleading, servile. Love me and have a good day! Those are the characteristics of people who have nothing to say. That fearful middle-class gentility of the Anglo-Saxons. They compare lawnmowers, homemade marmalade, so-called Italian restaurants. The Americans are invariably nice and friendly but they tend to compare prices. With great objectivity."

But what a lot of crap. His best friends were Bimmy, a German, and Sterling, an American. Giles Pollock, now an English baronet.

All things considered though he'd rather be in France than anywhere. He was never one for the easy environment. The fact is, and Laure knew it best, he was an in-between person, happiest when travelling, at home in a city he didn't know with a language he didn't understand. Unfixed. So long as he had a home base, back on the ranch, in Paris.

Still, there were days when he needed to get away from the French. When the war and the Occupation came up.

When his father-in-law talked about the hardships they endured. They construct historical narratives that are of questionable objectivity and often simply untrue. *'France liberated herself.'* Don't bother me with the facts. Well, yes, but don't convert cowardly behavior into heroics.

In fact, he despised them a lot of the time. Especially when he flashed back to the war. Still, being a mite cantankerous himself, Dermot enjoyed their cuts and thrusts.

He had a theory. The Irish and the French get along together not only because the Irish aren't English but because they are both cantankerous races. Cantankerousness in the Irish is genetic. It developed as an allergy to the potato over centuries of having the common spud as the staple diet. Then in the seventeenth century there were thousands of Irishmen in the service of the king of France. Mercenaries forced by the Brits to flee Ireland. With the liberated Irishman's eager propensity to copulate with the immoral mademoisclles, there was an injection of bloody-mindedness into the French blood. Irish sperm is highly potent. And mildly toxic.

The French have a different set of priorities. They put writers and painters above the mercantile spivs and forgive them their tresspasses. Being a bit of a painter and a bit of a writer, he appreciated this positioning statement. No, he thought, they're not 'nice,' the French. They're unscrupulous. But they're passionate. That suited him when he doffed his mental combat uniform. He was not much of a one for reasonable things. His abiding fear was to be detached from the French environment, to have the *carte de séjour* revoked, to be hurled back among the blinkered puritans and the do-gooders. For the second time in twenty years it seemed a likely prospect.

The first was the death of his daughter, Penelope. She was the glue that held the elements of life together: the marriage, his job, Paris. When she went, he slipped and went off the rails and took another cure for the booze. Laure lost herself in intensive research into the lives of long-dead painters. And in an art expert who flattered and charmed her. He lost himself in his yacht, externalized the pain, converted it into an obsessive interest in an object of beauty. Lived in the Swedish yard. Travelled, couldn't stand still, couldn't rest. The death of Penelope was the pivotal point in his life. Constant movement was an antidote to the pain. He couldn't go to the house in Provence. The Pavilion had been done up for Penelope. Her easel stood there, another reminder of her bubbly presence.

After Laure's affair with Marcel, he sought solace again in Nana the Troll. A sexual tranquillizer. But a powerful one.

Already, long before he left for Mexico, communications between Dermot and Laure had broken down. They were strangers. The cultural gap opened up and they fell into it.

Laure said, "Why don't you go away for good? I don't mind. I'm better off without you."

A nice thing to say to your husband when he's off to dangerous parts. It cut like a knife.

Now she had read the letter. Detailed. Clinical, except that it had been written in the heat of body love and his genius for verbalizing the particular. He had photographed the particulars. God is in the details and the details are often, shall we say, private. Unvulgar close-ups, expressions of adoration.

He protested to himself, I took them for painting reference. Like Rodin, Maillol, Egon Schiele. People didn't understand that. Especially wives. Even French wives. The word made flesh. Not the way it's meant in the bible. It's the Irishness. Upwelling verbosity. Sensuousness. Flaws in the character. His last poem:

> *Yes, I am a twisted vine*
> *But if you cultivate me*
> *I may give a heady wine*

Suddenly he had a forlorn sense of drift. The ballast keel had fallen off. He was unstable. Philanderer that he was, and he hadn't been one until after the rift and her betrayal, he didn't want to be unshackled from the marital anchor. Total freedom leads to insanity. He had spent his life looking for an identity and the nearest he came was as a *père de famille* for a limited time when Penelope was alive. He didn't want to think about that. Laure had cut him adrift. His love for her was deep and she had repelled it. It was sacred, sanctified by marriage. Meant to endure. She had shown him that it was not important. He was floating free, with no direction, and, as your man said, 'Pleasant it is, when over a great sea the winds trouble the water, to gaze from shore.' His shoreline was being undermined. The undertow was fearful. No solid ground under the size twelves. He talked to himself. He did go on. He was one for the words. And the images. He saw what he wanted to see, not the reality of what was there. This could lead to trouble. Sometimes the images came together like the split screen in the camera, a perfect fit, but that was rare.

He said to Nana, "The French? Well, perhaps they're a trifle more sophisticated than the Irish. Maybe my countrymen have changed. Buck Mulligan and the sow that eats its farrow. *Be the holy man, God bless us all.* Are they still be talking like that? Had they ever? Oh, yes. And why not? Language is not for computer instruction books. Living off the Words, the only Irish export apart from your American politicians. Words, as Robertson Davies said, are only farts from people who've swallowed too many books, but wasn't he a Canadian?"

"You do know a lot," she remarked, already bored.

"Yes, knowledge but not wisdom. Still and all. If you want to know where you're going you have to know where you come from. I know that one all right. Another gem of purest corn serene. I'm thinking about it as I circle the birthplace, like an Indian scout around the wagon train, delaying the arrival as long as possible. Born there, I am a stranger in a strange land. Me, an alien now, a man without a country, I came from Piltown, County Kilkenny, but I'm not of it. Was I ever? Do I belong here? That's what I want to find out."

"What's so special about it?" she asked.

"Ah, well now, alannah, Kilkenny is famed in song and dance for nothing except cats tearing each other to pieces. 'Fighting like two Kilkenny cats'. Not altogether inappropriate when applied to the human species. That's meself, certainly. All rage and fury at times. What others are for, I'm against; what others are against, I'm for."

"Just like your father," she said.

"'Fraid so. And I'm thinking the other wordy fella from Asheville, North Carolina, was probably right: You can't go home again. I'm a displaced person. A hotel man, airline man, autoroute man. *Homo transiens*. My best line: *'I'm just a skidmark on a runway. That's all."*

He thought, 'Not like Laure, permanently fixed in France.'

Madness threatened so he went back to the madhouse. The place where he was born. 'Whelped' was The Boss's word for it. The old elephant now returning to the cemetery? Not quite. Maybe he could go another round with life, yet.

She complained, "When will we get somewhere civilized? Where we can have a good lunch and go to bed for the afternoon? I'm dead."

"Not for a while, I'm afraid".

He stood on the clutch (heavy as a tractor and distinctly anti-feminist) and crashed down through the steel gate into second gear and the big Michelins with the twelve cylinders driving them at 6,000 revs gripped the patchy tarmac and the four exhausts played Enzo's unmistakeable *Maranello Concerto* and blasted off the hills and the three-double-barrelled Weber carburetors and the valves and tappets bounced off the banks and the cow near the hedge jumped over the moon.

Apprehensive about going direct to Fiddown and Piltown he decided to approach it from the north and went up to Inistioge and down through Thomastown.

He thought, 'It must have been near here that The Boss was picked up during the Troubles.'

They sat there stopped on the road while a herd of cattle slowly swayed across from one field to another. The farm laborer, his trousers tied up with string and a potato sack wrapped around his shoulders to keep him dry, slapped the rearguard cow on the rump and waved his blackthorn stick at them as he turned to close the gate after him.

"Where are we now?" Nana asked.

"Near Piltown. As I told you it means 'a hole.' Out of one hole into another. I think you know when you first poke your head out into the world that life there is not going to be like a strawberry tart."

"Did you live on a farm?"

"No. We owned a farm but we didn't work it. We had very little property left in Ireland. What started as a vast tract of land between Carrick and Piltown, with a big house, was lost by my great-grandfather with quadrupeds that were insufficiently motivated and women who were too eager. Slow horses and fast women, the downfall of many an Irishman. Plus a family predisposition to the sauce. His only claim to fame the fact that he had a horse in the Grand National which is still running. My grandfather was the Land Agent for the Earl of Bessborough. All gone up in smoke with the Big House in 1922. Cromwell's colonel had had a good run for his money."

"I don't know any Irish history. Is it interesting?"

"Not really. Rather boring. Failed rebellion after failed rebellion. Famine after eviction. Cry-babies, all of us. Complaining because the English took all our land. Benevolently, of course. Because we were too ignorant to farm it properly. We ourselves lived in a form of genteel poverty from the rent of the farm which The Boss couldn't work due to his war wounds and this modest income was supplemented by his 100% disability pension. A few rich aunts subsidized my education. Waste of money, of course. A no-man's land between the British professional class and the poor Irish tenants. Flotsam of the gentry. The Boss had just passed his exams as a Quantity Surveyor in England and was in Wales on his way back from Piltown when the war broke out. He joined up and found himself in the 3rd Welch Regiment, a six-foot-three tone-deaf Irishman who

187

could read and write in the midst of a bunch of five-foot nothing singing miners. Indeed to goodness, Bach, it was not a happy conjunction. He transferred out of it, was commissioned and went to Belgium with the Royal Irish. Mons, the Somme, Passchendaele. Piltown. The End."

"My father-in-law was in the Resistance. I have a photograph of him in his Resistance uniform."

"You don't say? Looked like an SS Cavalry uniform to me. I thought he was a military govenor in the Channel Islands?"

"I don't know. He was a show jumper. Maybe I got it wrong."

"Ah, well, never mind. We're all agin the government here. Our genetic heritage they keep telling us is schizophrenia and repressed sexuality. Different now."

"I noticed."

"Thank you, ma'am. You liberated me. But this valley bred them all. The high incidence of insanity in Ireland was certainly due to the fact that they didn't fuck enough. No condoms and God help the girl who got in the family way. Off to England to work as a 'maid.' There was, of course, no such thing as homosexuality in Holy Ireland. The fact that the postmaster blew his brains out with a 12-bore the day after his marriage must have been due to a Ruskin-like fright when he saw her beard. And don't be telling me about the priests and the altar boys of today: I don't believe a word of it even if it is true. It's a valley but not at all like Vaucluse in Provence where I have a house and the sun shines and the melons ripen and other succulent things represented in myth by the fig add to the sensuality which the natives of Piltown in my day thought could only be discovered through the bottom of a glass of stout."

"But you left when you were young."

"Twelve. I was confined in the place before I was despatched to school in England. That wasn't a barrel of laughs but it was on the way to France—the dream of art and fair women—and freedom. Unfortunately, Hitler thought so too and he beat me to it. I didn't get to live there for a long time but I stayed longer than Herr Schickelgruber. Paris, the Mecca for all souls that want to sing. In the meantime I saw the world at His Majesty's expense and had fun bombing and firing rockets at the Huns and Japs. A good war and worth a guinea a minute, as The Boss used to say. He was an irreverent character."

"Tell me about him."

"More? He was a card. The old man at a wake. Derry was a hunchback, a farm laborer. When they laid his corpse out, they put a heavy weight on his chest to keep him in a more or less horizontal position. The weight was tied by baling twine to both sides of the bed to keep it in position. At some point in the proceedings, with all the keening and boozing, The Boss cut the twine and the weight fell off. The corpse sat up and exhaled, making a loud "Ahhh!" as the wind was expelled. This scattered them like St. Jerome's lion in the monastery. Laugh? I thought I'd die when I heard it for the hundreth time. Oh, dear God, give me patience."

"What's on the other side of the river?"

"Curraghmore. Seat of the Lords Waterford. Beresfords. Admiral Lord Charles Beresford and all that."

They were on the hill overlooking the valley. The Comeragh Mountains were a blue-green wash obscured from time to time by the rain that lashed across the windscreen. It was not an Irish *Autoroute du Soleil*. The weather had lightened up a bit and shafts of white light spread from breaks in the clouds. The river was a silver snake down below. Distances are nothing, five miles from Piltown but a world apart for a loner. It was his secret place. A lonely place but not so lonely as being in the middle of a bunch of yahoos with tide marks on their necks and talking about Michael Collins and DeValera and the grand days when their fathers fought for Irish freedom. He envied them. He was a mongrel, half Irish, half English. Isolated.

"Here's another tale. They evicted an old woman from her cottage. She put a curse on them. Three generations would die a violent death, she said. And they did. That's a true fact, as we say in Ireland. Her cottage was overgrown with brambles and we gave it a wide berth. It was said no dog would go near it. No hound would follow a fox into the undergrowth. And that's another true fact."

They went down to Waterford and on to Portlaw and continued to Carrick-on-Suir, across the bridge, missing Mount Saint Nicholas, the Christian Brothers school.

He said, "That's where I was given six of the best on each hand to warm me up of a winter's morning. Sadistic bastards. Pedophiles. I regret not having a bomb to plant there. Being of forgiving nature I wish only that most of the Brothers would be roasting in hell and turning on a spit with red-hot pokers rammed up their arses. I must be mellowing in my old age. The milk of human kindness was not flowing in that place when I was there. The bowels of compassion seldom opened but I would still like to shit on them from a great height."

"Doesn't sound much like Aiglon College in Switzerland."

"No, I suppose not. Nor were holidays at Tramore or Clonmel like Capri and Cap Ferrat, where you spent your summers."

Up past Kilkieran, Ahenny, Tullaghought, Kilmagganny, Newmarket to Knocktopher. Empty villages, forlorn, the bold peasantry no doubt at their roast lamb and mint sauce. Or checking up on the price of beef on the hoof or the stock market results more likely.

He said, "I wouldn't mind a 'welch' in the Café de Flore meself. What am I doing in this God-forsaken place, at all? Well, you're not interested in a geography lesson but the names are vaguely familiar to me even if the road isn't."

"How did you get around?" she asked.

"Usually in a pony and trap. But we were plutocrats by local standards. We had an old Fiat. We called it the Bluebird. We used to take it on its weekly outing to Tramore Strand every Sunday and I would ask The Boss to stop at the quay in Waterford so I could look at the small freighters tied up alongside. Dreaming of being on the bridge with Captain MacWhirr in the South China Sea. Escape!"

"Who was Captain MacWhirr?"

"Nobody important. A Conrad type."

"Thanks for the information."

"We used the Bluebird if by some miracle we could get it to start. It went so slow that any slower and it would have gone in reverse. Too often I was obliged to go on the backs of horses that have a usefulness confined to supplying manure for the strawberry beds. No power steering. Horses. For hunting the fox. The unspeakable chasing the uneatable."

"We have our own riding horses for the family apart from the stud."

"Naturally you would. Why wouldn't you?"

"Stop it!"

"The Fiat (it must have been one of the few in Ireland at the time) was a soft-top old jalopy with side windows and brass legs that you stuck in slots in the doors, the thick mica yellowed and cracked and almost opaque. There were flaps at the front so the driver could stick his arm out to signal his steering intentions. This innovation could have been dispensed with as no Irish driver ever had intentions or considered it necessary to exert such wasteful energy which in those days was conserved for lifting glasses of porter or John Jameson whiskey. Even now French drivers whose traffic indicators demand just a flick of the finger save them for Christmas or use them *after* they have made some exciting manoeuver."

"What a strange childhood. And you do admire the French."

"Yes. I'm afraid they're not disciplined like the Germans or the Swedes. Still, the trains run on time, when they're not on strike. No, my childhood didn't fit me for the cosmopolitan life."

"You learned quite well."

"Perhaps too well. I'm a peasant at heart. Mind you, the country has gone to the dogs. Today the Irish are way down on alcohol consumption by comparison with the rest of Europe. AA meetings in all the villages. The hell-for-leather boys are now commuting to Brussels and Strasbourg in their Armani suits and delicately sipping their Mouton Rothschild with their low-cal meals. Busy trying to shake the cow-dung off their Gucci loafers. The ferry at Rosslare decanted nothing but Mercedes tanks and those on the road often had calves heads sticking out of the back windows. Give us our EEC subsidies, O Lord, we beseech thee."

"I'm hungry. It's brunch-time. Will we be able to eat soon?"

"Hold your horses till I find the local *Taillevent*. Let me remember the old Bluebird. The 1926 vintage car's head-lamps were carbide, and seldom worked. Many a time have I held a flashlight out of the passenger's window as the only method of illumination on the road to Clonmel. This combined with a certain zig-zag course (the John Jameson automatic pilot) made for an exciting form of locomotion. The starting handle was iron with a brass sleeve and it was brutal. I remember once we passed a car that had rolled and was on its top, probably with someone inside it. The Boss wasn't going to stop but my uncle insisted. As the uncle ran back to the scene, the Boss shouted 'Take the starting handle in case he's in agony!' Yes, he was a card. The tube-patching kit and the tire-pump were the most-used acces-sories. Patchwork tubes they were, more holey than right-eous. There was a thermometer (broken) on the nickel-plated radiator but the steam that issued forth was usually the first and only acceptable evidence of overheating. It took as much water to top it up per mile as a steam loco-motive on the Canadian Pacific Railway going up the Kicking Horse Pass in the Rockies.

"The road down to Waterford was always straighter than the road back. The Boss was not obsessively interested in beaches and disappeared for the best part of the day to relieve the boredom in some way which seemed to relax his normally stiff driving style but gave the car a certain drift. It sort of fell off the bumps and the furrows in the road and the drastic over-corrections from them led to series of corkscrew turns unless the car took over and you spun off and came to a lurching halt with the front wheels in the ditch. This was not an infrequent occurrence. In those days you were unlikely to meet another car on the road and any Civic Guard was likely to be pursuing an equally erratic course before falling off his bicycle. The only obstruction was the bridge at Waterford which opened up to let ships through, much like that one at Copenhagen that's always up when you're rushing in from Kastrup airport to commit a mortal sin in Gilleleje or Nyhavn 71, and God save the mark but weren't they the great days, at all at all? Stage Irish intrudes, my dear."

"I'd like to have met your father. And I'm still hungry."

"I have to make one stop. An important pilgrimage. Let me rave on about the Boss. He was better with horses. His brother-in-law, Colonel Grover, who used to come over to fish and drink with him every year, gave his annual version of how the old man, arriving in Belgium during the early part of the first war, and finding the locals shouting to no effect in some strange tongue at the remounts shipped over from England, set to and taught them the commands in English which the horses, not like most of us being bilingual in Flemish, obeyed. He seldom missed a point-to-point or a meet of the South Kilkenny hounds and appeared to need a constant sip from the hip flash to keep out the cold. Having been gassed at Passchendaele he needed a lot of lubricant. This partiality for high-proof booze he passed on to me together with certain other self-destructive characteristics. The Irish virus is a powerful imagination which is fueled by alcohol. Am I boring you?"

"A little."

"Well, I understand it. To be honest, that's all about the Ireland of fifty years ago. Today the modern Irishman is beating the best in the world. Factories assembling computers, Moulinex at Clonmel, and dozens of Japanese and German firms finding a good labor force and intelligent. We're there. Last stop but one before lunch."

Dermot stopped at the one-track station of Fiddown, built for the Earl of Bessborough's convenience like everything else around there since Cromwell planted him on thirty thousand acres of the best land in Ireland. He left from that station on the Rosslare Express in 1938 to be civilized at school in England. It didn't take. A subsequent veneer of cultural sophistication covered a multitude of sins. Mixing Flaubert with O'Flaherty and Synge with Saramago is what got him into this screwed-up situation.

Every night, he'd sit on the stairs, just above the visible part, when they played whist with Paddy and Dermot Malone and wait for the whistle of the Rosslare Express as it passed through the valley. It was a sort of barometer.

"She's loud tonight, there'll be rain." And: "She's on time tonight!"

Nothing drove him up the wall more than the predictability of it. Talk about boredom.

The whistle of the Rosslare Express came to symbolize escape. When it was time to leave Ireland, he was petrified in case he missed it. The big excitement was when the Empire flying boats passed overhead on their way to Foyne, carrying a seaplane piggyback. All his life he was at airports and stations hours before time. Another legacy of Piltown. When he was lying awake in the house in the Luberon and he heard the freight train that goes through the valley of the Durance he heard again the Rosslare Express. But nostalgia had set in. He was beginning to miss the whistle that echoed through the valley of the Suir.

He said, "I can't pass Fiddown without looking at the river."

"Why, is it special? Looks like an ordinary river to me. Not like the Rhone at Avignon."

"No. But it figures in my past."

The bridge spans the wide river, the Suir. The odor from the low tide is not like anything that comes from a French perfumer. Suir is pronounced 'shewir.' After a few quick ones it was slurred phonetically and appropriately into 'sewer.'

The steep mud banks and rivulets trickle down to the narrow, slow-moving stream. There was a new bridge, a nondescript concrete heap, but they had left part of the old wooden bridge alongside it. His bridge. It had a 'Danger, No Entry' sign and someone had made a half-hearted attempt to block it off. They should have done that years ago.

"This is the scene of two traumatic events of my childhood."

"Yes?"

"Yes. We had been to Curraghmore. Riding back across the bridge, my pony shied at a flash of the sun on the metal strip where that bridge opened to let vessels through at high tide. She then put her front legs up on the low rail and tried to climb over it. The drop to the quay below was considerable and the rail was not that solid. I was petrified. The horse and I had an uneasy relationship at the best of times. I shouted. The old man turned and leaned out of his saddle. He grabbed the bridle. He succeeded in holding the pony, still reared up in panic on the guard-rail, while I slid off in a most unorthodox way. When he had restored everything to an even keel and quieted the pony, he led her off the bridge and ordered me to remount. I refused. Too much was enough. I never put my leg across a horse again. And the old man wrote me off as a dead loss. I was not fit for the society of the Kilkenny quadruped set. A bunch of horses' asses looking at a bunch of horses' asses, is how I thought of the horse shows to which I was subjected."

"Darling, can't we go and find a restaurant?"

"Yes. Next stop Clonmel. County Tipperary. It's not a long way. Just let me get out and have a look."

Nana the Troll was restive. Next stop real anger. Then violent recriminations. 'Why did you make me come here? My husband—' And so on. He knew that Nana found Ireland deficient and his childhood tales monotonous. Unless he managed to stir up some sexual interest in her soon she'd discover that she'd forgotten some important duty in Denmark. There was a marked shortage of fashion boutiques with names like Chloe and Sonia Rykiel and Armani in the main street of Carrick on Suir and it wasn't at all like Sloane Street or Strøget in Copenhagen.

He drove on to Piltown, slowing down and stopping for a few minutes outside the cemetery. She looked at him with total incomprehension. She didn't like cemeteries. He sighed and drove on. No point in telling her all his ancestors were buried there under a large horizontal gravestone that he and his friends used to sit on before confession. It had been covered in moss and he had once scraped away the moss to read the names and the dates.

He slowed again passing the gates to the Bessborough estate and Anthony's pub in which his father had spent so much time and what was left of the family fortune.

At the top end of the village he pulled into a driveway and stopped at the gate leading to a courtyard. It was not now an impressive entry. Broken walls, pools of liquid cowshit, the outbuildings in a state of collapse, the house itself looking shabby. An old Georgian rectory inhabited now by an insensitive farmer. Whitewash turned yellowwash, bare patches with moss growing out of the cracks. Wooden fences broken, all sad. He thought about her showplace of a Danish farmhouse outside Skagen. As featured in *Interiors* that he called *Inferiors*.

"Why are we stopping at this ruin?" she sulked.

"Oh, we're not staying long. That's where the friends of my youth grew up."

"It's a bit decrepit."

"Yes, it's Irish. Not like a model farm in Scandinavia. We owned it but my father thought all money not spent on booze or horses was wasted. Still, he kept the house in good condition when he lived here. But that's forty years ago."

"Are we going to your house?"

"I think not, if you don't mind. I'd prefer to go there alone. It's out of the village. Where the peasants live."

"Well, you're not a peasant any longer."

"No, I'm a ball of fire. Up with the lark and up with the whatnot. International fireman, in fact. Putting out fires all over the world. Milan today, Hamburg tomorrow. Ferraris, yachts, Savile Row suits . . ."

"Women."

"Only two."

"Yes? How does Laure like it here?"

"She's never been here. Not interested in Ireland. She's French."

"Sorry, I forgot. They're so sophisticated."

"Yes."

"Where does she like?"

"Which places? Oh, Italy, Greece."

"But not Capri or Mykonos."

"Not exactly her cup of tea. Delphi, Crete, Urbino, Sansepolcro, Parma. Places where there are interesting pictures or buildings or Greek ruins or remnants of ancient civilizations. Viterbo, Tarquinia, the Palazzo Te in Mantua. That sort of thing."

"All very cultural."

"Yes, she's no ignoramus."

"Meaning me, I suppose."

"Don't be silly, Nana."

"I think you should be with her."

"Me? I'm just an Irish country boy."

"You're just as much a snob as she is. You go together."

For a moment he thought so too but he didn't answer. The snide remarks were getting to him. It was the beginning of the usual row. Could it be avoided? Probably not. When she got her teeth into something she wouldn't let go.

Sometimes sex was the key to amiability. He reached over and ran his hand up her thigh. She slid down in the seat and opened her legs and smiled. Maybe it would be all right.

He felt in an extremely vulgar mood.

He backed out and went on up the hill. On the right was the village school with its carved inscription: 'Donated by the Countess of Bessborough.'

He wondered why it didn't say 'generously.' Cromwell gave them thirty thousand acres, and they gave back a small village schoolhouse.

He removed his hand to change up as they topped the hill. She sat up and switched to a cold, conversational mode. She had remembered that it was time to fight. It would not be all right after all.

"What's that tower?" she asked.

"An Irish erection. Half up. A monument to a young Ponsonby. That's the Bessborough family name. He went missing at Waterloo but turned up a year later so they never completed it. Ireland as you may have noticed is full of ruins."

"Yes, I had noticed. The walls around the estate are impressive."

"Paid for by one loaf of bread a day, and glad the workers were to get it."

"Is it all like that?"

"Like what?"

"Poverty."

"This is the richest part of Ireland. You should see it in the west. Remember, in 1845, at the time of the Famine, only five percent of the country was owned by the native Irish. All the rest, the best part, was owned by Plantation English and Scots. Baronets were created by the Brits if they could raise and pay two hundred soldiers to keep down the wild Irish."

"Ulla's husband is a baronet."

"Yes, an Irish baronet. Sir Simon MacOgden. Good old Simon. But his ancestors must have taken the habits of the natives. I hear he's broke and that he had to pawn the family silver recently. Ulla no doubt helped relieve him of his inheritence."

"You never liked her."

"No, never liked gold-diggers."

"She had to look after her old age."

"Yes. Married one rich man and got a house out of it. Married another for a title. Left him with nothing but the family silver. Which he had to pawn. Who has she lined up as the next victim?"

"She's my best friend."

"Ah, well, *pecunia non olet*."

"What does that mean?"

"Money has no smell."

"Look, can we get to wherever we're going? I'm starving. And I think I want to go back."

"Fine. But the nearest airport is Cork. There's an excellent hotel near there. Ballymaloe House at Middleton. Let us at least have a decent dinner there. We can have lunch in Clonmel and make arrangements to get a flight from Cork tomorrow. We can stay at Ballymaloe and if you insist on going I'll take you to Cork airport in the morning. In the meantime, can we try to get along?"

Without waiting for an answer he slammed the gear lever across the gate and double-declutched down into third, pushed the revs up to six thousand and the noise precluded any further arguments.

He was furious. Now he could not meander about the countryside, visiting his boyhood places. Couldn't walk over the fields to the quai where they used to fish and swim. Couldn't linger on the Limerick-Rosslare railway line where they used to put pennies and see them flattened. Couldn't trace the little stream that they used to dam. Couldn't recapture the drives to Dungarvan over the Knockmealdown Mountains past Mount Melleray, the monastery where his alcoholic family went on retreat but really to dry out and keep the peace, to Youghal, Ballycotton.

He wanted nothing so much as to be alone. The purpose of his search was wasted. Yet, he thought, one lesson stood out. Neither Laure nor Nana could ever live in Ireland. Neither one had the antenna to pick up the special strangeness of the land and its mysticism. Its poetry and its sadness and its intensely human relationships were outside the ken of both the followers of fashion and the intellectuals. They were overdeveloped. Overexposed. Mentally overcooked. Not knowing that raw vegetables are more sustaining than those with the goodness boiled out of them.

Of the two, Nana the Troll, being a wild gypsy sensualist, would adapt easier but she would miss exposure in the right places. She was someone for the fashionable places of the world. The hotels with hot and cold running chambermaids. Where the smart people gather. Even the Dublin Horse Show wouldn't appeal as much as Smith's Lawn and the polo. There would be no one in Ireland to lust after her.

She would much rather be in the Eden Roc at Antibes or the Mill Reef Club at Antigua or the Pelicano in Porto Ercole. Showing off her finery.

There was only one room available at Ballymaloe, a single. Dermot was relieved. He said she would stay there and he would go back to Youghal and then to the family house at Piltown. Nana went upstairs without saying goodby and he left. A dinner together would have been intolerable.

Once more he couldn't help thinking how superior was Laure. He couldn't get away fast enough. He roared over the Comeragh Mountains to Clonmel and was back at Grove House in Piltown tucking into fresh eggs and rashers and honest black pudding by six o'clock.

Glad to be shed of Nana, the Swedish Troll.

25. Mouse Works the Angles

I HAD A PREMONITION. Never fails, if it's a very bad one. Dermot was going to Ireland and that's where I should be. He had to be induced to finish the job. The client had spent a lot of money and the results, so far as I could see, were catastrophic. The photographer would take the film to Paris and get it processed at Picto. Then he would make a first selection and take the negatives on to the studio in Zurich where the art director had the scribbles and the headlines. Out of the hundreds of shots there might just be a half dozen acceptable ones. It was by no means certain.

But Dermot, if he came back into the act, might be able to talk his way out of it. They thought the light of God shone out of his backside. The prize bullshitter. He would stage a rapid recovery and go to Cologne by way of Paris, Colonfay and Zurich in a week or so. If he decided to be the faithful son-in-law.

I knew of no way of getting in touch with him unless he showed up at Grove House. So I got a flight to New York and an Aer Lingus connection on to Shannon, arriving early Thursday afternoon. I rented a Ford Escort and headed east. Unbeknownst to me, our boy was even then headed up to Clonmel from Dungarvan and would arrive in Piltown an hour before me. When I stopped for coffee at the West Gate in Clonmel, he had just departed. He said he had felt fine as he drove through the Knockmealdown Mountains, past the monastery of Mount Melleray where the professional drinkers went on retreat.

I bowled into the courtyard at Grove House at about six and the first thing I saw was the red car with the Reggio Emilia numberplate. I barged in the kitchen door and there he was being fed a high tea of bacon and eggs and sausages and toast and marmalade and Eileen O'Connor fussing over him like an old hen. He looked up and then continued eating as if it was the most normal thing in the world to meet after Morelia, Mexico, in Piltown, County Kilkenny, Ireland.

Dermot asked, in between mouthfuls, "All buttoned up then? Film in the can? Avedon shaking in his shoes? The Marlboro Man falling out of the saddle? You going on to Paris tonight then?"

I said, "Eileen, get me some rashers and eggs and don't be treating this fellow like the prodigal son. He's a spoiled brat. A miserable specimen. Wait till I tell you. By the way, Lothario, what happened to Nana the Troll? That must have been a fast fix."

He said, "She came to Ireland with me but I sent her back. Sex and Ireland didn't mix somehow."

"You actually brought her here? To this house?"

"No. I took her to Cork and we went through this village like a dose of salts. Couldn't find the Hermès shop. I didn't want her to intrude on my reverie."

"Well, that shows the first bit of good sense. Fell out of love with her beard. I suppose we'd better lock up the sheep."

Eileen said, "Ah, sure 'tis great to see the two of you here at last. Back where you belong and none of that gallivanting about the world. And arguing!"

I said, "You're dreaming, Eileen. He's off tomorrow, if not today, to fulfill his marital duties."

He looked up with a quizzical smile.

"You've lost your marbles at last. I always thought you were two bangers short of a barbecue. Where did you get that idea? Listen, Mouse. I've just got here after an arduous and traumatic experience. Consider that I've had a heart bypass operation. Feels like a heart transplant. I need to recover. First, I've lost Laure—and my whole lifestyle. Then, I chucked Nana, my comforter. Now I'm back in the bosom of my departed family. Familiar and friendly landscape. Compatible people. Using words instead of calculators. It's just the cultural shock I needed. I've seen the Luberon and Mont Ventoux. I've seen Fujiyama. Seen the Canadian Rockies from Lake Louise. The Himalayas from Simla. They're all the same because finally when you've seen one you've seen them all. Well, maybe I'll hang on to the Appenines and Amiata.

"But did you see the purple shadows on Slievenamon this morning? Did you see the mist in the Golden Vale? Ever see anything like the silver river at Clonmel? Ever have anything that tasted as good as this food in Freddy Girardet's near Lausanne? The gnat's piss that passes for tea in the Flore in Paris? No. It's a vacuum-packed world out there, processed and conformist. Like the books they write. Battery books. Passed fit for consumption by the Food and Drug Administration. Without passion. Precious texts published by poncey Etonian publishers with double-barreled names. Fearful formula politically correct gutless wonders. So cute. Dear God, you hear better stories in one night in the bar at Buswell's in Dublin than you'll ever read in the parochial books from the literary mafia in London. Mini skirts, mini talents. Trendy. No, this is the place where they're not afraid to go over the top. Oh, 'tis wild! I'm home, Mouse, home."

"Not for long. Call *Maître* Alain de Malherbe right away. He's at Colonfay. Waiting for your call. You've got the number. It's not a matter of pictures or cigarette ads. Or romantic illusions. Up with you!"

Eileen said, "Ah, let him finish his tea."

I sat down and took the new toast. Dermot kicked back his chair. He sighed with contentment. For the moment he was at peace.

I said, "There's no peace for the wicked. The telephone, Dermot. Save the loquaciousness."

He said, "Did you see all the Mercedes and BMWs on the road? Satellite dishes sprouting like mushrooms. Thank God the old trap is still in the barn. And the rowing boat's varnished. It would take an outboard. *'Come away, o human child, to the waters and the wild, for the world is more full of pain than you can ever understand . . .'*"

I insisted, "Never mind the Yeats. The telephone, Dermot. It's a matter of life and death."

That got him. A look of fear crossed his face.

"Laure?"

I said, "No, her father. Armand. He's dying. Needs you urgently. A dying man's wishes not to be ignored, Dermot. The telephone's in the hall."

He poured a cup of tea from the pot. Sighed and went to the telephone. I heard him clearly. Listening for a long time. Then the voice of efficiency. The Dermot that inspired confidence, especially when he was trotting out the old blarney.

"Yes, *maître*. As soon as I can get a flight out of Dublin or Cork. Probably not before tomorrow morning. There's one which arrives at Roissy at about ten. Yes, I'll confirm it. You'll pick me up? Great. Tell him I'm on my way. And Mouse, that's my cousin, will go to work on Laure. We'll be there come hell or high water. Tell him I'll never forgive him if he kicks the bucket before I get to tell him about the butterflies of Mexico."

He came out and sat down. He took another slice of toast, carefully buttered it and stared at his plate for a few minutes before looking up and smiling.

"You heard that, Mouse?"

"What was that all about, me going to work on Laure?"

"She's acting up. Refusing to go and see him. I can't talk to her. You can. You'll come with me to Paris. You can stay in the downstairs flat. When you've persuaded her to come up to Colonfay you can take a look at the pictures from Mexico."

"I suppose you'd like me to make the flight bookings?"

"Yes, and two rooms at the Shelbourne tonight."

"Is that all? You wouldn't like to take in the Abbey Theatre as well?"

"Good idea if there's a Brian Friel play on. But I'm afraid we won't be there till after ten. Talk about the Round Ireland Race in a day. You'll have to drive some of the time. I wouldn't want to run into a bullock in Wicklow."

"Now listen, boyo. One thing you're going to do because I'm not up for it is to finish the job. You're going to do the photo selection in Paris and then take the layouts up to Cologne. You can tell them to stuff them up their jumpers if you like, but they owe us half a million D-Marks. That buys a lot of potatoes."

"OK, Master."

I said, "Ouch!"

And went away to make the bookings.

We decided to drive the hire car to Dublin and to leave right away. Eileen was wringing her hands in the doorway as we left.

Dermot shouted, "Keep the kettle on the hob, Eileen. I'll be back in two shakes of a donkey's rudder."

Saturday

26. Armand Still Kicking

THE AMBULANCE ARRIVED from Guise. The surgeon emerged from the dining-room. He threw up his hands in surrender.

"He refuses absolutely to be moved. Says he isn't in pain. Wants to die in his own house. Wants to wait for his son and daughter. And Dermot."

"You know how stubborn he can be. Maybe he's right. I hope he can hold out until Dermot arrives. I wouldn't bet on Laure coming. Or Patrick. But I'll try."

"I'm going to need help to lift him on to another mattress on the table. Then we're wheeling in the mobile drip feed apparatus. Perhaps we can do as much here as in the hospital. In any case the journey might finish him. The road to St. Quentin isn't exactly an autoroute. I'll stay for a while but I have operations scheduled tomorrow. Maybe I can postpone them. I'd like to take him back to the clinic in Paris. See if you can talk him into it. He can afford a heli-copter air ambuleance."

Alain de Malherbe finally got Patrick on the telephone. He was not in a mood to plead.

He said, "Patrick, this is Alain de Malherbe. Your father's had an accident. He's dying. In pain. You should be here. He won't last much longer."

"Where's here?"

"Colonfay."

"No thanks."

"Listen, Patrick. There is a time to forget your animosity and this is it. Both you and Laure have a duty to respect your father's last wish. Now get up here!"

"*Maître*, I haven't spoken to him for years. I haven't anything to say to him."

"You could try saying you're sorry. And thanks."

"What for?"

"For not understanding his behaviour during the Occupation. It was heroic. Let your friends use the cabin in the wood."

"Yes, they got picked up and executed."

"Silly fools used a transmitter within half a kilometer of Colonfay. And they were turned in by your Uncle Didier. Your father risked his neck setting up another safe house in Puiseaux."

"Did he indeed? He's still an extreme right-wing monarchist, intolerant, anti-Semitic."

"And dying. It was nearly forty years ago. We all did what we were told to do. Besides your father was a supporter of the *Résistance* from 1943 onward. You know nothing of his record. He was too proud to tell you. You were full of venom towards him. Personally, I deplore your attitude. If you ignore this request, you will regret it for the rest of your life. You should come to him if only for the sake of your own conscience."

"Have you tried Laure?"

"Yes. And I wish you would try her. There is evidence which you both will see that will make you feel very small afterwards."

"Laure has never forgiven him for his part in Vichy. And I didn't like the fact that he had Didier executed. Didn't like him and Laure was petrified of him. But still."

"Your Uncle Didier deserved to be executed ten times over. You will learn that too. He was the worst of the worst. Shooting was too good for him."

"Are you serious?"

"I'm your father's lawyer. I have seen the proof."

"Has Dermot been told about my father's condition?"

"Dermot's in Ireland. He'll be here tomorrow."

"Have you got Laure's telephone number?"

"Yes, she's in the Luberon. 90083902. I'm at Colonfay. I'll wait for your call. 23609236. Take the train. I'll pick you up at St. Quentin."

"Maybe, *Maître*, just maybe."

27. Laure Tells All

ANDRÉ WALKED NERVOUSLY into the house at Maurepas the next morning. Laure was sitting at the kitchen table, looking out at the mountain. She had André's drawing lying on the table.

She said, "I'm going to Paris. Then, who knows, maybe I'll go to Italy."

André said, "I'll drive you to Marignane or Avignon."

She stood and picked up the drawing.

She said, "Let's compare it with the masters."

"That's not fair!"

So she opened up the vaulted room that ran the length of the main house, and took him in. This 'gallery' had no windows but was lit to spotlight the pictures individually. There were no pictures in evidence. Just bare walls. She pushed the button and the sections covering them slid back. It had cost almost as much as the complete renovation to install this hidden exhibition space. It was a fortress within a citadel. She was very proud of it.

"The temperature here stays constant right through the year. The old people knew how to handle climate. This was the original habitation. Walls two meters thick. Tiny openings for windows. Which I closed up."

She pinned André's drawing up on the easel which stood in the middle of the floor. He walked slowly around, stopping at each of the forty-three drawings. Most of them were without great value but they were nearly all sixteenth-century and mostly Mannerist. He stopped by a Guido Reni female saint.

He said, "That's how you saw yourself."

"Not any longer. A fallen angel. Dermot says the Renis are awful, all those posed types rolling their eyes up towards heaven."

"He's right. Ah, Agostino Carracci. Satyr copulating with a nymph. Not the artist Annibale was but Agostino was but a horny old bastard. Well, well. A del Porto monk approaching a nun with her skirts up and he with an enormous erection. And a Parmigianino Venus and Mars in the forge of Vulcan. Going at it, oblivious to the smith. I can't help but observe that you have a considerable number of erotic exhibits. A substitute? A stimulant? A wish-fulfilment thing? Some people are always looking at it and some people are always doing it."

"Doctor Wiseman is off on his Freudian flight of fancy. I do wish you'd drop it now, André. You've made your point. Let's revert to a more civilized form of conversation."

"You mean let's wrap it up in French *politesse* which is a cover for hypocrisy? Are there any gaps in your collection?"

"Oh, yes. I'd kill for a Correggio. I tracked one down recently. A woman in Paris had it. She promised to sell it to me. But she sold it to the Louvre. I think she was sleeping with the curator. It's his way of getting pictures. A more useful customer than me."

He drove her to Avignon. They stopped on the way to lunch at Goult. To lessen the tension, he asked her why she had married Dermot. She sighed.

"What does it matter?" she said, tiredly.

"I think there's not much wrong with it. Slightly out of synch. An adjustment to attitudes and it would work very well. How did it start?"

Laure said, "I had a big problem. I had worked hard at my studies and I had succeeded. But it was an escape. I was very uncomfortable. *Pas bien dans ma peau.* I had this terrible need to take my revenge. I'll be the best and it will let me do what I want. What I didn't want was the musty law. The cabinet of Chevalier was one of the oldest established in Paris and I was lucky (they all said) to be accepted there. But boring! Boring! Mesmerizing was the word. So dull. And the people! All programmed for lives of utter monotony. Let me out! I screamed inwardly. Yet I couldn't quite make the break.

"Until I met Charlotte Rubenstein, a psychiatrist friend of a Jewish girl I had known at *Sciences-Po*. Thereafter, I saw Charlotte three or four times a week at first, then once a week for two years after. I talked. It was a release.

She was a refugee from Austria and she had had a bad experience during the war. Her family had been wiped out and she was lucky to escape. She wound up in Holland where a Dutch family saved her. She reinforced my attitudes towards my family. She helped banish the residue of guilt towards them. Or more accurately hold it at bay."

André interposed, "It may be time to wash the record clean. Make peace. Your father did what most people did during the war. Probably he's less reprehensible than most. Maybe he played both sides against the middle. Time to stop punishing him. You haven't got a little illegal Nuremberg."

She continued without comment, "Then one day Chevalier became lawyer for certain questionable bigwigs in the armament business, and some Coriscan politicos. He had contacts because he was a *deputé*. A fixer. He promoted me to a special task in the cabinet. I was removed from the rest and given access to especially confidential information mostly relating to the affairs of a certain minister, financial and amatory. Chevalier himself started to pester me with his attentions. At first it was simply lunch to talk about certain delicate things and afterwards a walk in the Bois with his Briard. Then, calls to my apartment, ostensibly to discuss business matters. Finally, a direct offer to become his mistress. Or else.

"I was not too sophisticated but I could see it was an attempt to get me to compromise myself. I already knew too much. About insider trading by Chevalier. And payments to mistresses of politicians. Free apartments for functionaries. Kickbacks. I was shocked. That wasn't the worst. Bousquet was a constant visitor. So was Leguay. The worst types of Vichy, who were obviously pals of the president.

"There was talk of getting rid of an awkward customer who was asking embarrassing questions. There appeared to be no limit to the criminality of the ruling class. I decided to leave, but I knew Chevalier would make life difficult for me in the legal profession. He more or less said that if I joined another law firm something bad might happen to me. You think it's far-fetched? I understate it."

"How did you extricate yourself?" André asked.

"I married Dermot."

"Go on."

"I'm not sure I ought to tell you all this."

"Go on,"he said.

Laure mused, "I remember when Dermot came into my life. He called me and asked me to lunch to talk about representing his company as they were changing their legal counsel. He told me the story of his grandfather and Colonfay and my father's introduction. We had lunch. To cut a long story short, instead of asking the Chevalier cabinet to handle his company's business, he asked me to join the company as the corporation lawyer. So I did." She paused.

"I remember the day I met Dermot. Not grey like a French lawyer or an *inspecteur des finances*. Not sleek and dwarfish and Cardin-suited like the Latin edition of an advertising man or used-car salesman but six-foot two of dishevelled Irishman wearing what he called his Bertie Wooster sports coat and a salmon-pink shirt and dirty suede desert boots. With undisciplined hair and, I soon found, a reputation for brilliance and nonconformity. With what one of the girls called a soporific voice and a presence. He could sell any advertising campaign to the most antagonistic client. But he despised the business. He was a poet. Short story writer. Intuitive. The other side of the coin. Novel, in my experience. He was made to order. He had been married but it was a mistake. Didn't last long. He had almost forgotten it until it became necessary to satisfy his puritanical bosses in New York, so he got a divorce. The news that it had gone through had come through the day he asked me if I would work with him on an idea they had had in New York. To reorganize the Paris office. Would I be interested in helping him try to sort the legal problems and combining it with certain international coordination functions? Would I find it interesting? Would I!

"I remember the lunch and the dinner and sitting up all night at the Flore and how quickly we established a rapport. It was like opening the window in a musty room, and having an eagle fly in. At that moment he was living in London, a free soul, and the whole thing appealed to me. I went over there and saw his life and I wanted it. It was fun."

André asked, "So you married him?"

"Yes. I married him. Why did I do it? I asked myself. And others asked it from Geneva to New York. Escape. *Différence* was the answer. Contrast. Escape. Hope. Desperation. A role-changing act.

"Not like the rest of my circle. Removal from the squalor of the political-legal scene. Divorce from my mother's life and attitudes. Disillusionment, complete. Yes, commonplace though it is I was kicking against my background.

"Novelty, Dermot suggested, when I first met him. Novelty? Why did I do it? Why indeed? Well, look at the offers I had. The first from a buttoned-down American executive from the New York office, all Notre Dame and Brooks Brothers suits. The next from a Swiss client. Swiss! Chocolate and cuckoo clocks. The next a plummy Englishman, shooting grouse on the Twelfth of August. Then, a weasel of a Frenchman, dishonest, sucking up to the boss. And always my old *Sciences-Po* friend, Marcel. Plus a man in the *Conseil d'Etat*. He had wanted to marry me. My family wanted me to marry him. His parents were rich intellectuals though it was rumoured that his grandmother was illegitimate by a famous writer who was partly Jewish. But I could not bear to have him touch me. He had his problems and I had enough of my own. Later he was killed in a car accident. So much for the life of the privileged establishment. Prestige, perhaps, but not much fun. I wanted fun! I felt like committing a *bêtise*. I certainly achieved it.

"In comes a wild Irishman, ranting, irreverent, unclassified, out of the rut. I said, I want to be be happy. To be happy is to be different to them. To be modern and a success. I am not going to live like my mother! That's what I determined. And what bigger challenge than the wild Dermot?

"I'll tell you the real reason. He made me laugh. He took me out of myself.

"And he was acceptable to my mother. He was Irish. That meant Catholic. And anti-British. She would never have agreed to meet an Englishman. It seemed made in heaven."

She said, " Listen."

Maman: Laure, I don't understand you. Me: What don't you understand? That I don't agree with all this anti-de Gaulle, anti-Semitic, anti-English, anti-Socialist nonsense? That I don't want to live this kind of life? Boring, reactionary, royalist, for heaven's sake! I don't want any part of this family's past. Look, here in the book, Fascism in France *and in the American book,* Action Française, *your father's words, in 1935, about the new martial spirit of Mussolini's new army—don't you find that a joke now?— Listen:* 'Les âmes délicates sont parfois choquées par les violences qui accompagment cette immense opération de réveil national. Ha! Tant pis pour les âmes délicates! Il n'y a plus beaucoup de place pour elles dans le monde rude d'aujourd'hui.' *Tant pis pour les âmes délicate! Every day I see it. His support of the German moves against the Jews. OK, so I loved him. And I know you can make a mistake. But you go on believing Dreyfus was guilty. You go on about the English sinking the French fleet at Mers el Kebir. Grandfather killed untold thousands with his incitement to racial intolerance. It's mad! I don't want to be a part of it. You have no remorse. And you think the world begins and ends in the Sixteenth arrondissement or the Quai d'Orsay. Le Quai! Mother, that world has gone. It died in 1940 or before. I have no intention of living my life in a musty law cabinet with all those superannuated functionaries. Besides, you have lived all your life in the shadow of my father. He has no consideration. He goes off on his butterfly hunts whenever he has time. Ecuador, Madagascar, the Cameroons, Borneo! You only see him at meal-times. The rest of the time he's in his room playing with his moths. Whenever there's a crisis, he leaves for some exotic place. Where do you ever go? Colonfay. The Aisne. Not me, never. I'll have a life of my own."*

She went on, "It was like talking to the wall. So I got pleasure out of going into the vulgar publicity business. In those days it was not a business for well-educated, well-brought-up young ladies from the Sixteenth arrondissement. A business for vulgarians. It still is. And a woman was in it just for the false glamor and the opportunities it offered for diversions. I was delirious at the idea of marrying Dermot. I knew everyone was astounded and I enjoyed it. It was a funny business. The agency was a serious advertising company with big international accounts but it was also an office the purpose of which appeared to be to provide a cover for CIA people. Some had absolutely no knowledge of the advertising business. One was so ignorant he had to be a CIA man. All the men were unlettered and embarrassingly uncultured. When an art director showed an ad with a drawing of a nude with vulva and pubic hair prominent and suggested doing something similar and I pointed out that, after all, being by Gustav Klimt made it permissible, he looked at me and said, "Who is Gustav Klimt?" Hard to take. An interest in culture was seen to be detrimental to the business of making money.

"Fortunately I was insulated from most of that sort of contact by my legal standing. When it became known that I was going to marry Dermot, another admirer, the plummy type from the London office, said he was a crude colonial from Australia with the mud still on his boots. A womanizer. Improvident. Rude. He wasn't of course Australian. He'd been in the Sydney office for four years. But he couldn't have sold him higher. The trouble was he didn't behave with me the way they said he would. He was full of respect. I suppose I didn't explode people into an instant state of lust so much as make people want to talk to me.

"I would have preferred that they had the first impulse. I didn't want to be talked to: I wanted to be taken. That too like everybody else."

Laure went on. "When we became lovers, the sex part was awful but I thought that was to be expected at the beginning. The English have a joke about 'just lie back and close your eyes and think of England!' I moved out of the Rue Freycinet and took a small apartment on the Rue Visconti. He liked the Latin Quarter and stayed in the licentious Hotel d'Alsace just around the corner on the Rue des Beaux Arts. That was where it started. Decadence, he often said, is the highest form of culture. And he certainly seemed bent on proving it."

The Hotel d'Alsace. 13, rue des Beaux Arts. She looked at the plaque on the wall that said Oscar Wilde died there. She went in, tentatively. He had asked her to lunch there. It was all very odd. A strange venue for a business lunch. She was dressed for the Bristol or the Ritz, regulation Sixteenth arrondissement, ultra conservative, imprisoned in the regulations of the caste. Her manners matched her style. Correct.

The excitement hit her when she walked in the door. It was like opening up the shutters in Provence and letting the dazzling sunlight into a dark room. Light, bright, alive. It knocked the inherited conceit and assumed superiority out of her. It was as if she knew there was a forbidden world in here. There was an electrical charge of sensuality in the place. Baudelaire, Lautrec, Piaf. A scruffy fin de siècle look. Threadbare, heavy red velvet, decadence. Unimportant fripperies disdained. Even the furnishings had a look of anarchism.

Freedom, but not open to everyone. The girl in reception looked at her suspiciously. They looked after their guests there and they vetted the visitors. Who knows, it might be someone he didn't want to see. A wife? A pregnant girlfriend? A spy from his office? Laure carried herself with authority after all. In fact, she was not at ease, and compensated for it by being ultra 'correct,' almost officious. Her manners, too, were much too severe for that environment.

She led Laure through a dark lounge to the small courtyard at the back. There was a big table, the traditional table d'hôte, *where the lunch was being laid by a cross-eyed maid.*

He sat at the table by the fountain. A dishevelled character, looking as if he had been dragged through a hedge backwards. Fair, rough-hewn and laughing. Loud check sports coat, shirt open at the neck, hair falling over his lined forehead and in his blue eyes. He had, as they say, the map of Ireland on his face and he could have been a model for the Marlboro Man. He could never, ever be a French lawyer or bureaucrat. Point one in his favor.

The receptionist put her arm around his shoulders and kissed him lingeringly on the mouth when he turned his head. This was giving Laure the message.

She said, "I'm Laure de Coucy. You asked me to meet you here."

"Yes, indeed. But I should have warned you. This is a pretty strange place."

She was embarrassed, aware of the fact that she looked out of place. Inhibited, and she felt he knew it.

"I'm sorry. It seems pretty casual here. I like it."

"Casual's the word. Look around. See, there's an ocelot tied to the tree. And a pheasant. It has no tail because the dog got it. Look at the other tree. Yes, that's a python lying on the branch. Belongs to a Swedish girl who lives with a pop singer and invites people to watch it enjoying its supper of live rats."

"Ugh!"

"Yes, I agree. But we have others. There's a professor from Stanford who is here for the cure."

"The cure?"

"The cure. One week is all it takes to get rid of your neuroses. When he arrived he was all uptight and couldn't talk to anyone. Now he's mixing it with everyone. Normal. We have a car designer who does nice drawings. We have, let's see, all sorts of art experts, authors, American models, photographers, a doctor of medicine, an architect. Come this evening, we're having a party. We roll the carpet up in the lounge and let her rip."

"I'm afraid I'd be a liability. I don't drink or dance."

"Neither do I. But here nobody expects you to do anything except get along."

"Who was the girl who showed me in?"

"Oh, that was Astrid. One of six sisters of the owner. Look, we can't talk here. Come on up to my room after lunch."

She hesitated. The idea of going up to a man's room! Would he try . . .?

He noticed her hesitation.

"Relax. That's it up there. The open window looks over this courtyard. If I try to rape you just yell. I mean, nobody will take any notice but it will make you feel good! It happens to be the room in which Oscar Wilde died. It's worth a visit.

Lunch was full of laughter and the sound of friends. Everybody talked to her, put her at her ease. Warned her to look out for him, he was a real philanderer.

Afterwards they went up to his room. He didn't try anything. She was slightly disappointed. He told her the story of the company and its French problems. Said it wasn't normally in his line of work. He was a creative type but they made him a vice president and charged him with checking out the Paris office. He was a reluctant spy. A dishonest manager was cooking the books but they had no proof. They were going to fire him if they could find a way of doing so without paying the huge penalty that French law provided for. They suspected that he would backdate various contracts for his cronies and this would cost a lot. The job was permanent. Regardless of who was manager. Corporation lawyer. Was she interested?

Was she! She had never heard of advertising, 'la pub' as they called publicity in Paris, a very vulgar sort of métier in those days. And exactly the sort of occupation which would shock her family. Just as he, a wild Irishman, would cause consternation. How could she resist?

She went back to the office and resigned. Then she went shopping for a more liberated dress. Younger, more daring, more fun. To the hairdresser to get a looser style. A cliché, that. Change the lifestyle, change the hair-style, change the perfume.

She met him for dinner at la Coupole and he took one look and said, Wow! They talked. They went to Castel where he was admitted without trouble and all the model girls seemed to know him. The noise was too great and they left and sat outside the Flore until the small hours. He became less worldly as the night wore on. More innocent, if you like. Told her the story of how he was initiated into the free world of the Hotel d'Alsace and was liberated from the snobbish club of Mayfair, Eton and the Guards. He was practically a virgin when he came to the Hotel d'Alsace. The first day he was there he was invited to a partouze. He was ashamed to admit he didn't know what it meant so he said yes. He had hardly done it with the lights on. The two sisters in the reception giggled. An American girl checking in said, oh boy. She was playing hookey from le Rosey in Switzerland. At lunch in the courtyard someone told him a partouze was an orgy and he found an excuse not to go. It was in a barge on the Seine and all the rage in those days. He was tempted but not ready for it.

'I'll tell Father Tobin on you!'

They still had him in their grip. Not that you needed a special partouze. The hotel offered enough scope for variety and experiment. The air was laden with sexual excitement. It was a total immersion course in French, language and culture, as they say at the Alliance Française, pillow culture. It was good for what ailed you and it cost less than a shrink.

It was the nearest thing to a happy home that he had ever found. They said it was all happening in London but permissiveness had been around in Saint Germain des Prés for a long time. It wasn't so forced or desperate: it was normal. It got so permissive he used to send telexes from Madrid and places saying keep my room but there's no need to fill the bed. But that was later when he was properly run in. Swinging came with the room rent in the Hotel d'Alsace. He was the only one there who was gainfully employed so he had the Oscar Wilde suite. Thirty four francs a night including breakfast. The Immortal One had died in that room and his spirit was still around resisting everything except temptation. He must have been shocked at the heterosexual nature of the games. Not all, of course. Gallery owners from the street and the nearby Rue de Seine met there every day. There was a certain sexual ambiguity about them but they were polished.

Nowhere on earth offered such considerate abandon. Laure took to going there when he was in town and before she joined the company. He resisted taking it beyond the friendly stage.

She was too eager. He was obviously involved with a girl in London, apart from various casual affairs in Paris. Still, she had her target and she kept it in her sights. The sun shone every day even when it rained. They would walk up the Rue Bonaparte to the Café de Flore or down the Rue de Seine to the Quai de Conti and he would smoke a special pipe with Sterling Hayden in his Dutch barge. Sterling, and the hotel, and go out for a quick dinner in the Bistrot St. Benôit. With photographers or painters or booking girls from the model agencies. Or American girls having a fling. With the men the emphasis was rather homosexual and there were a few lesbians amongst the women. All sexes were gay in the good old-fashioned sense of the word. Knowing the men made him frequent the galleries.

Before he gave up the sauce he used to drink in the Colony Room in London with Francis Bacon. Suddenly he became fascinated by the history of art. He loitered around the Louvre. They went together to the Uffizi in Florence. Separate rooms. He found reasons to visit all the important exhibitions. Urbino, the Frick, the Prado, Ferrara, Mantua, Parma. He started to collect drawings. It became another obsession. It was at a time when contemporary art was going through the roof and people had forgotten that they weren't making old masters any more. Good drawings were cheap; mannerist paintings, too. The sexual license and the world of art was all an eye-opener to him. You didn't find it in the County Kilkenny.

He compressed a lifetime's lasciviousness into one year and an art education that started and continued and *provided a lifetime focus. They shared certain cultural interests but the gap was too wide. She knew he was afraid to touch her. He had her on a pedestal. She wanted to be on the bed. But someone else had that privilege. Like a fool she called on him one day and asked the girl at the reception not to announce her. His door was unlocked. She walked in thinking to give him a nice surprise. He was on the bed with Nana kneeling over him. She had never done that with him. She ran out in hysterics. But she didn't give up. He promised to stop seeing her and she believed him.*

Laure continued, "I suppose the letters did it. We would one day collect the letters as a sort of history of the affair. We both liked to write. He was going to be travelling a lot and life was short. We needed to close the culture gap. We needed, too, he said, a lightning conductor to help this electricity—do you feel it?—find a mutual earth. It would have to be a full-frontal exposure of the personality. Easier to put things in words than to say them face-to-face, especially since he wasn't fluent in French. My English was pretty good because I had polished it in England and read it since I was a child. My grandfather made me read his translations of Walter Scott and Stevenson. We had a Scottish governess for some time. But I wrote in French and translated the difficult parts when we met. It seemed a good idea.

"OK," I said.

"And that started it. What he called *The Confession Book*. Total exposure.

"Charlotte, the psychiatrist, said, 'He seems to have a fixation about confession and absolution.' Yes, it was all guilt. He was loaded with it. Acted tough but paid heavily for everything he did. 'Whatever you do you must not enjoy yourself!' That's the rule, and he never succeeded in breaking it. Except perhaps with Nana. And, I think, with Penelope. He had a habit of ending every letter with a little poem. They were entertaining. He wrote short stories.

"Well, you get the picture. Rather childish, I suppose, the game. Trite? Facile? Pretentious? Well, I suppose. But it was the kind of pet language you devise as a substitute for deep communication. An act. It was a verbal contact, not of the senses. It spoiled the future. I was impatient, all right. The impatience was rewarded.

"One day, he called from Paros. He'd had a row with Nana. I didn't know that at the time, of course. He asked me to marry him. I said yes.

"We were married in the church of Saint-Sulpice. Settled into a flat in the Rue Madame. He continued to travel. Of course people were shocked when I married him. They could see the excitement of an affair but marriage!

"You married him," the psychiatrist said later, "because he was the antithesis of all the men you were expected to marry. Because life with him would not be like that on the Rue Freycinet. He was your ticket to escape. Oh, yes, you were in love with him. But he wasn't the him you were in love with."

"Of course she was right. Now, please, I would like to hear all about you."

André said, "First tell me how it worked out."

"It was fraught from the beginning. Oil and water. Celtic dreamer and Gallic intello. Improvident, impulsive, undisciplined—and no solid dependability. Me looking for a protector. A disaster. One hesitates to use a hackneyed simile but Dermot was like a bird that had just been caged. All of a flutter. Trying to sing but desperate to break out. I was stupid. I forgot he had just been divorced from his first wife. He had been hurt. She was an English county girl but, I think, wayward.

"They had been married in Bombay. He was sent to India for two years. Hated it. She went out to marry him. Absence makes the heart grow fonder, he said, as an explanation for that marriage. He couldn't stand the society and the snobbishness. There were few English girls there and the ones that were single were jumped-up bitches, he said. You weren't allowed to talk to the Anglo-Indians, the pariahs, but you could mix with the Parsees and the high-caste Indians. He said the day he arrived he was warned that if he was ever seen with an Anglo-Indian girl he would be on the next plane out. Fantastic. Apparently, he revolted.

"He wouldn't talk about the early days of the marriage but I gather she had an affair with an Anglo-Burmese on the ship going out and continued to see him after they were married. A real mess as a beginning and it destroyed his position out there. He really hit the bottle and the ego was badly bruised. When they went back to New York they broke up. It was a traumatic experience for him. He was still hungover from the Catholic past and it all seemed wrong. Marriage was for life.

"This was not the Dermot who was later in Annabel's and Tramp and Castel with all the top models, who went to dinner with Michael Caine and took out Anna-Maria Pierangeli. Not the Dermot who developed an aversion to domesticity and permanence and marital chains. Not the Dermot who ran away at all signs of entrapment. Who boasted of being of the senses and not the mind.

"But it worked until the death of Penelope. Then he looked for diversions. So did I. I had an affair with Marcel. Non-sexual but he didn't know that and I didn't disabuse him. That hurt him. Two marriages, two betrayals. Our relationship broke down completely. He was bitter, unforgiving. I was resentful. He moved into the downstairs flat and we met only at mealtimes. Finally there was hardly any attempt to disguise his affair with Nana.

"She called once, "Why don't you let him go? He's bored with you."

"She sent me a packet of his letters, very steamy, when they had a row once. Not a nice person. I knew when he started to come to Paris that he was not ready to settle down.

"Even when I first met him in the Hotel d'Alsace he used to play with other girls there. As I told you, even Nana. Oh, yes, I was jealous. After all, how could I compete with all those free souls? I had no experience at all. I was not wild. I tried to wear short skirts but I could never be like his London birds. The Sixteenth is not Chelsea. The Avenue Montaigne not Knightsbridge. But I said yes to marriage.

Of course I did. I wanted him. And naturally I thought he'd be happy when we had an apartment in Paris. He does love Paris. So we settled into the Rue Madame.

"After Penelope died he was forced to move to Zurich, though I always suspected that he asked for the job. They made him head of the European creative side—he was never an administrator. Later they set up a company in Lausanne and he took an apartment there, in Pully. So he was always back and forth and I never knew where he was sleeping. Or with whom. After a while he started to spend more time away than in Paris. I was nervous.

"He will tell you suicidal. Perhaps. It was the big failure. We had next to nothing in common. My whole background was alien to him and all my friends patronized him. He had no culture as we knew it. Soon I was going out to social functions with my old escort, Marcel. To Versailles. Dermot minded, I think. He couldn't very well object. And he couldn't participate. The language for one thing. It was a disaster. I was seeing more and more of Marcel. It was never physical, as I told you. Only once, after the awful treatment of him by Uncle René. He taught me a lot about Mannerism.

"I left the agency. Set up an agency with a girl who was one of the best creative types in France. Of a similar background. She had connections. We got a lot of business which we handled efficiently. I sold out after five years.

"Started dealing in drawings. Things got better with Dermot. On a friendly basis. I was interested in art and so was he. But whereas mine was classical, Renaissance, his was modern and contemporary. He used to get drunk with Francis Bacon every day at the Colony Room before he quit drinking. I hadn't realized it but now his need for oral gratification seemed to turn to sex. Nana satisfied that, if his recent letters are anything to go by. Our relationship, unfortunately, began as mental communication. It was unsatisfying. He started to come to exhibitions with me. Because we had a lot of spare money—the apartment was given to us by my aunt—one day we bought a Giulio Romano drawing on the Rue des Saints Pères. Five thousand francs! He started to read my books on the Mannerists. Of course I didn't know too much about them myself. Marcel taught me a lot later.

"Dermot and I went to Italy together. To Florence, to Bologna, often to Milan because he worked there a lot. The Duomo Hotel. There was always an excuse to go to Italy. A client in Rome. Stay at the Eden. The Accademia in Venice. The Continental in Florence, and when it opened, the Lungarno. The most important list we had was the list of telephone numbers of hotels and trattorias. We discovered Parma and Mantua and Modena, where he had his car serviced at the Ferrari factory. Pienza, Cremona, Brescia, Bergamo, the Palladian villas in the Veneto, we saw them all. No doubt about it, his interest was cursory. He was still a playboy at heart. Fast cars and fast women.

"I remember we went to Greece when I was pregnant with Penelope. I was so seasick on the ferry to Santorini. I hate the sea. He loves it. I thought we had a lot in common apart from the wine-dark sea. All camouflage. Yes, we liked being together, as long as it didn't lead to intimacy. Oh, I don't mean sex. We did that rather awkwardly, shyly, like children.

"He hated to be touched. At least by me. No, I mean we never actually communicated properly. I was trying too hard: he was petrified of being imprisoned. Loss of independence, it isn't just a psychological cliché. Yet he wanted to settle down, I think. Yes and no. He quite liked the idea of being married to me and living in Paris. He was proud of me, I see that now. He loved me, yes. Not passionately but deeply. The trouble was he always set me apart. I could never be like one of the other girls. I remained an ideal. Who wants to be an ideal?

"After Penelope, he found more and more excuses to be in Lausanne. I didn't find out until much later that Nana was living there too.

"More and more also his interests centered on Germany. His big clients were there and the German offices needed a lot of help. He was in Dusseldorf and Hamburg all the time. We still shared our interest in pictures but he didn't keep up with my knowledge. I remain a student. He looks with an intuitive eye. First, the Giulio Romano. Then, a Bonnard, for seven hundred and fifty thousand francs! A painting, not just a drawing. We sold it later and bought three drawings. A Guercino. A Rosso Fiorentino. Then, because we couldn't really go up to expensive paintings, we concentrated on drawings, just because we liked them.

"Then Dermot bought a huge picture in Colnaghi's. A picture they had bought at Sotheby's that nobody knew who'd painted. Dermot had it cleaned. It was a Nicolo dell' Abate. He'll tell you how that started him on the detective trail. He's looking for another by the same painter. We were lucky. He was paid a big salary, in Switzerland, but he quit the company and became a consultant. He didn't become a resident of France for a long time. He had Swiss companies and a Gibraltar company. Big fees. Royalties on new products. I was making money with the drawings and I had a sizeable income too. My father kept giving me money. I didn't want it. I felt it was a form of bribe. To get me to see him. He pretended it would lessen the tax load when he died. Anyway, I said, he owes me.

"Penelope. Penelope came along. Then the May 1968 riots. Dermot was in Greece. He left after the riots began. He drove to Brussels for a meeting and couldn't get back. No *essence*. But I remember when they used the first tear gas and it came in the windows of the Rue Madame. He was nervous as hell. Fit to be tied. It was nothing to do with him. He was trapped. He could not accept it. He hated the students and the damage they were doing. The trees ripped up on the Boulevard Saint-Germain. The damage. The police breaking heads.

"He hated violence. I imagine he had seen enough of it in the war. I first noticed his hatred of that sort of thing in Athens. There was an explosion as we walked through Syntagma, that's Constitution Square, and a piece of brick flew past my head. He went white. He was shaking. I thought he was a coward at first but I didn't really know how dangerous it was.

"And I didn't really pay much attention to a story of two men killed next to him in Burma and the blood running over his gear. Another time we were in Bologna and there was that terrible bomb explosion that killed so many people. He simply could not accept any excuse for violence. Of course, he was a rather violent person but it was well suppressed.

"I think he was frightened for us. Especially after Penelope was born. I don't think he was afraid for himself. But he could not stand being in a position where he was not in control. Penelope. Look, it's hard to explain. He was so proud of her. He would have spoiled her if I hadn't prevented it. Then he accused me of being jealous of her. What a laugh. But it may have been partly true.

"We bought the house in the Luberon. Of course that was twenty years before the smart people discovered it. It was an old hunting lodge for the Château de Lourmarin. In fact, it was a joke. We needed a place to hang the big painting. And it was literally a fortress. A fortified farm. A big bastide with courtyard. Secure.

"Penelope grew up. She was very pretty. His coloring, my features, Irish but French. A volatile mix. She was quite a girl. He bought her the apartment downstairs so she would have a private place to paint and entertain her friends. He was so happy when she showed signs of artistic talent. She would be what he had always wanted to be. A painter in Paris. A foolish dream, but harmless. The trouble was he and I were drifting apart in other ways. We still shared the art scene and he was rapidly acquiring a French culture. Proust, Balzac, Baudelaire, Stendhal for a start, then Mallarmé and of course Flaubert and all the Russians.

"I wrote some articles for special art magazines. Pretty soon I was asked to edit art books and finally I became a recognized specialist in all aspects of mannerist art. I also set up a travel agency for art tours and architecture. My grandfather had instilled a reverence for Greece and the myths. I saw a Greek tragedy at Epidaurus and I took

Dermot there one day. You know if you stand on the stage and drop a coin it will be heard in the back row at the top of the theatre?

"Dermot sent me to the top, stood in the centre of the stage, and said—Fuck Sophocles! I must say he had a sense of humor. We were all growing up, I suppose."

Laure said, "God, was Dermot ignorant! Uncultured. But in the end I had to watch it. He soaked it up like a dry sponge. He never had the Greek or Latin background and had huge gaps in his general knowledge but he could trip me up on some things. I suppose we have to give him credit for the fact that he was travelling all the time and he was mixed up in some big projects. Very demanding. He was a one-man band. A sort of creative doctor. He gradually moved from multinational advertising to new product development and his fees were sometimes up to a million dollars. His clients liked him but he lost a lot because he could never suffer fools gladly. He could not learn to indulge the mediocre little men in the packaged-goods organizations. Dullards. He was not a corporate type. In and out. A fireman. A commando. Dermot was not—how do you say it?—a stayer. He was always a sprinter.

"Look, the marriage became an arrangement. It couldn't work properly.

"He would not be tied down. He was an alien in France; my scene wasn't his. He was a forty-year-old playboy when he was let loose in London and afterwards the continent. He was a child in many ways. Easily flattered.

"There were all those young girls who chased him. I suppose he was fairly glamorous. Tearing around Europe and to the West Indies for shoots.

"Ferraris and yachts. A grownup's toys. But who wouldn't go off for a week in Verbier or Monte Carlo? And who can blame an Irish country boy, deprived in his youth, from being impressed by fast girls and powerful cars? The fact was he could only loosen up with someone who didn't pose a threat. Someone impermanent. He always said he felt just like the horse he used to try and get a bridle on as a boy. He didn't want to be caught".

Laure hesitated. "The explosion on the Rue de Rennes. Penny's death. No, I can't talk about it.

"That's the story. Up to the time I read the letter he left lying around. The absolute end of the marriage. Enough. That's enough about me. Now you."

28. André's Story

ANDRÉ SAID, "THAT won't take long. We used to live on the Rue de Varennes. In a *hotel particulier*. The Weinrebs."

"Ah, yes, the name change."

"My mother's name was Wiseman. I assumed it after all the Weinrebs were killed. Didn't want to be the only one left. Can't explain it. In 1940, my father sent us to the house on Cap d'Antibes. My mother was American and I and my sister had American nationality. When France fell, we had a phone call to tell us to leave. We took a train to Madrid and then on to Lisbon. We took a ship to New York. I guess we owned the shipping line. We had a lot of companies apart from the bank. When we were staying at the Ritz in Lisbon, waiting to embark, one of my father's men arrived. He asked for our passports.

"The childrens' passports. My mother was reluctant to hand them over. He smiled and reassured her".

He said, "You won't need them. But two other children do." So they were used to get two children out of France. Everyone did it. That's about all there is to the story except for the fact that the maid who was entrusted with a lot of jewelry disappeared with it in Madrid. We never saw it or her again. My father had three brothers. One ran the bank in Hamburg, another in Frankfurt, and the one in Paris. The two in Germany were picked up in 1940. My uncle left in 1942 when the Germans occupied southern France. My father thought he would be safe if he stayed in France. Too many politicos owed him. He was picked up at the roundup of the Vélodrome d'Hiver.

"My step-sister, by his first wife, stayed with him. They were both deported. Weinrebs kaput. Lampshades. I escaped the clutches of your family's friends."

"Then what?"

"That's not enough? You want more?"

"Yes. It's too much and not enough. You have to go on."

"Oh, Groton, Princeton, Harvard post-grad, then three years with Kahn in Philadelphia. Big projects."

"He was the best of the modern architects. Did the Kimbell Museum."

"Yes."

"San Francisco?"

"Partnership with an old friend from Princeton. Married his sister. A Bellington. Owned Federated Foods in Minneapolis. She was living in Belvedere. Amusing herself with a gallery in Sausalito. Gave me shows."

"And the bank? The company?"

"My uncle came back and picked up the pieces. He's a genius. Built it up again from scratch. Didn't take a holiday for years. Collected reparations from the German government for the odd four hundred buildings we owned in Hamburg and Frankfurt. And the ships. The French kindly nationalized the bank after he'd built it up. Like the Rothschilds. Now we're out of it all. Clipping coupons all of us. In Gstaad, Paris, Aix, Belvedere."

"Are you still married?

"No. Divorced and now engaged."

"Children?"

"Only one. A son. Harry. He's taken over his mother's gallery in Sausalito. Not a great success, I'm afraid. Hasn't got the balls, if you'll forgive me, of his step sister. Tatiana. You saw her at l'Isle sur la Sorgue. She left that day for London. The Courtauld Institute. Harry's a bearded hippie type. Typical Marin County boy. But hetero, I think. Spoiled rotten. I gave up on him long ago. But I'll do anything for Tatty."

"Your wife was married before?"

"Yes. To a lush. He married her for her money. Was paid off. Still a menace. Has the right to see Tatiana, of course.

Always looking for the main chance. Trying to make money. Unfortunately, Tatty can be influenced by him. Thinks he had a raw deal. Maybe he had."

"What went wrong with the marriage?"

"Money. Too much of it. Indolence. Selfishness. Trying to buy people. Like me."

"You wouldn't be bought?"

"No. I had enough of my own. And I had a job. And, perhaps, a certain small talent. We'll see when I finish that painting of you."

"Is that it?"

"That's it. At least, that's all I want to talk about."

"You mean, all I would understand?"

"Perhaps."

"What about your sister?"

"Had two. I told you. My step-sister killed by the Germans, with a little help from the French. The other, Sarah, who came to America, killed herself as a result of it."

"Sorry."

"Don't be sorry. Not to be born at all is best, as the man said."

They crossed the Pont Edouard Daladier at Avignon.

He remarked, "Ah, Daladier, 'The bull of Vaucluse.'"

"Yes, they had a bakery in Carpentras."

"As some prescient gent said at the time of Munich, he had horns more like a snail than a bull. Described him as a dirty little man smelling of absinthe with a cigarette hanging out of his mouth."

"We don't like our politicians to be distinguished. Except Giscard. Look at how they lionized Daladier when he came back from Munich. At Le Bourget he said, The fools are cheering me!"

"They did the same in England when the umbrella man came back waving his bit of paper and said, Peace in our time!"

"Who knows? Maybe they were right, the appeasers."

"Pity they didn't ask the Jews in the camps. My uncle and aunt in Vienna. My cousins in Hamburg and Frankfurt."

"Yes, but if the Germans had won, if the English hadn't had that extra year to build Spitfires, there wouldn't be a Jew left in Europe."

"That's why they're all in the U.S."

29. Laure Says Goodbye

WAITING ON THE QUAI at the station of Avignon, she realized that she knew André's history and she knew the topography of his lean body. That she had been using him as a confessor. That he had been a sympathetic listener. And that he had encouraged her to talk about the Montriveau. That he painted. That he was painting her in a rather surreal compromising pose. Who would see it? Who cares? She knew that he had a surreal appendage. The hot sun warmed up the memory of his body. She was mesmerized by it. There was no embarrassment, no play-acting, no hangups. It was pure. He released her from all her inhibitions. All her shyness had gone. All her warped sense of sin disappeared. She had become a sexual animal, a female woman. His penis was playful, tantalizing, forceful. It was a magic wand that completely banished the oppressive pictures of Ventoux, of violence, of death.

She thought, They're right. There is a connection between violence and the orgasm. *La petite mort.* She wanted it to penetrate her in every way every day. She couldn't imagine being deprived of it. That was the beginning of fear. The idea of losing her liberated sexuality was worse than the fear of losing André. Much worse. He had switched her on. Now she needed a deeper relationship which included sex. Funnily enough, she thought of Dermot.

When the train for Paris pulled in and she stepped up to board it, André lifted her hand and kissed it.

He said, "Thank you, Laure."

She said, "Think nothing of it. It was a pleasure."

And they both laughed.

30. Armand & Dermot

THE LAWYER, ALAIN DE MALHERBE, picked Dermot up at Paris Charles de Gaulle airport. They drove north. The lawyer briefed him. Dermot was not in a receptive mood. Both wife and mistress galloping off into the distance.

He said, "*Maître*, I don't believe it. Last year, he was in a Land Rover that rolled in Turkey, breaking four vertebrae. He was supposed to die that time. Then he went off to Sarawak. You can't kill him."

Alain said, "*Oui, oui. Bien sûr.*"

Lawyers everywhere have a genius for saying something without saying anything. Dermot was a little frayed at the edges.

He said, "Listen. This marriage is all washed up. It's up to Laure. I have no interest in the family. Leave me out of it."

"But you're a joint heir."

"I renounce all claims."

"You can't. We went through all that rearranging of the marriage agreement. To avoid taxes if one spouse died? You can't undo that before the old man passes on. You say you don't want it. Neither does Laure. Besides, there's something he wants you to have, outside the normal inheritance."

"What's that?"

"I don't know. He'll tell you. If he's still conscious."

"And if he's not?"

"I have a letter for you. And I can fill in the gaps."

The relationship with Alain was a nervous one. He was an old friend of Dermot's father-in-law. Brother in the dangerous hunt for the elusive butterfly. Fellow tracker in the night in the jungles of Africa, defiant in the face of crocodiles and tigers in Sumatra and head-hunters in the Admiralty Islands. You did not get much change out of him. They started up the autoroute towards Péronne, St. Quentin and Guise. The lawyer was of an age when most people are driving wheelchairs in rest homes but he was French. They know two speeds. Flat out and stop. Dermot was too spaced out to care. But he looked at the man and thought: This chap was defending French people against the Germans during the war. He's no chicken.

They lapsed into silence and he could feel the mind beginning to slip, first into neutral and then the images of the past started to blur and come clear as they overtook the huge trucks with '80' on the back doing 160 kph going to Düsseldorf. Dutch cars each with a trailer. The odd DK plate, off to Frederickshavn, no doubt. Belgians. It was late afternoon and the sun cast long shadows over everything. It hid behind a cloud. Everything went suddenly dark.

Over the top and the best of luck

The image slipped completely. Another double exposure. It faded out the calm fields of wheat and faded in the churned-up fields of battle. Death stalked the haunted country, Picardy, Flanders, the Somme. Péronne, St. Quentin. Guise. The ghosts rose up out of the mist and came towards him through the yellow mustard gas. Péronne: the battle. Péronne, where there was an Irish monastery and the patron saint is an Irish monk, Fursey, who died in 650. St. Quentin—'*Champs de bataille de la Somme*'—blood and guts, with the old man dragging himself wounded through the mud. The 'Aisne'. It's bloody country. The images persisted. Von Kluck's gun carriages. Guderian's panzers. War cemeteries. His father spluttering with the gas. Wounded first not far from Colonfay, at Le Cateau in August 1914. Derek, his cousin, three classes above him, a captain in the Norfolks, killed by an impersonal mortar bomb in Normandy in 1944. The neutral Irish. Wasted by that Scotch whisky murderer Haig. The whisky distilled from dead soldiers. Shove in another four hundred thousand. And General 'Butcher' Gough from Tipperary with his shells dropping on the advance troops and not cutting the wire at all. Slipping in and out of the memories were reminders of his wife and her family. His father-in-law and he had enjoyed a remote but friendly relationship. Dermot hardly knew him. Probably only the butterflies knew him.

After Péronne the long road to St. Quentin rose and fell

like an ocean swell. A roller-coaster with hidden troughs. Endless trees flickering past the windscreen, with blinding light when they turned to the west into the low sun, and synchronized shadows. Sound bouncing off the trees as the car passed, swish, swish, Maître Alain guiding it with fingers resting lazily on the bottom of the steering wheel. The road running parallel to the River Sambre, the British army's extreme right in Nivelle's lunatic plan of advance in the hopeless battle of the Aisne. April 1917. Had his father perhaps fought here, precisely here? Was it here he got the bullet wound in the leg? Before the gas at Passchendaele.

Guise. All red-black brick and gloom. Sad cafés. Deserted squares. An impression that nothing has happened here since Démoulins, the native son, lost his head during the French Revolution. Désmoulins, married like Dermot in Saint-Sulpice, with Robespierre as a witness. Both guillotined. One factory, Godin stoves, an old ruined castle, decrepitude all round. The bridge piled high with German dead. So they said, but it was a morale booster. The melancholy of The Last Post. Hear the lone bugle.

Memories. Driving rain, leaden clouds, winter days when he went alone up to the château. Into Guise, and the bridge over the weedy stream. Imagined sounds under: galloping horses, gun carriages, Uhlans, spiked helmets. The empty road to the house, up the hill and turn left to Audigny. Nothing in sight but the house at the turnoff. Rolling fields. Sparse trees. Lonely. Wait.

Before the turnoff, the French war cemetery, *La Désolation*. A walled barracks for dead soldiers. All lined up in good order. A square with four battalions and a center saluting base.

And, yes, '*Dulce et decorum est pro Patria mori.*'

Each sweetly dead planted in line with the others. Forgotten. A short battle, Guise, August 29, 1914. Talk about lunacy.

The Château at Colonfay. The old man dying in the middle of the killing fields. Oh, yes. Dermot has a morbid interest in war. Why wouldn't he? His grandfather, his cousin. His father, finished. Nothing left but to drink and argue the toss and take the piss out of the Irish heroes. And a bullet in the back of the head for it in 1938.

Everything is connected.

They went over the bridge at St. Quentin. Another bridge. More symbolism.

Alain said, "You know he was a cavalry officer, your father-in-law?"

He said, "Yes. There's a picture of him mounted at the school at Saumur. He told me he never saw action and withdrew to Tours where he was demobilized in 1940. I often wondered what he did after that."

"He may tell you now. Remember, nothing was clear in 1940."

"I know."

"We are none of us pure, Dermot. What did your own father do?"

"He was a professional drinker. A rider when he was young. Point-to-point. Cavalryman, too. Fisherman. Layabout. But he was here for three years. Near enough. Mons. The Somme. Passchendaele. Murdered in Ireland in 1938."

"Did he talk about the war?"

"Never. Except to make macabre jokes."

"Tell me about him. We have all wondered about your background."

"Later. Maybe."

But he knew he would never tell. The French didn't really want to know. They added up their own casualties and sneered at the smaller British figures. They blamed perfidious Albion for all the defeats. The war fought on French soil from beginning to end. Two million dead or totally disabled. More than twice as many as the British. A third more than the Germans. Sixty times more than the Americans. 800,000 buildings and 40,000 miles of roads destroyed. How could he say he had more ties to this particular piece of France than had the lawyer himself? The names come back. *The Somme. La Bassée Canal. Béthune. Poperinge. The Ypres Salient. Mons. Menin. Auchy-au-bois. Colonfay.*

Dermot murmured, "Father, grandfather, cousin, all left their blood to fertilize Belgian and French soil."

The lawyer said, "Ah, yes. Your grandfather. That's how you met Armand, I believe?"

"Right. I'm drawn back to it. Remember Sassoon? No, you wouldn't."

You smug-faced crowds with kindling eye
Who cheer when soldier lads march by
Sneak home and pray you'll never know
The hell where youth and laughter go.

He looked out the window.

He said, "The rolling fields. 'The poor sheep, driven innocent to death.'"

He said, "There was this man Pilditch. He wrote about Auchy-au-bois. He was looking through his binoculars from the O.P. That's an Observation Post. All he could see was a high chalk parapet with a green strip of No Man's Land sloping up towards it. He made out what seemed to be a flock of sheep grazing all over it. He got a powerful telescope and made out clearly what they were. They were hundreds of khaki bodies lying where they had fallen in the September attack on the Hohenzollern Redoubt, and now beyond reach of friend and foe alike. They would lie there between the trenches until one side or the other advanced."

The lawyer said, "I don't understand how they could have gone on. That war was *effroyable*."

Dermot said, "Yes. The last one was a picnic. 60,000 British casualties the first day of the Somme. 3,000 Americans on D-Day, 1944. A piece of cake. Unless you were one of the 3,000."

"Were you there?"

"No. I was in a wood in Hampshire standing by as a reserve but not needed. I was ticketed for Burma with a one-day excursion to Greece. Then off to the Pacific in the Forgotten Fleet. Ishigaki and Miyako and Formosa. Then Japan. Great fun. Not as exciting as writing copy about cigarettes but still. You can't enjoy yourself all the time."

It was dusk, *entre chien et loup,* the French say, meaning you can't tell the difference between a dog and a wolf, when Dermot and Alain came to the deserted village. A crossroads around the war memorial, a small shop which combined the functions of Poste, bar, bakery, *maison de la presse*, and the road up past the small church to the high wall of the château. The huge iron gates open, rusting, askew. The sweep of drive up through the dense shrubs and the trees and the classical house, long and narrow, with the main door complete with coat of arms above it. Suddenly Dermot noticed that it was run-down. Paint peeling, shutters rotting. Weeds growing through the gravel. It was not the way he remembered it. Then all had been well-kept. Reminded him of the house in Ireland.

They pulled up at the kitchen door. He went in with heavy heart. It was not going to be a barrel of laughs. He was not much of a hand at deathbed scenes, especially when he's close to the subject. He reacts with nervous hilarity. Well, at least he wouldn't have his skull shattered by a bullet, like Dermot's own father when he found him. Still, he had an idea he was in for some final confidences.

They now had him on a bed in the library, tied down so he couldn't move. His doctor from Paris was there, and a local nurse. The doctor came out when he saw them at the door, and gave the lawyer the picture.

"We don't know how much damage there is. The two broken vertebrae at the neck were repaired and may be broken again. Then there are the two at the base of the spine. They can't be repaired and have almost certainly been added to by other fractures. I guess his back is broken beyond repair. He hasn't broken any ribs that I can see, and his ankle is sprained but not, I think, broken. Hip broken. I have strapped everything I can. Legs OK, left arm fractured. Until he can be taken to the hospital for X-rays, we won't know for sure the extent of the damage. He refuses absolutely to be moved from here. His heart's as good as can be expected. Breathing hard. Perhaps a lung punctured. Weak. I'd say he might last a few days. A week at the most.

He's taken too much punishment. The last accident nearly finished him. He doesn't seem to care very much one way or another. But there's something worrying him. He wants to talk to his son-in-law. That's you?"

He turned to Dermot.

Dermot said, "Yes."

"Don't tire him out. I'll give him a shot when you've finished. He needs sleep. See if you can get him to agree to be hospitalized. I don't think there's much point in it, but he could be looked after better there."

Dermot went in and sat by his father-in-law's bed. In profile, he looked like an old knight on an English tomb, lying immobile, looking up at the ceiling. He took his hand. He squeezed it. He could see him without turning his head. A faint smile flickered. His eyes were glassy. He turned them towards the nurse. He motioned her away. He went into his act.

Dermot said, "You never learn, do you? Up a tree in a corset. At your age. Undignified. You're like your daughter. She's always up a tree, too. On a shaky ladder. What a family! And I suppose it only hurts when you laugh."

Armand tried to laugh but it didn't work. His voice was rasping but Dermot could understand it. His English was better than Dermot's French and as a courtesy he insisted on using it but lapsed into French from time to time. He had an urgency about him as if he knew he had to talk in shorthand to be sure Dermot got it fast.

"In the *grenier*, a box. For you. The key in my desk. Laure. She must understand. *Je voudrais la voir une fois.*"

His eyes filled. He was distressed.

Dermot worried. He stood and put his face next to the old man's. He held his hand and went into his sincere routine. Which he meant.

"I'll get her. I promise. Hold on. We both need you."

The old man smiled. He wanted to say something more. The nurse was standing next to him, trying to drag him away.

Armand said, "You must look after Laure. She should be happy. Make her understand."

It was a heavy legacy. A lifetime of ballast.

Dermot said, "Yes. Now you must agree to be taken to hospital."

"Yes."

What else could you say? He kissed his father-in-law on the forehead and left.

Later the doctor came out and said he'd take Armand to his own clinic in Paris where he'd already been operated on for the broken vertabrae. He would accompany him to ensure that the journey was comfortable.

The lawyer went to the kitchen. Martha, the woman from the village who had looked after Armand since his wife, Oriane, died, had prepared dinner. She was weeping. It was all very emotional. She couldn't understand why Laure or Patrick weren't there.

But where are they? Why?

Alain said he was waiting for them to call. She said it had better be quick. To shut her up, he asked her to bring the keys from the desk, find a lamp and open up the *grenier*. She pointed out that the Germans had installed electricity up there. They used it as an observation post or something. Then he remembered. It had big iron T-bars across the house under the roof to reinforce the structure. The house had been an OP, observation post for artillery.

The doors to the rooms up to the *grenier* still had pencilled on them the names of various occupants:'*Ober-Leutnant Specht,*' '*Feldwebel Theis*',,and so on.

A corner of the long *grenier*—it stretched the full length of the house—was partitioned off. It was locked, and padlocked. He found the two keys.

Inside there was a desk and chair. In the middle of the desk, an old leather suitcase. On one side, a folding frame with two facing photographs. Oriane as a bride, and Laure as a child, holding her father's butterfly net. She in turn was holding the hand of an older boy. Not Patrick because he was much older.

Another sibling? There was a picture of his mother-in-law and a man about her own age. Laure's uncle? Didier? They had never talked of him. On the wall above the desk, a photograph of a man standing with a high brick wall behind him. The same man, but older. It looked like the wall to the kitchen garden of the house, with the cedar of Lebanon in the park towering above. It was a serious picture. The young man looked hangdog. He had reason to be. He was about to be executed.

Dermot sat at the desk. There was was a swan-neck table lamp. With trepidation, he unlocked the suitcase. Then he looked at the portfolio lying there propped against the wall. Being an artist, well, aspiring, he couldn't resist the temptation of looking inside that first. He extracted the drawings, which were carefully protected by flimsy interleaves and mounted in hard cardboard with flaps.

Dermot looked at the top one.

He exclaimed, "Jesus, Mary and Joseph!"

He put everything back and tied up the portfolio.

Finally he got to the letter he should have read first. The one given to him by Alain de Malherbe, the lawyer. There was a sheet written in Armand de Coucy's small clear writing.

Dear Dermot, The suitcase to which you have the key contains perhaps the key also to the happiness of Laure. The documents and newspaper cuttings are self-explanatory. I think that when you have explained and shown them to her she may forgive me. I hope so. I only did my duty. She had a fixation on her uncle, my brother-in-law, Didier, who was executed on my orders in 1945. She hated him, with good reason, which I did not appreciate at the time. She holds me responsible for his execution, rightly, even though she knows he deserved it. I could not have prevented it, at least not without sacrificing myself. I was playing a dangerous game and he suspected it. Perhaps I should have saved him, but I didn't. I had responsibilities. He had none. He deserved to die but so did a lot of people who are still around here today. Laure also blames me for the death of her great-uncle, who was also shot in 1945, for collaboration with the Germans. That, too, I was powerless to

prevent. You will see the evidence against both. Read care-
fully, please, the statement I have for your eyes only, and
destroy it immediately after. There are some drawings
which I wish you to have. They are in the portfolio in the
cupboard in the office in the grenier. *Alain de Malherbe has*
a notarized Certificate of Ownership and Gift to you
personally, made out some years ago when you were
married. There is also the history of the drawings and the
recent provenance. This was the property of Max Farber. So
far as I know, none of that family survived the war. I kept the
drawings in case one of them should turn up. What you do
with these drawings is entirely up to you but I make one
condition by which I hope you will abide. You are not to
allow them to be appropriated by the French Ministry of
Culture and those disreputable curators of the Louvre.
They are unknown and thus not part of the national patri-
mony. There's a medal. I'd like Patrick to have it. I leave my
main bequest, Laure, in your hands, in the hope that you
will find a way to make her happy.
    Your affectionate father-in-law, Armand de Coucy

He opened the suitcase. It contained various official documents. And newspaper and magazine articles.

The top one showed a photograph of one 'Didier de Montriveau,' in a strange uniform, and the headline to the effect that he had been in charge of the police under Leguay in Paris and in charge of the Milice in the Department of Aisne in 1943 and was executed on January 25, 1945.

It listed his crimes, which were considerable. Another feature article showed the face of her paternal grandfather, the industrialist, Marcel de Coucy, with Marshal Pétain, when he was in charge of press and publications for the 'New Order.' He died in 1944. There was a neat stack of the magazine *L'Illustration,* and a quick scan showed that this grandfather and her Uncle Didier had been prominent members of the Vichy élite.

There was another envelope addressed to Dermot McManus, and sealed with sealing wax. It was marked,

'Destroy after reading.' He opened it. It was a statement, notarised and witnessed, in the form of an accusation, borne out by the witnesses, that Didier de Montriveau, the milicien, has been observed sexually abusing his nephew, Henri, who has died in hospital in Laon, and that he has also abused one Bernard Dupont, aged ten, whose father he shot when the latter attacked him. Due to his position, no charges were laid, and it is certain that anyone raising the issue would have disappeared. When accused by his brother, Armand, he had threatened to have him watched, as it was suspected (rightly) that Armand de Coucy was engaged in subversive activities.

Attached to the statement was the note:

'Dermot: I could not explain this to Laure. Her brother and her uncle. I didn't have the heart for it.'

Initialled by his father-in-law. Another mystery. Laure had another brother. She never talked about him. He did not destroy the document. He replaced it in the suitcase, which he locked. What a can of worms. The plot, as they say, had certainly thickened.

He almost missed an envelope addressed to Armand. It contained a letter from the Présidence. It said, *'Thank you, my dear de Coucy, for keeping the* Resistance *network, Guise, operating throughout, and for your constant supply of information in my 'letter-box' in the wood. It was invaluable and provided at enormous risk to yourself.'* It was signed, Charles de Gaulle.

He carried everything downstairs and resolved not to let it out of his sight until Laure and Patrick had seen it and it was safely locked away. He decided to study the history of the drawings at his leisure. Alain and the doctor were in the drawing-room. The doctor was sleeping in the house and driving back to Paris in the morning. Now that he had talked to Dermot, the old man seemed resigned to being moved to the clinic in Paris where he was patched up after his accident the other year. An ambulance was booked and would arrive first thing in the morning.

Dermot needed to get out of there. He asked Alain if he intended to drive back to Paris. He said yes.

He decided to telephone Laure, and to leave with the lawyer. He would try to soften her up. The telephone was in a small room under the stairs. There was no reply in Provence. So he tried Paris. She answered, in a small, breathless voice, so slow he wondered whether she was all right.

"It's me," he said. "Your ubiquitous husband, who misses you."

A silence, then, "What do you want?"

"I'm in Colonfay."

More silence, then, "I know. Mouse told me."

"I was sent for by *Maître* de Malherbe. Apparently you refused to come."

"Oh, please, don't start. (Pause) How is he?"

"Almost certainly dying. He needs you."

"No!" she cried. "*Je ne peux pas! Je ne peux pas!* Leave me alone!"

"Laure, I understand. Honest. I know you can't do it. Only I promised to try. You will hate yourself afterwards. You can't go on blaming him. You are totally wrong about him."

"What do you know about it?"

She was breathing rapidly. Excited. Nervous.

"Enough. I have the evidence."

"It's none of your business. Has he been talking to you? He had no right."

"No, no. Can I come and see you? I'll be in Paris tonight. Can Mouse sleep in the upstairs spare bedroom?"

"No, yes. If you want. Dermot?"

"Yes?"

"I hope you'll be understanding when you get here. Things have changed. Be nice."

"Yes, I will. *Je vous aime.*"

"You don't mean it. You never loved me. And it's too late."

The lawyer was driving back to Paris and Dermot went with him, taking the suitcase. He decided not to speak to Laure that evening but to stay in the downstairs flat and call her first thing in the morning.

Sunday

31. Mouse, the Shrink

PARIS. I MET LAURE in the apartment in the Rue Madame.

I said to her, "Laure, you can have lots of lovers but only one father."

She said, "That's one too many."

"Well, too late now baby. You can't put his sperm back in his balls."

She laughed. A good sign. Mouse, the therapist.

"Oh, Mouse, how lucky you are! No men to worry about."

"Jaysus, girl, do you think women are easier? Now listen to me—"

"Wait, Mouse. No lectures, please."

"No. Only this. Never mind being kind to your father. Be kind to yourself. When he's dead you don't want to suffer the remorse. I don't understand how an intelligent person can't accept that parents should be judged in the context of their upbringing and their time. I've met Armand and I don't believe he's capable of doing anything nasty. Well, if he did slip one day, it was a sin of omission. He's incapable of doing anything dirty."

"You think so? Have you any idea what he did? Allowed me to be violated."

"Oh, I think so, Laure. There's very little in the behavior of the male animal that I don't understand. Nothing much shocks me. And there always seems to me to be too big a song and dance about it."

"And Dermot?"

"Ah, Dermot's not bad. If he didn't give you what you expected maybe you weren't the most receptive wife? He too suffered from parental abuse, no, not sexual. Wrongheadedness by a father who was blocked in his time. He couldn't help it either. Nobody's blameless, Laure. And nobody should play God."

"Thanks, Mouse!"

"Think nothing of it, Laure. Can I use your telephone? I must call Gwendoline, my better half. My stabilizer. I need to talk to someone who understands the essential truth."

"What's that?"
"Nothing matters."

32. Laure & Dermot & Mouse

IT WAS NOON ON Sunday by the time Dermot decided to ask Laure to come down to him rather than to intrude on her space. He asked Mouse to go up and get her. Laure came in looking antagonistic, or perhaps defensive.

First he had opened the portfolio and spread the drawings out on the floor. It was a good strategy. It defused what looked like an embarrassing meeting.

The reaction was considerable.

Mouse said, "Oh, good. We're into pornography. But why all those unnecessary appendages?"

Laure was stunned.

Dermot said, "That should take your mind off things for a while."

She had recently been up the coupole of St. Giovanni Evangelista in Parma and had seen the Correggios close to. And two years before up the cupole of the Duomo. She has seen the *Zeus as a cloud* in the Kunsthistorische Museum in Vienna and almost all the other Correggios around the world. These are just drawings, and erotic, even pornographic, but what drawings.

"Fakes? They must be. The unknown Correggios," she said.

"Right, of course. But maybe not fakes. You're going to do a book about them if they're real."

"Am I?"

"Of course you are. Give us a chance to go to Emilia Romagna again. And why don't we try to trace the paintings? Even the one that Farber's grandfather owned. We know that it exists. Unless it was destroyed in the war. Here, read the story . . ."

Dermot went to the desk and handed her the paper called *The Unknown Correggios*. It was dated and signed by

Maximilian Farber, Dealer in Antiquarian Books and Old Master Drawings. It was a long and persuasive document and would be sure to interest Laure who would readily insert it into her own knowledge of Correggio and his time in Parma.

There was the report from Armand de Coucy, showing how the portfolio of drawings came into his possession, and a 'Bill of Sale,' made out to him, in the amount of five hundred francs, for 'Six Drawings in the style of the Parma Mannerists.'

It did not make good reading but Laure would have to read it. He told her to sit down and handed her the report.

Laure said, "How disgusting they were!"

Dermot said, "Yes, the attitudes were deplorable. But your father did his best to protect the Farbers' property. Had he tried to hide them he would have been for the high jump. I think if you read it properly you get a sense of the man's innate decency. The influences of the period, the fear, the danger, made it quite impossible for him to do more. Not without compromising the entire family. You would have wound up in Auschwitz yourself."

"Maybe. I'll reserve judgment."

"You do that."

"You certainly seem to have involved yourself in my family's business."

"Most reluctantly. By your own default. It seems to have become my business. Alain dragged me across from Ireland. I didn't want to come but Mouse insisted. I had enough trouble understanding my own father."

Mouse said, "I wouldn't have insisted had I known I was going to be exposed to these drawings. The cult of the penis! Rampant males making like gods!"

Dermot said to Laure, "Your father left me a rather delicate legacy. Care to look over these?"

He handed her the documents.

There was the evidence that her father had been playing a dangerous double game. A functionary of Vichy, and an informer for a *Résistance* network. The proof that Uncle

Didier was not only on the side of the Nazis and responsible for the murder of thousands, but a sexual deviant as well.

She sat there a long time.

He went over and put his arm around her. She shook it off.

Mouse said, "Lighten up, Laure."

She sat down. Read parts of the papers again. She broke down. It was the last straw. The bottled up emotions of years made the dam give way. She sobbed noisily. Mouse held her. She shook and shuddered and Dermot waited until she was all wept out.

Dermot said, "Let it all out."

"Sorry."

"Why be sorry? For being human? I cry inwardly all the time. Come on."

She said, "It's an over-reaction. All this talk of his *Résistance* work is unsubstantiated. It doesn't compensate for his Vichy sins. And other things. More personal. I can't forgive him."

"You must, Laure. He's your father. You are very alike."

"Alike?"

"Yes. I know you don't think much of my powers of discernment but it has always been obvious to me. You are both locked in the de Coucy pride. Unable to let down your defenses. You decided long ago that he was inhuman. It's not true. Any one of us could have behaved as he did. Not quite as well. He's a war hero. Pretending to be a Pétainist while sabotaging the regime. He's an honorable man. In order to defend your honor he would have had to sacrifice the entire family. So he denied that it happened. It was a heavy price to pay and he spent his life paying it. Do you think it would have been easy for him to allow his little daughter to be sexually assaulted by that monster, Didier, had he known the full extent of your suffering? And he loves you. He asks little except to see you once before he dies. You are not judge and jury after all. He had a few laspses. We are all full of sin. And we find out too late that we have done wrong."

"Are you speaking of yourself?"

"Yes, I am. But I'm hoping it isn't too late."

"I'm afraid it is. Maybe not. I can't think straight."

She saw the hurt look on his face as he turned away. She touched his arm.

He said quietly, "I didn't know you had another brother, Henri."

She looked at him in abject desolation.

She murmured, "I can't talk about him. He was not all right. I thought he had been put in a special home for boys like him. Uncle Didier arranged it."

Laure looked again at the drawings and read the story of Farber's arrest.

She said, "These belong to Sarah."

He said, "Look. Suppose Sarah Farber is still alive. Aren't we going to try and trace her? Isn't that something worth doing?"

Laure said, "Yes. It's an obligation. I hope we find her."

Dermot said, "So do I. The glory of discovering the drawings is enough for us. And you will do the book."

"I'll think about it."

He said, "Laure, you must forgive your father. In fact, you have nothing to forgive him for. He has things to forgive you for, depriving him of your love all these years. You must see him. You will never be able to live with it if you don't. He did not know—all right, maybe he didn't want to know—what happened to you."

"I'll call him. Then we'll see."

Dermot called Alain. He got the number of the private room in the clinic in Paris and dialed it. He handed her the phone. The nurse answered.

"It's Laure, his daughter. Is my father still alive?"

"Yes, Madame. But weaker."

"Can he talk?"

"If I hold the phone near his ear, he can probably hear you. Wait."

"*Papa? C'est Laure.* I'm coming to see you. I understand everything. Oh, I'm so sorry. I will come and look after you. *Je vous embrasse très tendrement.*"

The nurse said, "He understood. He smiled. Please hurry, Madame."

"I'll be there this afternoon."

And she collapsed again.

33. Armand & Daughter

LAURE IS WITH HER father. He's weak but smiling. The X-Rays show that he has broken again the vertebrae that were on the mend and added another three. His hip is broken, and his right thigh. At eighty, the shock to his system was severe. Only the fact that he's lean and has climbed mountains and kept fit saved him. The doctor says he still hasn't much chance. He lies there, flat on his back, immobile, strapped down. Laure holds his hand. The old man is half-doped, of course, but you could imagine that he was thinking, Better late than never. Now I can go on and join Oriane. Laure is crying.

Armand whispers, "Don't."

Laure says, "You must get better. We'll look after you."

He squeezes her hand. Tears are in his eyes too.

He croaks, "It's difficult."

Laure says, "*Impossible n'est pas français.*"

The old joke. Slightly threadbare now. She replaced his hand on top of the other one, arms crossed upon his chest, a smile of contentment on his ravaged face. She was going out the door to the ordered taxi when the nurse caught up with her.

She went back.

Dermot was talking to the studio in Zurich when Laure came in.

She said, "My father died just after I left the clinic. The doctor said he died happy. As though he had completed his task on this earth."

She was calm.

He asked, "What about the funeral arrangements?"

"Alain will make them. He will be buried in the cemetery at Colonfay. Next to my mother. On Tuesday. We'll take the body up to the church tomorrow and have a special Mass."

"Will I come up?"

"I'd rather you didn't."

"Why? I liked him and he liked me."

"I know. But it seems wrong. A burial and then a divorce."

The door slammed in his face. With finality.

"What about the Sarah business and the book about the drawings?"

"Mouse and Alain will handle it. I can't think about the book right now."

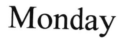

Monday

34. Laure at Colonfay

COLONFAY. ONE WEEK since the fall. Picardy weather. Low clouds, leaden sky, driven showers.

A small gathering. Laure and Patrick and Alain and Hervé and the farmer and his wife. The *maire* of Colonfay. A mass before the burial. Now on Monday to suit the convenience of the priest. By strange irony, he is a diehard communist who has raved about the bourgeois élite, using the pulpit as a political platform and taking Armand as his prototype. Complained about to the bishop and finally removed but now back for his revenge. Hiding behind the cloth. Threatened by Alain that if he dares to say anything untoward he will find himself in court and defrocked.

A simple ceremony. Laid to rest with the other de Coucys. In the bloody plot over which the guns have boomed and the barbarians tramped.

To the château for the conventional lunch. Awkward, embarrassing, everyone glad when it ends. Laure asking Alain and Hervé to choose a butterfly book from the collection. Protests. Too valuable. Choosing instead a box of moths each. Rushing away.

The house empty. The wind rattling the windows. The mongrel whining in the dining-room.

Laure floats along the corridor on the second floor. It's lined with bookshelves. Overflow from the library. She picks some out. Leather-bound editions of her grandfather's and her father's work.

There's the 1913 edition of Proust. The Grasset. Only 1700 in existence. She puts it on the window ledge. With unconscious reverence.

She wanders back along to the stairs up to the *grenier*, passing through the small rooms in the west tower which she had occupied as a lonely child, the room that looks out on the park and the killing tree. As she climbs, slowly, it all seems so remote. The past seems a fiction. Incidents lost in the mist of antiquity. She climbs up to the huge space under the roof, enters the 'office.' It's unlocked. Sits at his desk.

Looks at the photographs. Her mother, her brother, her uncle, her father in his cavalry officer's uniform, mounted.

She pulls open a drawer, not looking for anything in particular. There's a pistol. There's a vial of cyanide. Armand got it from the museum to dampen a sponge to kill the butterflies. There's enough to kill a regiment.

She holds the tube of white powder. Puts it back. Picks up the pistol. She remembers how an old suitor had killed himself with one shot to the heart.

That must be the way to do it.

She throws the pistol back in the drawer. Violent rejection of more death and melodrama. And hurt for Dermot.

She weeps. She spins out of control. She's overcome with guilt, all the affection withheld, all the rejections, Dermot's deprivation, all the the conceit and the superciliousness. The vengeful acts perpetrated. The anger. The pride, envy, covetousness, lust, and all the other seven deadly sins.

She decides to call Dermot, to stay anchored in the world. She needs him if she is to go on living. To compensate him. She needs a fix on reality. She goes downstairs to the telephone in the little room off the hall. She dials the number of the downstairs flat in Paris.

Mouse answers. She's just come back from Provence.

"Dermot's on his way to the airport."

"Oh, no! Can you stop him?"

"No, but I can get him tonight in Dublin."

Laure's hysterical, too bright, not making much sense.

She says, "Oh, Mouse, it was all a terrible mistake. I've been so stupid."

She's on an unnatural high. Mouse is imperturbable. She calms.

"Are you all right?"

"Yes, perfectly. Resolved. Will you tell him it's going to be all right? Everything will work out. I want to see him. To please come back soon. We go together, we must forget the rest, look at what we have, and now the paintings, something to work on together, if he can forget Nana—"

"He was never unfaithful to you really."

She laughs.

"What do you call infidelity?"

"What do *you* call it?"

"I call it unimportant now. It was silly. a misunderstanding."

"Nana never meant anything to him. He actually never liked her. He actively disliked her. She has no principles. But she didn't give him a hard time *all* the time."

"Yes, I asked for that."

"He never saw her without wanting to leave and be with you."

"Honestly?"

"Yes. He needed to feel wanted. But he always felt you were a virginal type, a sort of Mother Superior. You always made him seem like an oaf. He made the mistake of putting you a pedestal. The physical side seemed almost sinful. Incestuous."

Mouse gently steers the conversation towards less emotional and more mundane things.

"What are you going to do about Colonfay?"

"We'll get rid of it. It would always be haunted. Some memories will not go away. Alain can dispose of the butterfly collection and the library."

"Dermot talks about selling his boat."

"He mustn't do that. The old yawl is his escape symbol."

"You think he'll want to escape again?"

"Don't you?"

"No comment, Laure. Ride him with a loose rein. A bit of illicit copulation never hurt anyone. Adultery may be next to godliness. The folly is in confusing lust with love."

Laure breaks into wild laughter.

"But what's sauce for the goose is sauce for the gander."

"Don't tell me more. I'm not old enough. But, Laure, you know there's no chance of it working unless you lay down some rules and stick to them. I have heard it said that you have to work at it. Personally, thank God, I was not motivated to make marriage work. It's an altogether unnatural state."

"Oh, Mouse, you're lucky. You have the strength to survive alone."

"Huh! Little do you know. Me and the donkeys for company. The lonely nights and the itch. Sublimation in work. Right now I must get Sarah and the porno drawing sorted out."

"Yes, work's the substitute. But it's not enough for me."

"Well, good luck Laure. Give it a go."

Laure goes out the back door and stands on the terrace. She looks down on the park. It's still a battlefield after the battle. As though a great hand had come down and swept away the shrubs, the trees, parts of the wall and the greenhouse. It all seems strange.

She walks down the park. Stands by the cedar of Lebanon. The mongrel has followed her down and sniffs around. She looks up at Laure and growls.

The branch is still hanging down, held by the white tendons. It creaks in the wind. The slippery ladder still lies next to the trunk. The grass is flattened where Armand lay and the overgrown crater is still there where the shell landed in 1914.

She reaches out and touches the bark of the tree. To connect?

The killing tree. The monument to the innocent and the guilty. Didier, Armand. Dermot's grandfather. Sundry unimportant collaborators. An execution post, an unmarked war memorial, a center of death from which spread out ripples from the grave to drown the living in a sea of breaking memories.

The de Coucys. The McManuses. Contrasts. Joined together like the planks butted up or scarfed like the strakes of mahogany on Dermot's wooden yawl. Break the joint and the whole body falls to pieces, lies around, a rotten hulk.

Within a radius of a hundred meters, a neglected spot in an unknown corner in France, a geographical location unremarked, as wanting in meaning as a bridge over a lesser river in Ireland.

Crossed lives. Parallel lives? Diverging lives? No! *Converging* lives. It will work.

She goes through the broken wall into the wood and up the rough cart track to the front of the house. She picks up the broken arm of a doll that's lying in a bush, its pink plastic and string of elastic spoiling the verdant nature.

Penelope's? Possibly. She carries it with her and drops it onto the front seat of the car. Why? She doesn't know.

She goes back into the mausoleum.

She gives certain instructions to the faithful retainer. Mostly about guarding the house and especially the library and butterfly collection until *Maître* de Malherbe arranges for both to be collected. He would continue to pay her and she should take her orders from him

She sees the mongrel bitch sitting by the car. She opens the back door and the dog jumps in.

She drives through the huge gates without once looking back.

"*Pax*" she says, for no good reason.

35. Irish Mud

DERMOT'S IN IRELAND. He stays the night in the Shelbourne in Dublin and drives down to Piltown in a rented car early the next morning.

Mouse calls him. Gives him Laure's message. The invitation. She's noncommital. Refuses to elaborate or to comment. She's saying, Keep me out of it.

Great peace descends upon him. There's a future. He's very tired. But happy.

He seems to be floating about it all, looking down on himself as he drives through Inistioge down to the village of Piltown. He needs a few days to pick the pieces up, to make himself whole again—for Laure.

He turns left to Fiddown and the river.

He stands there like the man in the Caspar David Friedrich painting, looking out over the desolate scene.

Nothing's happened since he left the village years ago. Nothing. It was all a dream. Unreal.

Mud, flats of wet mud with rivulets. Mud banks that slope down to the channel where the last of the ebb flows in a narrow stream and the dark water swirls around the concrete pillars. There's the smell of a low tide, fishy.

Upstream, under the bridge, the dark mass of Slievenamon broods over the valley and he seems to hear the whistle of the Rosslare Express as it echoes off the lonely mountain.

It's evening now. A soft evening. The hour of the incarnation, the time of Angelus. The setting sun throws long shadows over the woods across the river on the Waterford hills. The tops of the trees are a lumpy quilt of blue velvet with dark green folds and the gathering clouds piled up above the ridge.

He stands at the edge of the quay, surveying the empty scene. More pictures. Image slippage. Fade out.

He thinks, No linnet's wings. And no wooden bridge. Well it hadn't been the Pont Alexandre Trois, or the Palladio in Bassano, much less the Ponta di Santa Trinità in Florence. Just a small bridge. But fine. Big enough to take a pony and trap or three riders abreast.

Under the bridge, swinging to the tide, a rowing boat tied to an iron ring in the wall. In it, a red-headed girl with a beauty mark high up her thigh. And an old soldier floating in the weeds . . . .

Yesterday. It was yesterday. Nothing has happened since.

Nothing ever happens.

He turns and is about to get back in the car when he spots the pile of lumber under a forest of nettles. Planks and piles from the old bridge. Burma teak. White now like bleached bones.

He finds a short length and detaches it from the rest.

This time he throws it onto the passenger seat of the

A chunk of dried mud has fallen off on the fabric. He's going to scrape it up and keep it. Why? He doesn't know. It's just mud. Everything's clear as mud.

Irish mud.

Epilogue

SINCE THIS IS A true story, with maybe a few liberties taken here and there, I have to say that Mouse, with the skills developed during her time with the library service of the British Council, a sometime cover for spooky business, tracked down Sarah. Laure and Dermot went off like sniffer dogs afer the paintings. They discovered them in a castle in the Maremma of Tuscany. It caused a lot of commotion in the art world when both drawings and some paintings were exhibited. The nature of them restricted entry to the galleries and, of course, there were 'correct' places were they could not be shown. People do not like seeing life in the raw. It is writ: there's only birth, sex and death. Ask Laure. Or Dermot.

Acknowledgements

I owe a considerable debt to Dr. Margaret Reinhold for her constant encouragement and for advising me on the subject of 'denial' of child abuse when it has been perpetuated by another member of the family. Without David Malouf's critical reading of the early draft of the book and his suggestions, it would be a much more confused text, though you may think that would be difficult. My father-in-law, an eminent entomologist, whose wartime behavior was irreproachable and the very opposite of that of Armand in the book, helped me about lepidoptera and its literature.

Patrick's story (Chapter 17) was taken word for word from the much-decorated François Paliard, and is of how he was arrested and subsequently escaped over the mountains to Spain, arriving in London and working in intelligence with the Free French under de Gaulle throughout the war. My thanks to him for information and a long friendship.

I have consulted too many sources to list them all here and any errors of interpretation of historical fact are mine alone.